Messianic Reveal

Advance Praise for *Messianic Reveal*

In *Messianic Reveal*, Ethan Burroughs draws on a deep wellspring of expertise about the modern Middle East in all its extraordinary color and complexity to craft a tale of intrigue that is exciting and suspenseful. Though a novel, Burroughs writes about U.S. actors in the Middle East—from soldiers on the battlefield to the men and women who staff our diplomatic missions —from the perspective of one who has, himself, both worn a uniform and served inside an embassy or two. *Messianic Reveal* is a riveting read, but it's also very much an insider's guide to the people, places, cultures, and institutions that drive events in the world's most volatile region.

　　—Peter O'Donohue, retired foreign service officer

Ethan Burroughs's *Messianic Reveal* is a *potpourri* of culture, images, flavors, aromas, and sounds of the Middle East. Burroughs's descriptive story-telling authentically and artfully transports the reader to the region and accurately depicts ex-pat and local life. I was delighted by the well-paced unfolding of the plot and stayed up late many nights reading on to discover how the pieces fit together. I have lived, worked and traveled in many of the countries depicted in *Messianic Reveal*; yet, Burroughs provides an insightful and thought-provoking hypothesis of how history, religion and cultural variations within the Middle East interplay that I found to be very innovative. Overall, *Messianic Reveal* was a page-turning, exciting and intellectual adventure. I can't wait to see what trouble Clayton Haley unearths in the sequel!

　　—Paula Winchester Rank, author of *Best Interest of the*
　　　　　　　　　　　　Child: a Parker and Price Adventure

I just finished *Messianic Reveal* and believe it's a winner. Once I got into it, I was hooked. The historical background really set the stage for understanding the story. I enjoyed the characters; the author obviously has much experience interacting with those types of individuals and knows them. Government activities both at home and abroad were real and believable. What really caught my attention was Ethan Burroughs's effort to inform concerning the complexities and real problems associated with the Muslim communities and real historical events with potential ones—that was awesome. Now I need to read book two and find out what happens to Clayton Haley. Mr. Burroughs successfully baited the hook!

—**Bob Riddell**, high school Bible and history teacher

MESSIANIC REVEAL

A Clayton Haley Novel

Ethan T. Burroughs

NEW YORK

LONDON • NASHVILLE • MELBOURNE • VANCOUVER

Messianic Reveal

A Clayton Haley Novel

Published in New York, New York, by Morgan James Publishing. Morgan James is a trademark of Morgan James, LLC. www.MorganJamesPublishing.com

ISBN 9781631951459 paperback
ISBN 9781631951466 eBook
Library of Congress Control Number: 2020936618

Cover Concept by:
Saltdesign

Cover and Interior Design by:
Chris Treccani
www.3dogcreative.net

Morgan James is a proud partner of Habitat for Humanity Peninsula and Greater Williamsburg. Partners in building since 2006.

Get involved today! Visit
MorganJamesPublishing.com/giving-back

To my wife,
who encouraged me to chronicle
the amazing life we've built together.

Acknowledgments

Writing this novel, my first, proved an exhilarating journey and challenge, which I gladly share with an audience eager to gain an understanding of Middle Eastern developments beyond sensational and often misleading headlines. Though fictional, it reflects on an extraordinary region that is home to some refreshingly ordinary people who want the same things out of life that we do—stability and a secure environment in which to raise a family. Sadly though, the region also hosts some all too real villains and spoilers. I hope that insights laid out in this book shed light for the reader on a region that has mystified the West for nearly fifteen hundred years.

In some ways, this account and my own sojourn in the Middle East was inspired by a book I read as a teenager, Louis L'Amour's *The Walking Drum*, set in the 1100s. L'Amour, of course, was known for his Westerns, but decided to explore the Middle East in the guise of his protagonist Mathurin Kerbouchard, who also marveled at the region's gracious nobility.

I am enormously grateful for my friendship with a number of U.S. foreign service officers, who loyally serve the United States in advancing our interests abroad. They do this often under trying circumstances. They are true patriots who deserve our respect and appreciation. I equally admire and appreciate the fierce defense of our principles by our servicemen and women, and am in eternal debt to my friends in the Green Berets who helped me capture their humor, fun, and deadly seriousness in their spread of democracy.

I am also grateful to a support base that has encouraged me to write, my wife, of course, and family members who read early drafts and provided helpful guidance and pointers that I used in developing Clayton Haley's narrative. And, I'm grateful to my brother who linked me to a kind, encouraging, and patient editor and the kind folks at Morgan James Publishing, who believed in me and found young Mr. Haley's incredible journey credible.

Author's Note

Names, characters, businesses, places, events, locales, and incidents mentioned in *Messianic Reveal* are either the products of the author's imagination or used in a fictitious manner. Aside from historical facts in the prologue, any resemblance to actual persons, living or dead, or actual events is purely coincidental. Furthermore, the author intends only the highest respect and affection for the people of the various faiths listed in this book and provides his personal opinion in this narrative that distortions in these faiths have proved motivating factors in contributing to the furtherance of Middle East unrest, surely an outcome undeserving for many who have needlessly suffered.

Haley continues to pull on threads of conspiracy and suspense in the sequel, *Writ Reveal,* coming soon.

Cast of Characters:

Clayton Haley: Protagonist and United States foreign service officer assigned to Embassy Paris.

Paula Abrams: Foreign service officer assigned to Embassy Paris, covering the Middle East, and mentor to Haley.

Dr. Ibrahim Mustafa: Palestinian professor who lives in Paris and teaches at the Sorbonne University.

Nate Philson: U.S. Army Captain and commander of Operational Detachment Alpha team of "18 series" Green Berets. Haley as an enlisted soldier served with Philson during previous tours in Iraq.

Wilson Edger: Intelligence officer stationed in Paris.

Sami Yacoub and Ghada al-Jibouri: Locally hired political experts at U.S. Embassy Baghdad.

Mohammed Abdullah al-Qahtani: Yemeni/Saudi exiled and self-proclaimed Messiah implicated in 1979 siege of Mecca.

Ali al-Sadr: Iraqi Shia connected to events surrounding the 1979 siege of Mecca.

Dr. Abdulaziz al-Onezi: Iraqi *in vitro* specialist recruited by Ali al-Sadr.

Abdullah Mohammed al-Otaybi and Ali Mehdi al-Qahtani: Young cousins and relatives of Mohammed Abdullah al-Qahtani.

Muhsin Bin Laden: Half-brother of Osama Bin Laden and construction empire scion.

Prologue

1979–Chaos in the Middle East

Iran 1979.

On November 4, 1979, an angry mob of Iranian students, stoked by the Iranian Islamic Revolution that took place earlier in the year, ransacked the U.S. Embassy in Tehran and held sixty-six American diplomats and citizens hostage for 444 days. The "Iran Hostage Crisis" became emblazoned on the American psyche as an unprovoked attack on our compatriots and national dignity. The Iranian revolutionaries, however, regarded the event simply as the "Conquest of the American Spy Den" and therefore, an appropriate response to years of perceived U.S. support for an installed corrupt puppet regime in the Iranian capital.

The inability—both diplomatically and militarily—to retrieve the hostages in a timely manner resulted in the loss of U.S. standing in the region, cost President Jimmy Carter dearly in his re-election bid, and bolstered Iran's fervent Islamic revolutionaries, led by Ayatollah Ruhollah Khomeini. It became clear soon enough that the recently overthrown, U.S.-backed Shah Mohammed Pahlavi and his family would not return to power. The following April, the United States launched an accident-ridden rescue attempt, Operation Eagle Claw, which resulted in the deaths of eight American servicemen and an Iranian and the loss of two aircraft. The former Shah died a few months later, in July 1980. These events only solidified Iranian beliefs that *Allah* was on the side of the revolutionaries, and the American hostages continued to languish as guests of their Persian hosts.

Egypt, 1979.

Predating Iran's Islamic Revolution by only seven months, Egypt became the first Arab Sunni country to sign a peace treaty with Israel. For his bravery in pursuing an elusive peace, Egyptian President Anwar Sadat was awarded the Nobel Peace Prize in 1979 and then assassinated by young military officer and fellow Egyptian Khalid al-Islambouli in 1981. The death of Sadat, who provided temporary refuge in Egypt to Iran's deposed Shah, was celebrated as a victory to a new generation of Islamists, those opting for conservative, political, and occasionally violent interpretations of the tenets of Islam. The new theocratic leadership in Iran, for example, quickly declared al-Islambouli an exalted martyr upon his subsequent execution for Sadat's assassination, making him an inspirational symbol and a first among many to be recognized for devotion to political and militant efforts to promote an Islamic religious agenda. Iran's *Persian* and *Shia* leadership also adorned the memory of the *Arab Sunni* assassin by issuing a postage stamp in 1982 in his honor, and until 2004, Tehran memorialized him with the eponymous *Khalid Islambuli* [sic] *Avenue.*

Saudi Arabia, 1979.

Also in November 1979, was the largely lesser-known seizure of the Grand Mosque in Mecca, Saudi Arabia by young Saudi militant Juhayman al-Otaybi. Al-Otaybi and several hundred followers believed his brother-in-law Mohammed Abdullah al-Qahtani to be the *Mehdi* (Islam's prophesied Messiah, some thought to be a resurrected Mohammed, or perhaps Jesus, returned to earth to issue in the final days). The al-Otaybi group's taking of the mosque, aimed at unseating the House of Saud, resulted in the deaths of hundreds, including militants, the Saudi National Guard, and still unknown numbers of religious pilgrims amassed for the annual hajj. Al-Qahtani and most of the armed militants were reportedly killed during the storming of the mosque by Saudi military and Pakistani and French mercenaries, and al-Otaybi and most of his surviving followers were publicly beheaded in cities throughout Saudi Arabia in January 1980. Ever the opportunist, Ayatollah Khomeini publicly blamed "American imperialism and international Zionism" for supporting this attack on Islam's holiest city and incited anti-American demonstrations around the Muslim world. Mobs overran and burned the U.S. Embassies in Islamabad, Pakistan, and Tripoli, Libya over the following days.

Iraq, 1980.

Meanwhile, next door in Iraq, Saddam Hussain, head of a secular political movement, the *Ba'ath* party, perceived the time ripe to emerge from the yoke of Ottoman and Western colonialism and return Iraq to glory not witnessed since the Islamic golden age and rule of the *Abbasid Caliphate* in Baghdad from 750–1258 AD. Hussain believed that Iraq, though much smaller than Iran, could exploit ongoing Iranian turmoil and appeal to newly found Shia religious zeal, much of which adhered to theocratic beliefs established in *marja'iyat*—the holiest of Shia cities and institutions, located in southern Iraq and under Arab control. He also believed the some six million Iranian *Arabs* living on the eastern shores of the *Arabian* (vice *Persian*) Gulf would readily rise up and join Iraq's return to glory. He miscalculated and underestimated Iranian unity and/or the iron fist of control the Iranian revolutionaries fervently wielded over their newly bolstered countrymen.

Hussain's invasion of Iran in September 1980 embroiled both countries in an eight-year war that cost around one million lives and resulted in untold destruction. This conflict re-introduced chemical warfare to the world and induced the shameful use of children as mine detectors. It also led to Iraq's ill-fated 1990 invasion of Kuwait, largely an attempt to recoup war damages lost in the useless conflict that resulted in no border changes, just death and the destruction of both economies.

United States, 1981.

It was the death of the Shah and subsequent Iraqi invasion of Iran that led the Iranian government to negotiate with the United States over the hostages. With Algeria's mediation, and via Canadian intervention, the Iranians released the sixty-six captives on January 20, 1981, just minutes after the swearing in of President Ronald Reagan. Khomeini's defiance of what he perceived was American regional hegemony ensconced him and his theocratic, anti-Western rule as a new regional power and wedged a deeper schism between the Arab/Persian and Sunni/Shia worlds that sent ripples and then waves of conflict and unrest through Syria,

Lebanon, Israel, Egypt, Yemen, and beyond. It also launched a forty-year U.S.-Iranian grudge match and a cold war characterized by embargoes, sanctions, and proxy conflicts.

These factual events contributed to the rise of Saudi Arabia's Osama Bin Laden and his Al-Qaeda terror group, multiple Israeli-Palestinian conflicts, the Taliban in Afghanistan, recurring Gulf Wars, 9/11, and even the Arab Spring, and *Daesh* or ISIS. They also serve as the backdrop to our story, covering up stirrings that threaten an apocalypse with a reach far beyond that of the Arabian/Persian Gulf.

Part I

Chapter 1

Paris, France. Spring.

Clayton Haley couldn't believe his luck. Embassy Paris for his first tour. Somehow, he got the position over twenty of his State Department classmates, many of whom actually spoke French and had listed Paris as their top bid. Haley, alas, could only recall an *un peu* smattering of a course he took in high school, which was mostly comprised of the first few lines of *La Marseillaise,* the French national anthem. Since then, he had seen little need to announce to the *"children of the revolution that the day of glory had arrived,"* if his recollection of the song was correct. There had not been a high demand for French proficiency in his small high school in upstate South Carolina.

Ironically, he had placed Paris third on his wishlist after Beirut, Lebanon, and Tripoli, Libya, but given recent security drawdowns at those missions, he understood options were no longer available for first or second tour officers in the department. Embassy Paris—the United States' oldest diplomatic mission in the world—was a

3

nice consolation prize, however, for Haley as he embarked on his new civilian career, a far cry from his prior military service. He certainly appreciated his freedom to choose how he attired himself each day and did not miss the days in which the Army dictated all his fashion and haircut choices.

Haley had been in country all of a few weeks and was just getting to know his colleagues and his way around town. He essentially knew how to get back and forth from his small flat, located near the La Garenne Colombes Train Station in Northwest Paris, to the stately embassy chancery on 2 Avenue Gabriel Street. The embassy somewhat reminded him of the Eisenhower Executive Office Building or other edifices found in Washington, DC. He figured that the same architects had designed many of the imposing and monumental structures in the capitals of both countries and supposed they shared the same inspiration, or perhaps the same building codes.

Haley felt honored to be among the select of pedestrians granted access to the fortress. Simply waving familiarly at the guards, flashing his badge, and inputting his passcode on a numbered keypad ensured his entrance into the U.S. government facility, leaving those less privileged outside the secured building. Prior to joining the department, he too had the experience of standing on the outside of the forbidding entrance, iron bars, gates, fences, rope lines and stanchions, and barricades, including those aesthetically adorned with plants, wondering what it must be like to enter a bureaucratic holy of holies. Outside the embassy, he kept his badge out of sight, mindful of security precautions but also embarrassed by his photo. Since the taking of the photo, Haley sought to try out a non-military regulation haircut and was pleased his dusty, light brown hair had grown to lengths not enjoyed since his college days, albeit still conservatively short.

He learned the embassy was located near the tourist traps around the Place de la Concorde, a public square made famous for executions during the revolution, thus the tourists and their fascination for the *macabre*. He perceived the traffic a bit manic, but manageable, and dreaded his first driving attempt navigating the large roundabouts in the Parisian intersections, wondering if he would be able to make it out of the many layers of circles in an effort to simply take a right turn. Good thing his car wouldn't arrive for another few weeks. And true to Hollywood portrayals, he found the sirens of the police more amusing than alarming and marveled at how their tones dropped in pitch as they moved off into the distance.

***

Haley was off for the day so he could unpack his household effects, receipt of which was a major milestone in the transient life of a foreign service officer. As he rifled through boxes in his small flat, he reflected on the twists and turns thrown his way over the last few years...

He'd dreamed of becoming a diplomat since his participation in high school Model UN classes. He enjoyed researching and debating how governmental policy intertwined with personality politics and how countries notionally could join efforts to address real humanitarian crises. A self-admitted idealist, and inspired to save the world via flexing the United States' diplomatic muscle, he enrolled at the University of South Carolina as a government and international studies major, eschewing the obnoxiously orange, nearby Clemson University. He found out soon enough, however, that a humanities degree wasn't enough to net him a job to save even himself. He met with former FSOs and even took the Foreign Service Exam, but he failed to pass it and came away from the experience disappointed, perceiving that State lived down to its reputation as an exclusive *pale, male, and Yale* club. Not financially able to wait around for something better and contending with a mountain of student debt upon graduation, Haley enlisted in the Army to pay off his bills.

Given his degree and his apparent natural language aptitude, which failed to show itself during high school French, Uncle Sam saw fit to place him in military intelligence, or MI, in military parlance due to the compulsion to incorporate more TWAs (Two or Three Word Acronyms), and train him in Arabic. Arabic, even more so than French, was part of a very rare skill set among those Haley grew up with in South Carolina. His kinsmen and friends typically looked askance at anyone who spoke a language other than *"Amarrkan."* This often included folks from up north with their funny accents.

Haley's enlistment lasted just over five years, delayed by long-term Arabic language training followed by two tours in Iraq. As an MI "eavesdropper," he often found himself behind enemy lines and exposed to danger. His second tour was cut violently short due to a leg injury he suffered courtesy of an improvised explosive device he stumbled upon while on patrol. While recovering from his wounds, he studied for the Foreign Service Exam and finally passed it in a sitting at U.S. Embassy Baghdad proctored by FSOs.

Given his veterans' hiring preference, language proficiency, and military-required security clearance, Haley's State Department processing went quickly, even by government standards. He joined

A-100 orientation, a two-month training that launched people into the foreign service, in the fall and was slotted for a six-month Arabic refresher in the run-up to an assignment in Beirut or Tripoli (working out of Embassy Tunis). Given the aforementioned drawdowns, however, and all FSOs' "availability for worldwide assignments," Haley was moved unexpectedly to a Paris consular job, recently vacated by the incumbent due to curtailment. As he finished unpacking, he looked forward to getting into a work routine, meeting his colleagues at the Embassy, and learning how the State Department ran.

***

Like nearly all first-tour officers, Haley worked in the bustling consular section, a seeming rite of passage for State. He found it quite interesting so far, working with the large number of American and local immigration experts who comprised Embassy Paris' consular team.

As he learned the ropes, he moved across the cubicle farms from section to section, covering non-immigration (NIV) and immigration visas (IV), passports and naturalization, and American citizen services. His supervisor, the deputy consul, informed him he would work NIVs in the mornings and IVs in the afternoon. Given that France and the United States have reciprocal visa waiver programs, most of his NIV and some of his IV work focused on that of third-country nationals, many from Middle Eastern countries, and afforded him the opportunity to keep up his Arabic, which ranged from rudimentary to passable, depending on the day.

Chapter 2

As the weeks zipped by, Haley's comfort at "the window"—pitched by the State Department as the "last three feet of diplomacy"—grew, as did that of his relationships with his colleagues. The department inspired and counseled consular officers that the engagement with visa applicants, in many cases, was the first or only interaction much of the world would have with the United States. While putting U.S. national interests and security first, dictates reminded those at the window to demonstrate courtesy and hospitality in their interactions with host country residents. Haley saw this as a tall order given the time constraints; visa interviews took on average less than three minutes. Even so, his good manners, famed southern hospitality, and ingrained affinity toward people made him an affable and effective interviewer. He took enormous pride in implementing U.S. law in refusing visas for insincere applicants or those who would otherwise exploit the United States' weak immigration laws. Conversely, he proudly and warmly welcomed visa issuance for those who presented themselves as ideal and law abiding travelers, who would return to their country of origin in a timely manner. He doubted his great-great-grandparents, who hailed from a mix of Scottish, and perhaps a little Huguenot ancestry, enjoyed similar customer service in their efforts to travel to the new world.

***

Boutique Sandwich and Crêpe Restaurant, near U.S. Embassy, Paris.

Over lunch one day at a sidewalk sandwich shop next to the embassy, Haley discussed a recent IV misadventure with a political officer with whom he had grown chummy.

"I had the weirdest case today at the window. Do you know the U.S. government recognizes proxy marriages?" Haley queried while looking down the street in the direction of a police car, catching the offkey dropping of pitch as it sailed out of sight. The busy-ness of the downtown traffic entertained him. Though a "country boy" at heart, he liked seeing the hustle and bustle of the city and listening to the cacophony of horns, bells, silverware clatter, and chatter of fellow diners.

Haley found his keen observation skills a bit overstimulated when out in public, given there was simply too much to see, and he struggled occasionally to focus on singular items. The Paris sky showcased its typical shades of drab and gray, seemingly always on the edge of a drizzle. He didn't mind, though. When gray presented itself as the dominant hue in the sky, roads, buildings, and moods of people, other colors clamored for and won attention, showing their brilliance. As such, colored signage, street lights, plants, flamboyant clothing, and the fluorescent hair of tourists and locals alike, expressing their individuality, seized his notice.

"Yes. I adjudicated a few of those in my time in consular. They're kind of rare, though," responded Paula Abrams, a fourth-tour officer who covered the Middle East file in the Political section. "What's the backstory?" she asked, reaching for some *pomme frites,* known jokingly as "Freedom Fries" in the embassy.

Haley set down his sandwich, his absolute favorite; it was called *jambon beurre* and consisted of layers of ham on a baguette with a French cheese he couldn't pronounce. It was a far cry from his standard fare of ham from the Bi-Lo grocery store with Duke's mayonnaise on Sunbeam bread. Never in a hundred years would his buddies back home have pictured him living in France, or for that matter any other *"farren country"* north of the Mason-Dixon Line. Nor would they imagine anyone ever putting butter on a ham sandwich, which essentially is what a jambon beurre is. And they would only imagine a funeral setting as explanation for him wearing a dark Jos. A. Bank's suit and tie and sporting black, wingtip dress shoes. Nope. His old civilian wardrobe consisted primarily of jeans or cargo shorts and t-shirts. His pals would not recognize him.

"I interviewed a young lady whose AMCIT husband—though I still am not convinced he's actually a U.S. citizen—filed a petition for her citizenship. Turns out she's an Eritrean who only speaks Tigrinya. We have some Arabic, and even Amharic speakers, in the consular section but no one who speaks a common language with her," quipped Haley, combing his short dirty blonde hair with his fingers, as he often did when thinking.

"Where is her husband and why is she applying in this consular district?" asked Abrams, sipping from a green Perrier bottle, and dusting crumbs from her own sandwich off the table cloth onto the sidewalk. Coming from work, she too was dressed in business attire, a dark pantsuit with a peach colored blouse. She had short dark hair, complemented by the suit, and, as always, a sparkle in her eye. She enjoyed the role of mentoring Haley. Though he was serving in a consular position, he aspired to do political reporting. Abrams was kind enough to chat about her work with him from time to time.

"Well that's the problem," said Haley. "She's here on some type of refugee status under the UN, but her husband is still in Eritrea. And what's really strange is his father apparently stood in for him at the wedding ceremony, which took place some twelve months ago."

"That's not unheard of. Proxy weddings allow for and even assume stand-ins."

"That's not the worst of it. Turns out, if you'll recall from your consular days, we have to ascertain physical . . . um . . . joint presence of the groom and bride . . . after the wedding, to confirm, um . . . consummation, so to speak," fidgeted Haley while clearly becoming hot under the collar. "It's been over a year and a half since she last saw her betrothed husband."

"Oh, I see. That's a different story. What did you do?" inquired Abrams, amused, but not discomfited by Haley's awkwardness.

"Oh, it gets better. She has a baby that's about three months old. All we can do is report this to the fraud unit. At some point, I'll have to break it to her that she'll not be becoming an American citizen. I'll leave it to her and her father-in-law to explain the child to the husband. The embarrassing thing is that our microphones at the window were down, and we had to shout back and forth through the small aperture. And since we shared no common language, much of our conversation . . . ascertaining proof of consummation . . . was managed via gestures. Not my proudest day. It would have been hilarious if not so embarrassing," mulled Haley.

Abrams chuckled. "That reminds me of an immigration case I had a few years ago in which an applicant swore up and down that her pregnancy lasted fourteen months. She even brought a note from her quack of a doctor verifying her eventual delivery as an "immaculate gestation." Like you, I left it to the applicant to explain to the AMCIT petitioner the unnatural circumstances of the pregnancy. And, don't get me started on the crazy cases I saw when adjudicating Diversity Visa Lottery entries. I think each Congressman who supports this odd program should spend just one day at the window processing applications. That will change their minds about how we recruit citizens." After a pause, she added, "Why would the United States employ a lottery system to attract new citizens? Why don't we simply recruit the talent we need?"

Haley rolled his eyes in agreement, mentally reminding himself he needed to follow up later in the day with analyzing the validity of high school diplomas for Somali applicants for this program, essentially establishing the intending immigrants had the equivalence of a U.S. high school education, the primary requirement for qualifying. He had already refused several applicants for forging their diplomas. One, he noted with exasperation had clearly created at stamp for his diploma with a carved potato half dipped into an inkwell. One had to admire the creativity of the applicants, he thought.

Chapter 3

Abrams and Haley swapped a few more stories about IV work and AMCIT stories, most sadly involving alcohol and poor judgment. Consular officers and embassies writ large, prioritized the care of American citizens abroad, and provided a number of services ranging from credentialing births and deaths of Americans, loaning emergency funds for repatriation, and checking on the welfare of those in detention for breaking local laws. Haley marveled at the capacity for bad decisions exhibited by seemingly normal Americans when they traveled to foreign countries. They must somehow believe the Marines posted at each embassy were on standby to rescue them from their own life choices.

After a few minutes, they motioned to the waiter for service. They each ordered *"café, s'il vous plaît."* The waiter's subtle eyebrow lift indicated he was not at all impressed with Haley's French. Upon his sauntering off, Haley moved on to an NIV interview he had that morning. "So I interviewed two Yemeni cousins today," he said. "Both early twenties, passable English, trying to travel with their older "relative" to the U.S. for medical treatment.

They've lived here in Paris all their lives and said their grandfather, or uncle, or whoever, has been here close to forty years. It's unclear if he ever learned French or English. He was reportedly too sick to come in for the interview. They said interview arrangements for him would be made once their visas were approved."

Abrams cocked her head in thought and shrugged, "That's not that unheard of. There have been waves of Arab immigrants here for generations from Morocco, Tunisia, Lebanon, Palestinian Territories and elsewhere, and sadly, they don't assimilate as well in Europe, notoriously in France, as well as they do in the States. Quite often, they stay in isolated neighborhoods and communities, travel little, only going to and from home and the mosque. A pretty simple lifestyle. Not that unusual. Even though we pride ourselves on welcoming immigrants, I would say recent waves have shown less desire to integrate into our society."

As the waiter unceremoniously dropped two coffees on the table, Abrams continued. "Look at Detroit, for example. I understand there are communities where everyone speaks only Arabic, and even the street signs are in Arabic. And last time I was in DC, I heard that some 300,000 immigrants from El Salvador live there. Many of them haven't bothered to learn English. And ever since the so-called Islamic revolution in Iran, the Iranian community in Los Angeles is well into the hundreds of thousands as well, if not more. That's why people call it *Tehran-geles*."

"No, no, I get that," said Haley. "What's weird about this is the funding for the medical care. The older man they wish to accompany—sorry, but it's not clear to me if he's an uncle, cousin, or grandfather, or a combination of all three. I find some of the family heritage structures of these folks similar to those of trailer parks back home, more kudzu than trees, and mostly covered in moss, if you know what I mean. Anyhow, it's about the money. The young men showed me bank statements. Turns out, they're loaded. In just two of the HSBC financial accounts they have here in Paris, they have over $14 million, certainly enough to cover medical expenses in the U.S."

"What's he suffering from?" asked Abrams.

"According to the note from his doctor, epilepsy. The embassy health unit reports there are plenty of good places here in Paris that treat epilepsy. I told the applicants, but they insisted they had the money and could get more, if needed, and they want to see a certain geneticist at the Mayo Clinic, apparently an old friend of the family."

"Where would they get more money?" inquired Abrams.

"That's what I asked them. They simply said they have plenty of family members who would help out if needed. Of course, this wasn't enough to satisfy me, but, honestly, it's hard to 214b someone with millions in the bank."

"214b?" asked Abrams.

"Sorry for the shorthand. Surely you remember from your consular days the nomenclature for the visa refusal for suspicion that the applicants are intending immigrants or would incur public charges or fees they can't pay. Why should the taxpayers pay for folks who shouldn't be in our country?" Haley paused, registering a nod from Abrams, and they both took a sip of coffee. He had never really drunk coffee much until his time in the Army. While he was deployed to Iraq he developed a slight addiction. It would have been worse if the coffee he drank there tasted half as good as that in a French cafe with a kind and generous friend.

"So, here are some very rich Yemenis, with no record of working or jobs, who have lived here in Paris, yet never really assimilated, and there's no way of knowing how they got their money," Haley pondered out loud.

"To my questions about where their wealth came from, they both simply said from their grandfather, *'who is very rich man,'*" he mimicked, overly pronouncing his 'r's in thick Arabic tones. Haley continued, "This clearly bothered me, so I googled them. In many Arab countries, you can tell a lot about someone's lineage if you know their father's and grandfather's names. The two young men's names are", glancing at a notepad he had stashed in his pocket, "*Abdullah Mohammed Juhayman al-Otaybi* and *Ali Mehdi Mohammed Abdullah al-Qahtani,*" he said rhythmically, as if in cadence. "Given their full names, I can trace these guys back a couple generations. If you drop the first few names, you can determine who their grandfathers were. According to online sites, *Juhayman* al-Otaybi and *Mohammed* Abdullah al-Qahtani, their grandfathers or individuals with similar names, were killed by the Saudis for leading a religious cult in a violent storming of the Grand Mosque of Mecca in 1979. And, they weren't Yemenis, they were Saudis."

Abrams mused, "This is pretty strange. It's not unusual to have Yemenis represent themselves as Saudis, but I've never come across Saudis portraying themselves as Yemeni. You'll recall when the Saudis finally disowned their most famous son, Osama Bin Laden, they identified him as Yemeni, because his father hailed from Yemen. Very convenient. It's likely not a big deal, though, and you should realize there are probably a few thousand people with these names. They're pretty common."

Abrams signaled to the waiter to tally the check. The server impatiently eyed the table as prime real estate, worthy of patrons perhaps less American, and haughtily delivered the bill, which he had already prepared in anticipation of their departure. His mannerisms exuded sarcasm, "as if he was one giant eye-roll," thought Haley.

"Agreed," said Haley as he grabbed the check before Abrams could reach for it, "I ran this by Evan in the fraud unit to check their bona fides, but given his backlog, he thinks it will take a few weeks, if ever, before he can get back to me. What do you think about asking one of your Middle East academic contacts if they know anything about these characters—al-Otaybi and al-Qahtani?"

"Sure," said Abrams, "happy to. I know a number of scholars who are quite open to talking to us about Arab world affairs. They usually like to harangue us on our Palestinian-Israeli policy. They often have some sharp criticism of our liberation of Iraq, Syria, and other regional entanglements. I know one guy, Dr. Ibrahim Mustafa, who has long straddled the Middle East and Europe. He's very smart, fair, and generous with his time. Plus, if I recall, he's a Palestinian who lived for a while in Saudi Arabia. What part of France are the applicants from?"

"Let me see." Haley flipped through his notes. "Sorry, but I'm going to butcher the pronunciation, but they live on *Rue Shevrose, Nu-ful le Shatow.*"

"You're kidding, right? Neauphle-le-Château is a city about an hour west of here. Nothing special about the place other than it served as a temporary home—also back in the seventies—to one of the most famous villains in recent history. How about you join me in speaking to my historian friend? And, your French pronunciation is horrendous. How did they ever teach Arabic to a bumpkin like you?"

Chapter 4

Mysterious mobile call, a few days later, somewhere in France.

"Kaif halak, ustath, [How are you, sir]?" said a weathered but sonorous voice. *"Bismallah al-Rahman al-Raheem. [In the name of God, the most gracious and merciful.]"*

"Kul shai ala ma yaram, [All is as it should be]." The respondent on the other end of the phone replied. "All is well, and Allah's blessings on you as well. Please, if you'll allow, let's continue in English. It's been decades since I used Arabic, and I've allowed my skills to fall into disrepair, and sadly, my dependence on Iraqi dialect makes it difficult to speak with other Arab nationalities."

"Tayyeb, insha allah. Bas biltakeed, Farsak masboot. [Fine, God Willing, but for sure, your Persian is perfect]."

"Of course, it's my mother tongue but also a language in disuse for me. I've been out of Iran and in the West for many years now. How may I assist you?"

"I need you make meeting with specialist alm al-wiratha [genetics] in Al-Urdon, [Jordan]" he continued in broken English.

"Of course, I have not met him yet, but I will travel next week to Amman to visit his clinic. I understand that he is very good, very professional, and he appreciates the sensitivity of the matter. And I understand that he has made very good progress."

"*Tayyeb*," the first man repeated. "*You give update to me when I arrive Amedika soon. I must take visa first, then travel. Will meet Dr. Farhan.*"

"Of course. *Ma salama, sidi. [Go in peace, sir].*" He pushed the red hang up button on his cellular phone, then swiped over to his contacts app. He quickly input the initials IVF and found contact details for Dr. Abdulaziz al-Onezi. Next to his name in Arabic was *al-Ikhsob fi al-Mukhtabr wa Alm al-Wiratha [genetics laboratory]*. His Arabic, though rusty, was good enough to know that Dr. al-Onezi worked in genetics and *in vitro* fertilization, but the science itself was a complete mystery to him. He was just the middleman, broker, and talent scout, and he had a proven record—over forty years—excelling in networking and finding just the right people for the jobs needing done. He wasn't afraid to get his own hands dirty and had great acumen for finding the pressure points in others to get them out of their comfort zones. He messaged Dr. al-Onezi via WhatsApp to re-confirm their appointment the following week and to remind him to be ready to travel, upon his instructions, to whatever location he dictated.

The original call's instigator had already removed the SIM card from his phone and broke it into pieces, depositing the phone in a nearby trash receptacle.

Chapter 5

American Cafe near the Sorbonne, Paris, France, the following week.

During a consular section admin day, Haley followed Abrams into an American coffee franchise located just off the Sorbonne University campus in downtown Paris. He had been looking forward to this, as his work never took him out of the consular section. He saw this as an opportunity to have a sneak peak at what political officers, or poloffs, did and hoped his next assignment would involve political reporting. Plus, it was nice being in a university environment.

An embassy motorpool driver dropped them off near the campus entrance, and they walked across the manicured grounds to the pedestrian entrance of the cafe. He was sure he was overplaying it in his mind, but he couldn't help feeling a tingle of excitement with his return to academia, especially that of the renowned Sorbonne, albeit for just a quick coffee.

As most days in Paris recently, atmospheric coloring hued drab with an extra dose of dreary. Haley mused that the clouds wanted to rain but were too lazy or stubborn to let go. He wondered if this reflected on American stereotypes of the French.

It was chilly but not enough for outerwear beyond the professional attire worn by Abrams and himself. Recalling the heat and blinding brilliance of summers in Iraq, Haley was content to never see the sun again.

Abrams gestured to Haley in the direction of the appointed cafe, and they made their way into the crowded shop, which was nearly at full occupancy. Most of the patrons were students, but judging by the clothes and ages of some, Haley assumed faculty also frequented the place. It was dimly lit, but given the level of activity in the place, seemed to have a glow about it. Haley was relieved the customers obeyed the no smoking signs as he did not want to have to dry clean his suit to get rid of any smell of cigarette smoke.

A gentleman who appeared to be in his sixties, dressed in a dark, slightly weathered suit, white dress shirt, and no tie sat at a small, round table in the corner. His hair was white and thin, and a tad unruly, but with just enough black in it to indicate he had once had very dark hair. He was clean shaven and offered a generous and sincere smile. He politely stood as they approached, reaching out to Abrams with a warm handshake, and turned to Haley. With an accent interlaced with French and Arabic tones he said, "You must be Mr. Haley. My dear friend Ms. Abrams spoke highly of you. I am honored to meet you."

"*Tasharafna [I am honored to meet you]*. It's good to meet you, sir, and please, call me Clayton. I'm very grateful for your taking the time to meet. Paula told me you're quite the expert on the Arab diaspora community here in Paris."

Abrams jumped in. "Clayton, as I mentioned in the car, Dr. Ibrahim Mustafa is a professor in Middle Eastern studies at the Sorbonne, but relevant to your questions last week, he has resided in Paris for a few decades. Having lived for a few years in Saudi

Arabia, I suspect he will be very familiar with the occurrence connected to Mr. al-Qahtani back in '79."

Dr. Ibrahim interjected, "I was pleased to get Ms. Abrams' call, and I'm quite intrigued by the reference to Mohammed al-Qahtani, a name I've not heard uttered in many decades. But first, I would be very rude to not offer you coffee. Alas, in your American cafes, we can't find a good *shai [tea]*, or even Arabic or Turkish coffee. We can, however, experience a nice rich Arabica coffee," he smiled, pleased with his play on words and knowing *Arabica* was standard coffee fare across the world, while *Arabic* coffee, made from cardamom, was popular among the Bedouin tribes of the Arabian peninsula. "And you must know though your young country excels at marketing coffee," he said, nodding toward the other patrons in the store. "It was the Arabs who first introduced this magical elixir to the world. The Yemenis, to be exact."

The barista took their coffee orders, with Dr. Ibrahim and Paula both requesting espresso, and Clayton an Americano, black, no sugar, while they settled into plush chairs. They moved the small table so they could lean into their conversation. Dr. Ibrahim insisted on paying. He was also patient and generous with his compliments as Clayton exchanged a few more courtesies in Arabic.

In response, Dr. Ibrahim said, "Mr. Haley, your Arabic is quite good. Your pronunciation clearly denotes some impressive exposure to *Fus-hah*, classical Arabic. Most Arabs struggle with this language. I consider myself quite educated, yet even I, from time to time, struggle with the very complex grammar. I don't wish to discourage you, but conventional wisdom says it takes some twenty years to really grasp the language. Most of us find it a bit more expedient to speak *Aamia,* or our local dialects. Being Palestinian but having been raised in Saudi Arabia, I tend to be most comfortable with the *Shami* or Levantine and Gulf dialects. Furthermore, do I detect what you Americans call a 'twing' in your accent when you speak English?"

Haley was starting to really like Dr. Ibrahim. "I believe you might mean a twang. And yes sir, it's our accent and good manners that distinguish us from the rest of America," Haley said, winking at Abrams.

"That, and living in the past, enjoying NASCAR, being rednecks, and eating boiled peanuts and whatever grits are," she shot back. "The rest of the U.S. somehow won and then moved past the civil war," she continued to jab.

"If you'll forgive me and my love of historical fantasy—it comes with growing up in the Middle East—you know that *Sham* is the name for greater Syria, or the Levant?" Dr. Ibrahim gently interrupted, politely ignoring the banter. "It also derives from the name of the Prophet Noah's son, Shem. Given that all Arabs and Jews source from him, we are Semites. I find it interesting when we Arabs are called anti-*Semitic* when we oppose European and American Zionist takeover by *Semites* of *Semitic* lands in *Semitic* Palestine."

That's for another and longer conversation, however," he quickly conjured, reading Abrams' and Haley's body language, which suggested a potential debate. "On to the topic at hand," Dr. Ibrahim continued, "Mohammed al-Qahtani. Again, not a name I've heard in a long time, and frankly, never uttered in more than a whisper since his fateful … how do you call it? Rampage? He and Juhayman al-Otaybi attacked the Grand Mosque in Mecca, Saudi Arabia in 1979. I remember this well. I was in my twenties at the time, and lived only 450 kilometers away in Medina, Saudi Arabia, where my father served as an accountant for the Saudi Ministry of Awqaf, which as you may know administers religious endowments and manages the employment and training of the nation's religious scholars."

Ever the professor, Dr. Ibrahim settled into story mode and recounted for Paula and Clayton that al-Otaybi was a restless and unsettled youth and how he met al-Qahtani while both were imprisoned by Saudi authorities for rabble rousing.

"Al-Otaybi, smitten by a misplaced reverence for al-Qahtani, was convinced in a vision that al-Qahtani was the long awaited *Mehdi [Messiah]*, and the two should lead a cause to usher in an Islamic apocalypse. If I recall correctly, they were related to each other by marriage. I certainly am not fortunate enough to have any relatives so close to God. I have some cousins, however, whom I am sure are in the service of *Shaitan [Satan]*," he chuckled.

"Al-Otaybi, like his father and grandfather before him, opposed what they perceived was the religious illegitimacy of the House of Saud in governing the kingdom, but more importantly, in being the protectors or custodians of the holy sites of Islam and the administration of the Islamic religion. In short, they believed the Saudis did not have the spiritual credentials to rule, and they were not puritanical or pious enough to enforce the very narrow interpretation espoused by the followers of an eighteenth century Muslim reformer named Mohammed ibn Abdulwahab. These 'Wahabis' preached a simple message: 'live today like Mohammed lived in the 600s'. This message resonated well on the remote Arabian Peninsula, detached from the industrial revolutions and modern developments in Europe, North America, and Asia.

The discovery of oil on the peninsula changed everything and introduced the world to this harsh and isolated land."

Dr. Ibrahim leaned back in his chair, taking a deep breath as he continued. At the same time, Haley settled into his own chair, mesmerized by the tale he was hearing. The muffled chatter of the coffee shop dissipated into background white noise. Abrams made occasional scratches in her notepad.

"Fearing the corruption of the west, the Wahabi message unified the many disparate tribes in the region, most often under the banner of a violent movement called the *Ikhwan*, or '*Brothers*'. In fact, the Saudis executed either al-Otaybi's father or grandfather for his role in an Ikhwan uprising. I can't remember which one. Employing the fear of western corruption, al-Otaybi and al-Qahtani targeted for recruitment the tribes previously united under the Ikhwan banner as well as disenfranchised students from the Islamic University, or Seminary, if you prefer, in Medina, Saudi Arabia where I lived at the time.

"And you know of course the importance of the three holy sites in Islam," he digressed and then explained. "For we Muslims, we have *Mecca al-Mukarramah*, or the Holy City of Mecca,—the birthplace of our Prophet Mohammed, *Medina al-Munawarrah*, or the Enlightened City,—the burial place of Mohammed, and Jerusalem, or as you know it, *al-Quds*—the Holy City,—the destination and launch point for Mohammed for his miraculous overnight trip to Paradise. I suppose we must share Jerusalem with our cousins the Jews and our adopted Christian relatives," he sighed and smiled in resignation. "We're quite the dysfunctional family, no?"

He didn't leave room for an answer. "Anyway," he returned to his narrative, "Al-Otaybi and al-Qahtani also recruited acolytes from Egypt, Kuwait, Yemen, Sudan, and as far away as Iraq, and, if I recall, an American or two. Not content to simply confront the existing religious establishment and what they saw was a corrupt regime built on newfound astronomical oil wealth, their cult worship urged them to undermine the Saudi Arabian seat of theological reference in Mecca, as marked by the presence of Islam's most holy structure, the Kaaba, the most sacred building in Islam and built by Abraham and his son Ishmael."

Haley chimed in. "That's right. If I remember from my university studies, the House of Saud—aka, the royal family—had only a geographical right to call itself the protectors of Islam. These guys have been the *Sharifs* of Islam for only about a hundred years."

"Rather coarsely put but somewhat correct," replied Dr. Ibrahim. "In fact, prior to the rise of the *Sa-oodis*, the Hashemites—now in Jordan—provided custodianship for all three of Islam's holiest sites, including the much disputed Al-Aqsa Mosque in Jerusalem. And I'm impressed you know the origin of the word you've so popularized in your cowboy movies, 'Sheriff,'" he jested.

Haley flashed Abrams a knowing, superior grin. She rolled her eyes in response.

Dr. Ibrahim pretended to ignore the exchange. "The Kaaba, otherwise known as the 'House of God', is referenced in the *Quran* as having been built by Ibrahim and his son, Ishmael. I believe your understanding is that Isaac was your *Abraham's* favored son, whom he nearly sacrificed? I'm afraid we'll have to disagree on that account, but we'll leave *that* story for another conversation," he smirked, noting again, Haley's desire to interject his own opinion on the matter. "You know once a year, we Muslims dedicate a week of holidays to commemorate Allah's provision of a ram so that Ibrahim would not have to sacrifice his son Ishmael," he instigated, enjoying a bit of Haley's discomfort over this account.

"According to Islamic lore, the Kaaba may have been built on an original place of worship dedicated by Adam and Eve. This theory, I don't put much stock in, but I do wonder at times about how intertwined Islamic, Christian, and Jewish histories are. I even recall my grandfather explaining to me that nearby Jeddah, gateway to both holy cities of Mecca and Medina, was named for *Howa*, whom you call Eve. And my father told me only a few years prior to the Grand Mosque seizure, he visited what the locals identified as the tomb of Eve. He described it as massive, as some believe Eve was a giantess. Her tomb was located in Jeddah, which by the way, as you know, means simply 'grandmother' in Arabic. A suitable title for the mother of humanity, no?"

Abrams looked up sharply from her notepad. She and Haley had never considered that there might be a tomb for Eve. Dr. Ibrahim clearly enjoyed himself. The three leaned in even closer as he continued. "Ironically, that very tomb of the world's 'Jeddah' was demolished in the 1970s by order of the then King of Saudi Arabia, King Khaled, if I have my Saudi lineage correct, because pilgrims were known to travel to the site to pray. The Saudi religious establishment couldn't have competing religious sites in the country, could they? Or so the story goes—

"Please forgive the digression, but it's important to know the vital spiritual importance of these cities and sites to the world's Muslims. That al-Otaybi successfully seized the Grand Mosque shook the House of *Sa-ood's* political establishment and its religious credentials to their core," he explained. "Some of his followers were former national guardsmen and knew their way around weapons. Additionally, the cult was well funded and had sympathizers, even in the religious establishment. As you earlier inferred," inserted Dr. Ibrahim, "the modern day Royal Kingdom of Saudi Arabia was less than fifty years old and only in its second generation of rulers. Control over the country was tentative at best and nearly entirely dependent on obeisance to the theologians and custodianship of the mosques in Mecca and Medina. The country was woven together by a fabric of religious fervor funded by massive and newfound oil wealth."

Dr. Ibrahim continued his narrative, but could not recall the number of militants who followed al-Otaybi and al-Qahtani in seizing the Grand Mosque. He estimated it was around 500. He recounted how the well-armed and frenzied attackers easily overpowered local policemen, armed only with clubs. The date of the attack was seared on his memory—November 20, 1979, the day his father was mortally injured in Medina under mysterious circumstances.

"Interesting side note," he added, "Rumor has it that the first call to the Saudi authorities after the seizure was made by an employee of what later became a household name in your country—the Bin Laden Group."

They each ordered another coffee.

Chapter 6

Amman, Jordan

The black Mercedes-Benz E-Class vehicle made its way through the Abdoun district of Amman, Jordan south to Deir Al-Ghbar. The luxury car, like its passenger, appeared anachronistic in the working class district of the capital city. The roads in the country, like the buildings, the landscape, and the people, seemed to the passenger a bit overwrought, and still suffering the consequences of Old Testament curses. He was familiar with Jordan, having spent a little time there, and knew that the country was in desperate need of a break. It had never completely absorbed the waves of Palestinian refugees, which now comprised some sixty percent of the population. Though many of the thousands of Iraqi refugees since 2003 brought with them vital talent and money for investment, they too were a strain on the educational, healthcare, and transportation infrastructure.

And since the beginning of the 2011 Arab spring, nearly a million Syrians joined the throngs of refugees already straining Jordan to its limits. One only had to look at economic forecasts to wonder at the short term outlook for the country. Yet, King

Abdullah II continued to remain popular with his constituents and due to his high intelligence and eloquence, he was viewed as a favorite of the west as well. It didn't hurt that Queen Rania, raised in Kuwait, was one of the most beautiful and regal women in the Middle East. The King, born to a British mother, and the Queen, to Palestinian parents, had non-standard geneological pedigrees but were raising a crown prince who was a direct descendant of Mohammed and would be expected one day to carry the Hashemite mantle in governing holy sites of Islam and Christianity.

The passenger's destination was a genetics laboratory in Deir Al-Ghbar, "house of dust," he loosely translated. It suited the backdrop—dusty. He didn't know the small district was also known for an ancient monastery, long destroyed, but originally built by Crusaders as a house of Christian worship and to protect those who stood watch over the Holy sites as laid out in the Bible. In fact, Mount Nebo, where Moses viewed the Promised Land, lay less than forty kilometers away.

But the passenger was on a different type of religious pilgrimage, one that would usher in a revival and restoration of spiritual order, not one to celebrate a bygone era. He ordered the driver to stop at the genetics laboratory of Iraqi expatriate to Jordan, Dr. Abdulaziz al-Onezi. He needed updates from the good doctor on progress made over the last few years.

***

American Cafe near the Sorbonne, Paris, France. Second round of coffee.

Haley couldn't wait to become a political officer. He found the conversation and Dr. Ibrahim's personalized lecture exhilarating, or maybe it was the caffeine coursing through his veins. He was aware there were other customers in the coffee shop, but they all seemed to him as if in a peripheral blur. He was enrapt in the account provided by Dr. Ibrahim. He had never had someone so neatly package the various viewpoints held by a fifth of the world's population, and he wondered why he had never heard of the siege of Mecca.

Dr. Ibrahim continued once the barista brought the second round of coffees.

"The Saudi authorities, of course, tried to storm and retake the mosque but were rebuffed by the militants, who tactically used the mosque's walls in their defense. The terrorists employed snipers to pick off the soldiers and repelled several assaults on the gates and through underground tunnels of the mosque by the National Guard. Al-Otaybi even used the loudspeakers, normally reserved for calls to prayer, to announce his demands—cutting oil exports to the United States and expelling Western expatriate workers from the entirety of the Arabian Peninsula, something you'll recall Osama Bin Laden uttered verbatim some twenty years later," he mused.

Dr. Ibrahim added it took two full weeks for the rebels to finally surrender, accounts of which were full of gaps. Some said French commandos—hastily required to convert to Islam so they could enter holy ground—were used in the attack, while others said it was Pakistani Special Forces, presumably already Muslims. Maybe both. Others believed the Saudi National Guard lobbed grenades into crowded areas killing hostages and terrorists alike. There were also allegations of the use of gas against the insurgents. Regardless, all sides suffered heavy casualties—certainly in the hundreds killed and wounded, and many of the militants presumed escaped.

"Al-Qahtani, the proclaimed Mehdi, reportedly died in the mosque's recapture, which definitively put to rest his Messianic claims," Dr. Ibrahim editorialized. "Al-Otaybi was captured along with some seventy followers, and nearly all of them, certainly the males in the group, were tried and publicly beheaded. Their charges included violating the mosque's sanctity and that of the first month of the Islamic calendar (known in Arabic as *Muharram*); killing Muslims; disrupting prayers at the holy site; and 'erring in identifying the Mehdi', a crime I find amusing and ironic."

Dr. Ibrahim looked around the cafe to ensure no one else was following his account of these events. Abrams and Clayton inadvertently also looked around conspiratorially to ensure they remained in a bubbled conversation. "The Saudi response, unpredictably, was not to crack down on radicalism, but instead bolster the *mutawaeen*, or ultra-religious conservatives, the so-called 'religious police'. The King shuttered cinemas and music shops, banned photos and TV appearances of women, increased rather narrow-minded religious curriculum in school, and rolled back the social and progressive clock on Saudi Arabia a few centuries. With the death of my father, and the life sucked out of Jeddah, I decided to seek a better life for myself in Europe."

Abrams checked her watch, but indicated no desire to break up the meeting. She drained her coffee, and readjusted in her seat, crossing her legs while Dr. Ibrahim posited, "Also unpredictable, especially for our hapless American friends, is that you were blamed for this. You'll recall that only two weeks before the attack on the Grand Mosque, Ayatollah Khomeini whipped Iranian students into a frenzy that led to the sacking of the U.S. Embassy in Tehran and the capture of your diplomats and probably not "just a few" spies, I suppose. Khomeini was quick to point his finger at American imperialism and Zionism. Very convenient timing, I suppose again. In response, you're too young to recall, anti-American protests erupted all over the Muslim world, Turkey, Bangladesh, the UAE, and even in the Philippines. They burned your embassies in Pakistan and Libya! *And, protests erupted even among the Shia in Eastern Saudi Arabia!* Why? I'll get to this later."

Haley's head spun as he tried to put in chronological mental order these significant details of events he knew very little about, and never dreamed they might somehow connect or overlap. He glanced at Abrams for help, but she seemed just as perplexed as he. Dr. Ibrahim, thoroughly enjoying himself barreled on, "I'm not one to defend American missteps in the Arab world, but I've always thought it irrational to blame you for the attack on the Grand Mosque. I must give you a bye on that particular conspiracy," he jabbed.

"Speaking of conspiracies," he added, "I've long been puzzled by the coincidental timing of such major events in the Muslim world, often perpetrated by Sunni and Shia elements alike, who have largely been at odds since the founding of Islam some 1400 years ago. Sadly, very much akin to the European wars between Catholics and Protestants—all in the name of God or Allah."

"And," he continued, "per my earlier reference to Eastern Saudi Arabia . . . one might suppose that anti-American sentiment there in the aftermath of the alleged American-orchestrated Grand Mosque seizure would source from discontent over the astronomical wealth generated for U.S. and Saudi oil magnates. This wealth went to deep Sunni pockets, while Saudi Shiites remained isolated and neglected, even persecuted in their own country. Why else would the Shiites rail against the Americans? One must also consider, however, that Saudi Shiites were mostly allegiant to Najaf, Kerbala, in Iraq, or other Arab, Shia *marja'iyat*—or sources of religious doctrine, not Mecca. I'm sure that Tehran's new turbaned seat of power in 1979 was well aware of that dynamic, and therefore played a strong hand in inflaming tensions and trying to drive a wedge between the Sunni stronghold in Riyadh and Washington. Tehran has long known how to stir the historical and metaphorical Sunni-Shia pots and resents to this day that the Islamic conquest of the historical empires of Persia came at the hands of Bedouin riffraff who traversed the Arabian deserts."

Haley inhaled. Having studied Arabic, and read up on the Middle East, he prided himself on not being a complete ignoramus on Arab and Muslim world happenings. Similarly, Abrams, as a Middle East watcher for the department also read up on current events. Neither, however, had ever had received such an encapsulated mix of history, geopolitics, religion, and conspiracy as doled out by Dr. Ibrahim. Abrams sat in her chair, mouth slightly agape. She wasn't taking any more notes.

"Please forgive my long winded narrative. You can take a professor out of the classroom, but not the classroom out of the professor—or so goes a similar saying. Now I wish to bring to your attention how personal this matter is to me, and why I am very grateful for Paula's reaching out to me.

"As I mentioned before, I lived in Medina, Saudi Arabia at the time of the attack on the Grand Mosque and remember the developments well for two reasons. One, I recall being caught up in al-Otaybi's fervor. I never met him, but his followers at the local university in Medina tried to add me to his numbers. Al-Qahtani must have been quite charismatic because he drummed up full throttle support from idealists there, even to the point of their trying to undermine Riyadh's power and religious custodianship. But secondly, it's all clear in my mind because of the unexpected death of my father. He was mysteriously and fatally injured on November 20, 1979, dying just a few days following the attack. He was the reason I didn't join the al-Qahtani cult."

As a Palestinian driven out from his ancestral home in Beit Safafa, now in the West Bank," Dr. Ibrahim regaled, "my father recalled all too well the betrayals of the *Nakba* and the *Naksa,* so he harbored no particular affinity for any particular political or religious movement."

Haley interjected, "Paula, the *Nakba*, Arabic for catastrophe, dates back to 1948 and the loss of the Palestinian homeland to perceived European Jewish occupiers—backed, of course, in the eyes of most Arabs, by the U.S. government. The 1967 *Naksa,* or 'calamity,' commemorates Palestinian displacement after Israel's victorious "Six-Day War,' when it reversed multiple attacks from Egypt, Jordan, and Syria into one of the most impressive military wins in history. Meanwhile, generations of Palestinians still live in limbo, as refugees or stateless residents in Jordan, Gaza, Syria, Lebanon, or simply floating around Egypt, Europe, the United States and Canada, or the Gulf. Many of them still claim the 'right of return' to "Palestine," sadly, an impossible hope, for which no practical bureaucratic or legal framework exists."

Dr. Ibrahim responded, "All too true. Pragmatists like myself have simply moved on. We accept our reality and have determined to live more prosperously in the present and future. Alas, many of my countrymen cannot move forward and continue to dwell in past unresolved grievances. That said, I would give my right arm to return to the Beit Safafa of my childhood, surrounded by my family, eating our traditional foods, *hummus, mutabbel, wara' aineb*, grilled lamb, with Turkish coffee, most of which was appropriated by the "Europeans" who set up shop next door. But no one, and I mean no one, can prepare the world's best dessert, *kanafeh*, like my cousins from Nablus. Apologies. Please forgive me for waxing nostalgic."

Haley chuckled, having enjoyed this sweet pastry soaked in sugary syrups. "It's my fault for arranging this appointment so close to lunchtime. Our next meeting will have to be over *shwarma*."

"Agreed," Dr. Ibrahim smiled. "But back to the story. My father was equally and roundly embittered at the Israelis, the Europeans, the Americans, and even the Arabs, all of whom contributed to his forced exodus from our land of "milk and honey." As a result, despite being a well-established engineer, he was forced into indentured servitude in Medina, working as an accountant for the religious authority there. I last saw him alive the night he went for evening prayers at *Al-Masjid Al-Nabawi*, the mosque of and final resting place of our prophet Mohammed and his successors *Abu* [Father of] Bakr and Omar. Plus, the mosque maintains an empty tomb for the return of the Mehdi, or Jesus, so some of our Shia brethren believe. I'll bet you were not aware of that!"

Abrams retorted, "I'm Jewish, so I have no comment on Jesus' final resting place."

"I'm Christian, so it doesn't matter how many empty tombs people carve out for him," smiled Haley.

Dr. Ibrahim rolled his eyes in jest. "The same night the fracas began in Mecca, the police came to our house and informed us that our father had fallen down stairs at the mosque and suffered traumatic brain damage. Oddly, his injury was on the back of his head, an unlikely wound for someone who falls headlong down the stairs, no? We ran to the hospital to see him, but he was already nearly gone. My mother and I held his hand as he passed away, his last words a garble and confusing to this day, only *'sari'oohu'*— they stole him, or it. You know, Mr. Haley, Arabic doesn't have a pronoun for *it*, just feminine and masculine markers. To this day, I don't know whom or what was stolen. This mystery continues to cause me great pain. My father was a good man, and his death was untimely and unjust." Dr. Ibrahim paused and gathered himself.

"I apologize for getting sentimental," he adjusted himself in his seat. "I've never talked about this. Your mentioning of al-Qahtani and al-Otaybi has taken me back forty years in time, to memories long dormant and never reconciled."

Paula placed her hand on Dr. Ibrahim's arm, saying, "Please Dr. Ibrahim, we're sorry for bringing up difficult memories. Don't feel like you need to go on. You've already been very kind and generous with your time."

"No, the wounds are there, but I have a purpose for my story and wish to continue," he responded. "The police were intensely focused on the Grand Mosque seizure, so there was no proper investigation, and my father's death was ruled an accident. You can tell by my tone that I've never been satisfied with this. I've always known there was more to this story, but the only lead I've ever been able to find is that a young Iraqi employee at the *Al-Masjid Al-Nabawi*, prophet's tomb, named Ali Hussain al-Sadr disappeared on November 20, the same day as my father's injury. Not much was known about him, other than that he had a violent criminal record in Iraq prior to arriving in Mecca. Turns out he had only been in Saudi Arabia for a few months. Prior to that, his only known residence was in Neauphle-le-Château, France."

Haley was stunned to hear the name of Neauphle-le-Château brought up again. "I'm sorry, but what is the significance of this town, Neauphle-le-Château? Paula, you mentioned this earlier, when I spoke of the two Saudi/Yemeni applicants and their elderly, wealthy relative. You mentioned something about a famous villain being from there as well?"

Abrams nodded. "Yes, I did, but let me allow Dr. Ibrahim to convey the significance of this town; he'll have more historical context. Not only do we have your young visa applicants hailing from this town, along with their uncle/grandfather who happens to have a name connected to the fabled wouldbe Mehdi of Grand Mosque fame, but now the Iraqi potentially connected to Dr. Ibrahim's father's death also lived there? The coincidences are stacking up too mysteriously."

Dr. Ibrahim agreed, "Indeed, I too am puzzled by the intersections of relationships that seem to define this otherwise unremarkable French 'commune.' I admit I am enjoying the suspense and the look of anticipation on your face, but I must excuse myself for a restroom break. Let me suggest that you simply do a quick Google search to solve your mystery."

Haley, dying for the big reveal, got out his State Department issued iPhone, and typed in N-E-A-U-P-H-L-E, misspelling it a couple of times before getting it right. A number of links appeared, but given his resorting to Wikipedia's assistance in helping him craft college papers, he clicked on its first entry. The contributor to the Wikipedia site noted in very simple terms that the "commune" of Neauphle-le-Château "gained international fame" on October 8, 1978 when a house there was rented by a very famous Iranian exile, someone initially deported to Iraq by the Shah of Iran. This deportee took refuge among Iraq's Shia devotees in southern Iraq, and then moved to France where he presumably linked to international Shia spiritual, political, military, and financial backers. It's also where he plotted his triumphant return and takeover of Iran. His former house on the corner of Chevreuse Road and Jardins Path has long been destroyed, but downtown Tehran, to this day, boasts *"Nofel Loshato"* Street in commemoration of the city's importance as a former residence of Ayatollah Ruhollah Khomeini.

"You've got to be kidding me," exclaimed Haley.

There was a brief pause in the conversation, as Dr. Ibrahim returned and settled into his chair.

"So," pondered Haley, "you're saying that Khomeini, '*The Khomeini*,' the man who upended the Iranian establishment and replaced it with a bunch of revolutionaries for the last forty years, which have been stirring up hornet nests in Arab Sunni countries and wreaked havoc in creating a Shia crescent of capitals from Tehran to Baghdad, to Damascus, to Beirut, and down to Sanaa— all the while poking the U.S. government in the eye—is from the same French town of the grandchildren of the Grand Mosque "rampagers," and an Iraqi man who may have had something to do with your father's death? Seems like some very convenient coincidences."

"First off, you came to me with the al-Qahtani/al-Otaybi story. I don't pretend to understand these connections," replied Dr. Ibrahim. "And I'm not a superstitious man, and I don't believe in coincidences. Being a professor has taught me one must use logic to interpret one's own perspective of truth. I only point out that the Ayatollah did indeed live for a short period in Neauphle-le-Château, where most believe he planned his return to Tehran and his overthrow of the corrupt Shah regime. Given the timing of the attack and that Mr. Ali al-Sadr also spent time in Neauphle-le-Château, I've long suspected the two must have known each other somehow. Who knows, maybe the events in Tehran and Mecca were somehow connected?

What is certain and factual is that the Ayatollah had deep Iraqi and Arab connections. Once he was expelled from Iran to Iraq, he took refuge among prominent Shia families in Najaf and Kerbala, Iraq. If you know your Islamic history, and per our previous reference, you'll know that the world's Shia Arabs look to the *Iraqi* holy cities as their *"Marja'iyat,"* or religious bases. Not to *Qom*, a contrived holy city set up in Iran in the 1920s in an attempt to hold spiritual sway over *Shia* faithful. You'll have to remember the British administered Iraq in those days, virtually shutting the Persians out of their holiest cities and sources of spiritual enlightenment. Given unrest and the destabilization of Iraq in the post-World War I and II eras, Iran's Arab Shia population was compelled to turn inward and to political aspirants for religious inspiration."

Abrams excused herself for the bathroom. Haley needed to go, but didn't want to risk missing out on even a word of Dr. Ibrahim, who continued, "And did you know there are some six to seven million *Arab* Iranians? In fact, nearly all the people who live on both sides of the Persian Gulf, including on the Iranian side, are Arabs! It should be called the Arabian Gulf!

You'll also recall the name of the mysterious employee at the Prophet's Mosque in Medina, *Ali Hussain al-Sadr,* is likely an Arab Shia name, one well connected to Iraqi Arab Shia religious royalty. Yes, religious royalty. You'll likely know of another very famous al-Sadr, Moqtada, who has been a thorn in the American side in Iraq since 2003. Do you know the black turbaned or *Sayyid*, Moqtada, claims to be a descendent of Mohammed's grandsons, Hassan and Hussain? That I can't speak to, but his father and father-in-law were both very famous and respected Grand Ayatollahs of the Shia faith. His father Mohammed Mohammed Sadeq al-Sadr was brutally executed, along with Moqtada's two brothers, by Saddam Hussein in 1999 while putting down a Shia uprising. I've long suspected Saddam harbored intense hatred for the al-Sadr family, or Sadrists, since the Shia took Khomeini in and possibly helped him seize power next door in Iran."

Haley interjected, "This is hard to take in, but it sounds like you're saying that by taking in Khomeini, Iraqi Shia Arabs may have inadvertently spawned the Islamic Revolution in Iran, which led to the horrific eight-year Iran-Iraq War against their own people?"

"It does indeed sound like I'm saying that," Dr. Ibrahim grinned. "But I defer to the many British and American historians and political . . . what do you call them? Winks? . . . who find other convenient truths behind many of our Middle Eastern conflicts—you know, oil, water, good, evil."

"They're 'wonks'," Haley quipped but hurriedly continued so as to stay on historical vice political point. "So what is a *Twelver*?"

"You are quite astute, my friend, and this is indeed a tie-in to consider, one that pulls our Sunni, Shia, Arab, and Persian friends together. Khomeini and the other Ayatollahs, and for that reason, most Shia around the world, identify as Twelvers. That is to say they believe in twelve divinely ordained leaders, much like how Issa al-Messih—your Jesus the Messiah—had twelve disciples, no? In Shia Islam, however, most weren't necessarily contemporaries; they succeeded each other in parallel leadership to that of Sunni Islam's political and often secular caliphates. After Mohammed came Ali, Hassan, Hussain, and here is where it becomes tricky, but then, if I recall from my 'Friday School,' *al-Sajjad, al-Baqir, al-Sadiq, al-Kadhim, al-Ridha, al-Taqi, al-Naqi,* and *al-Askari,*" he said counting on his fingers. "And then, the twelfth in line of succession was meant to be—"

"The Mehdi, or the Messiah," exclaimed Haley.

"*Bilthabit!*" Dr. Ibrahim pointed out. "Exactly! The last Imam, according to our Shia brethren, lives in *ghaibah*, or absence. I'm sure there's a more theological word for it, but essentially, most believe this Mehdi, or Messiah, was born then disappeared for some reason but will return to usher in peace, justice, new world order . . . you know, very much what you Christians believe about the second coming of your *Messih*. In fact, some theologians believe the Islamic *Mehdi* and Jesus are one in the same. You know we don't believe Jesus died on the cross, right?"

"Yes, I understand Islam teaches Jesus was never tortured, crucified, and executed. Those happenings and the resurrection are all pretty unavoidable pillars of our faith. Your belief is there was some type of body swap, no? The real *Issa* was whisked away in place of some sap who unwittingly bore all the hatred the Romans and Jews, or for that matter the sins of the world, could throw at him?" asked Haley.

"I wouldn't put it in those terms, but essentially, yes," said Dr. Ibrahim. "We couldn't have our greatest prophet, even above Mohammed, brutally tortured and executed like a common criminal. But let's leave theology aside and move back to superstition and conspiracy. Your Mr. al-Qahtani, a Sunni Muslim who led a cult that believed he was the Messiah, laid siege to Islam's holiest site only a few months after the Twelver cultists seized power in Iran, one of the world's ancient empires, with the potential backing by custodians of the holiest Shia sites in Iraq," surmised Dr. Ibrahim.

"And so the story ends. Even if there was anything beyond these tenuous connections, this fascinating tapestry unravels with al-Qahtani's death back in 1979. And to put the final nail in his coffin, al-Otaybi was beheaded publicly in 1980. Fascinating story, but one with finality," sighed Haley.

"I wouldn't be so sure about that," gestured Dr. Ibrahim. "What if Khomeini's grand scheme wasn't the Grand Mosque in Mecca after all? What if he sought something more powerful than just conspiring with al-Otaybi and al-Qahtani in grabbing Sunni Islam by the throat and making silly demands about Western intrusion on Islamic lands? What if he sought to unite the whole Umma [global Islamic community] of Islam in one glorious revival? I would caution you that while American leadership tends to suffer from attention deficit disorder, we in the Arab world remember everything and can wait forever."

"I'm not following you," whispered Haley.

"Please, let me keep my suspicions to myself for now, as they are quite irrational, but might I ask that you research through your intelligence and diplomatic archives to see if the Americans or French might know what it was that was stolen from Medina the night of my father's fatal accident?" implored a now observably anxious Dr. Ibrahim. "Meanwhile, I'll try to contact a distant relative who also lived in Medina at the time."

Part II

Chapter 7

U.S. Embassy Paris. A few days later.

"He's a nut job!" screamed Political Counselor Ellen Scrivens at both Abrams and Haley after they attempted to convey some of the more salient details of their meeting with Dr. Ibrahim.

Haley immediately regretted not making an appointment. Scrivens seemed the type who didn't welcome new developments or surprises. Haley imagined that as a child in kindergarten, her crayon drawings must have been well ordered, color coordinated, and always in the lines. Haley remembered his mother telling him he used to tear the coloring pages out of the book to make airplanes; clearly, he and Scrivens approached tasks from different perspectives. In fact, they hardly covered the al-Qahtani/al-Otaybi visa interviews before Scrivens interjected, "Why are you wasting my time with this nonsense? Have you never heard of coincidence? There are hundreds of thousands of Yemenis here in France, and I can't have my political officer following up in consular interviews and, with respect, Clayton, I don't want a vice consul playing political officer. If you wanted to do political work, you should have bid on a political job."

Scrivens turned to Abrams. "Paula, I don't mind if you meet with your professor friend for background and for relevant political reporting, but let's please focus on the Arab diaspora community in France or Arab League issues and forget this nonsense." Addressing them both again, she continued, "And, no, I won't clear on a cable, so please don't ask me if you can write this up. I don't want to hear anything further about this, OK?" she said while issuing a shooing gesture, inviting them to depart her office.

Haley and Abrams left her office and instinctively went their separate ways, both ashamed and indignant over what they perceived as an unjust jump to conclusions. For Haley, it wasn't as big a deal since he didn't have to work with Scrivens. He felt bad for Abrams, though, as this ordeal was clearly an embarrassment to her and had introduced tension in their working relationship.

***

An hour later, and back on his home turf, the consular section, Haley sought an ally in his boss, the consul, Steven Jeffries. He thought Jeffries would agree something simply wasn't right with this case and that the visa applications of al-Qahtani and al-Otaybi, and the elder Mr. al-Qahtani deserved more scrutiny. Haley struggled with making a rational recommendation on the disposition of the matter, but believed in his gut that something simply wasn't right.

He heard from Jeffries a message similar to that of Scrivens, albeit less caustic, "Let's just adjudicate the visas. Are these folks qualified for visas or not? We don't have time to sleuth every NIV case that comes along. Make the call. If you have any doubts, submit the files for administrative processing, and let the

Washington experts make the call. Remember, the burden for justifying a reason for travel is on the traveler, not on you. We have people in Washington who look into this, right?"

It was clear in Haley's mind, that no, people in Washington would not be able to put the various puzzle pieces together—certainly not the folks who sat in soulless offices rummaging through hundreds of visa clearance requests a day, as he perceived the process.

***

Haley re-submerged into his small desk in the consular cubicle farm and disobediently brought up on his desktop computer the electronic files on al-Qahtani and al-Otaybi, thumbing through his notes annotated in the Consular Affairs Bureau visa application software. The applicants were still in "administrative processing," code for undergoing interagency review, so he knew he likely had a few weeks before he would have to make a decision on issuance. He found it hard to stay focused, however. He had hundreds of other cases in the works and could not afford to spend time on these particular files. He felt ashamed and burned by his encounters with both Scrivens and his boss. He got along with Jeffries but recognized Jeffries would, nine times out of ten, like water, take the path of least resistance. To him, it was simply a matter of process over product.

Scrivens, according to an equally frustrated Abrams later in the day, operated with typical "inside-the-box" thinking, which defined so many in the State Department—averse to supporting "push the envelope" initiatives. Haley admitted his idealism, and in this case his curiosity, was over-amped but "it stuck in his craw"—as his Dad used to say—to simply leave this matter alone.

In this moment of despondent reflection, Haley thought back to what he perceived as a very unremarkable childhood and poor preparation for the sophistication of implementing U.S. foreign policy and dealing with big personalities like Scrivens. Walhalla, South Carolina is a small town not far from the North Carolina/South Carolina border, a pleasant enough place, which looked up at the Blue Ridge Mountains. He remembered his summers picking and shucking corn, bailing and hauling hay, fishing, and eating boiled peanuts and the world's best hickory smoked pork barbecue—God's gift to mankind, or at least to the gentiles. He also remembered how testy folks could be when discussing vinegar- versus mustard- versus ketchup-based barbecue sauces.

His time in college, the military, and the State Department had taken some of the twang out of his accent, giving him more cosmopolitan airs when back home. He grinned as he recalled his last trip to Walhalla when he ventured out shopping at a local flea market with his mother:

"Hey, hwhar you from?" queried the vendor in response to his greeting, which he must have enunciated correctly, triggering her probe. She was a young woman and toted one kid on her hip, had another in a stroller, and yet another tethered with twine to a booth. She carried herself with the resigned confidence of one proud of her right to have made poor choices in life and with matching esteem in her biological prowess in producing more progeny than she could afford. Haley guesstimated she was probably still shy of twenty years old and wondered at how generous her contributions had been to Walhalla's growing meth problem. Her ample curves distorted the images on her t-shirt devoted to NASCAR's Dale

Earnhardt, Jr. She tied her straight and bleach blond hair up in a ponytail, which whipped around considerably with her animated speech and gestures.

"I'm from right here. I grew up here in Walhalla." Haley responded.

"No you ain't. Yo-ain't from round heres. Hwhar you from, for real?" She pressed.

"I tell you, I'm from here. I grew up in north Walhalla, just off Pickens Highway. In fact, my father . . . apologies, 'diddy,' is a pastor in one of the churches over there . . . I mean, up yonder." He explained.

"You shore? Yo-unt tawk 'ike us!" She continued to doubt.

"I sure used to could," he grinned.

The recall of this particular encounter still brought a smile to his face. That and the juxtaposition of that episode with his current life. Haley was a long way from his idyllic childhood and ease that comes with a slower pace of life, and he marveled at how he was now surrounded by cerebral colleagues with master's degrees from Ivy League schools, all seemingly born and bred for the highbrow life of a diplomat. He doubted any of them hailed from a place like Walhalla, referred to jokingly by local denizens as "Hogwaller," despite its clear connection to Scandinavian paradise.

Haley glanced at his phone, seeing a message from Dr. Ibrahim asking to meet again. Abrams was heading out on annual leave soon and skittish about reigniting the ire of both Scrivens and Jeffries, so Haley knew better than to try to set up another meeting right away. "I'll wait until Paula gets back," he thought, and sent a message through WhatsApp telling Dr. Ibrahim that he was unable to meet due to pressing work concerns. He hated putting off the kind professor but believed he had no other option. The professor's response was gracious, but he seemed disappointed.

Haley returned to the files. The applications for the two young men and the older gentleman were in order. Reviewing his notes from the interview with the younger men, the purpose of travel was to see a geneticist at the Mayo Clinic. The documents in support of the file included a referral, of sorts, for the older gentleman to see one of the Mayo Clinic's many research scientists, Farhad Hassan, PhD. Jeffries would be highly annoyed Haley was spending this amount of time on this one case, but he couldn't resist Googling Dr. Hassan.

***

It took Haley a few minutes to find a brief bio on Farhad Hassan PhD, and then only after bouncing from link to link on the Mayo Clinic's website. The bio, accompanied by a photograph of a man in his late sixties or seventies included the following:

Farhad Hassan, PhD
Education
1998 Research Fellow Roslin Institute, University of Edinburgh, Scotland
1990 Research Fellow, Mayo Clinic in Rochester
1984 PhD, Genetic Research, Iranian Research Organization for Science and Technology, Tehran
1978 MS, Genetics, Institut Pasteur, France

In addition, the link indicated Dr. Hassan published a couple of papers on somatic cell nuclear transfer, something Haley knew nothing about. Given the unrest in the Middle East over the last hundred years, it was not odd that someone with talent and ambition would leave home and follow opportunities in the west to advance personal aims, so to Haley, Dr. Hassan's posting appeared unremarkable, if not bare compared to that of his colleagues.

Maybe Jeffries and Scrivens were right. Haley needed to stop sleuthing and simply adjudicate the case and move on.

Chapter 8

After a few weeks, however, the issue resurfaced. The consular inquiries on both Abdullah Mohammed Juhayman al-Otaybi and Ali Mehdi Mohammed Abdullah al-Qahtani came back, denoting no derogatory information, so Haley was clear to issue their visas. He asked his staff to call them back to the embassy to submit their passports for visa issuance. He noticed in his consular software that their elderly relative, Mr. Mohammed Abdullah al-Qahtani, scheduled his interview for later in the week.

Haley previewed Mr. al-Qahtani's application, which of course included variant spellings of the names Haley had on record. He took note of the bio information on the application and matched it with that on his Yemeni passport. The gentleman was reportedly born January 1, 1935 in Medina, Saudi Arabia. Haley had adjudicated enough visas to know that a January 1 birthday more often than not denoted a lack of knowledge of the real birthday, especially among developing countries or regions with poor public record keeping. "Travel to Minnesota seeking medical consultation" was indicated as the purpose of travel. The applicant listed an intended stay of two weeks with plans to stay in a nearby luxury hotel, to be booked upon visa issuance. It all checked out—nothing extraordinary, especially for travelers with means.

Out of curiosity, he googled the name Mohammed Abdullah al-Qahtani once again, annoyed with himself for his growing obsession. He skimmed through multiple online Wikipedia pages and articles devoted to Mr. al-Qahtani, some with grainy black and white photos of a dirty, bedraggled, and bearded young man with curly locks. Photos of the supposed assailant of the Grand Mosque showed a protruding incisor and unmistakably light colored eyes, even as depicted in death.

"Enough," demanded Haley of himself. He chided himself for getting carried away in the gruesome details of an irrelevant event four decades prior. He would interview tomorrow an applicant who coincidentally shared the name of a cult leader in the past. Nothing more, nothing less.

***

The following day, upon hearing his number called, Mr. al-Qahtani approached the window, accompanied by his younger relatives, whose visas had been issued and emplaced in their Yemeni passports. "Good morning, gentlemen," greeted Haley, "it's good to see you again." Haley then turned to Mr. al-Qahtani. "And, *sabah al-khair [Good morning]* sir. Welcome to the United States Embassy."

Mr. al-Qahtani, appearing in his mid-seventies, or possibly in his eighties, wore the traditional *khaleeji* Gulf garb, the white *thobe [robe]* and *ghutra [head scarf]*, with black *egal [rope]* keeping his head scarf in place. He stood tall, regal even, and thin with an impressively long, yet unkempt gray beard. He flashed a smile, one of acknowledgement and courtesy but not necessarily extending friendship. His left incisors were noticeably more prominent. His honey-colored eyes signaled sharpness and determined leadership qualities. He was clearly in charge of his faculties and that of his subjects, the two younger gentlemen. In a quick glance, Haley thought he detected a lack of fingernails on two of the gentleman's fingers. He also noticed a faded, but still prominent, red birthmark on his face.

Haley addressed the young men, "Please, if you don't mind, I'll need you to take your seat in the waiting room while I speak directly to Mr. al-Qahtani."

Ali and Abdullah were clearly unhappy with this directive but acquiesced immediately upon a look from their senior.

"Mr. al-Qahtani, *tahki inkleezia? Hal bihaja ila mutarjim? [Do you speak English? Do you need a translator?]*" Queried Haley, pleased to be able to brush off his rapidly deteriorating Arabic.

"I speak English too good. I no need translator." Al-Qahtani replied in a crisp, accented tone.

"Very well, sir. With your permission, we'll start the interview. This should take no more than three or four minutes. For starters, let me confirm that you are who you say you are—Mr. Mohammed Abdullah al-Qahtani, Yemeni national and resident of France, correct?"

"Yes. I am live in Paris more than thirty years."

"Sir, what do you do for a living?"

"I'm teach Arabic language and Islam religion to Arab Muslims immigrants to Paris."

"How do you account for your very substantial bank account?"

"I'm very rich. Allah bless me. My family rich for long time. Strong invest."

"What types of investments?"

"Islamic banks. Projects. Mosques. Business. I have experts manage invests."

"They seem to have done very well on your behalf. I congratulate you."

"You most welcome."

"What is the purpose of your travel?"

"I go Mahyoo. In Rochester Amedika. I get treatment."

"What type of treatment? And is this your first travel to the United States?"

"I have consultation with doctor. For *sara'*. Arabic word. Shake disease."

"Sir, can you please spell this word for me in Arabic? I'll look it up after the interview."

"*Saad-ra-'ain*," he spelled out three Arabic letters.

"Thank you, and again, is this your first travel to the United States?"

"First time. No travel to Amedika."

"OK, and per your application, I understand you will consult with a Dr. Farhad Hassan?"

"Dr. Farhad."

"Have you seen him before, and why this person?"

"Dr. Farhad good doctor. He expert in *sara'*."

"Have you seen him before?"

"First time travel to Mahyoo."

"Has Dr. Farhad traveled to Paris?"

"Dr. Farhad too famous. Travel to many countries—France, Amedika, many country."

"Per his bio, he's an American citizen originally from Iran."

"Many people from Iran."

"How long will you stay in Rochester?"

"I'm stay in Four Seasons hotel."

"For how long?"

"Two weeks, in sha allah."

"What will your appointments with Dr. Farhad entail?

"I'm no understand."

"What treatment from Dr. Farhad will you get?"

"Only opinion. No surgery. No medicine."

"When was the last time you were in Saudi Arabia?"

"I'm travel on Hajj and Umrah to Mecca and Medina."

"When did you travel?"

"Many times."

"When were you last in Yemen?"

"My family in France with me. I stay in France."

"Did you know Juhayman al-Otaybi?"

Al-Qahtani's eyes flared briefly. "I'm know too many al-Otaybi family. Very big tribe. Many thousands al-Otaybi tribe."

Chapter 9

"Welcome back, Paula. Good to see you," said Haley to Abrams upon her first day back in the office after her R&R. He gave her no time to answer. "So I interviewed Mohammed al-Qahtani."

"Really? How'd it go?" she asked.

"Frustrating. He played me the whole time," lamented Haley.

"How do you mean?"

Haley relayed the high and lowlights of the brief encounter, zooming in on how evasive al-Qahtani was during the interview. "I should have brought up a translator, but had I done that, I wouldn't have been able to raise some of the questions I did. I really botched it, though, and got nothing from him. The bottom line is he was more than qualified for the visa anyway. I had no grounds or desire to refuse him, but I had really hoped to learn more about his consultation and his connection to Saudi Arabia and Yemen. Turns out he has epilepsy; I had to look it up in my Hans Wehr Arabic dictionary to confirm. I also asked him about Juhayman al-Otaybi."

"What?" Abrams was incredulous. "Why would you do that? You don't really think he has any connection to anything that took place back in 1979, do you? Certainly, the Saudis wouldn't let this guy live out his life in peace here in France if there was really any connection to the attack on the Grand Mosque."

"I know, but he frustrated me. He had a ready-made non-answer to every question I raised. It's like he knew I would issue a visa no matter what, and he was simply humoring me by participating in the interview. Plus, I've got Scrivens in my head right now. I've spent way too much time on this case. By the way, did you hear Dr. Ibrahim is trying to meet with us again?"

"I did. Let me settle in and get caught up, and then I'll reach out to him. I better do this alone, however, so as not to get you in more trouble with Scrivens and Jeffries. I'd hate for them to complain about you to the Front Office."

Haley sighed. "Yeah. That's probably wise. Keep me posted?"

"Sure thing," said Abrams, adding "so when does al-Qahtani travel?"

"Soon," said Haley. "I need to get clearance to issue from Washington, but that won't take more than a couple of days or so."

***

"Yes, I'm trying to reach Dr. Farhad Hassan, please," queried Haley.

"I am Dr. Hassan. Who is this?" responded an accented, irritated voice. Haley immediately regretted the call. He had found Dr. Hassan's contact details on the Mayo Clinic website, and on impulse, dialed his number. In the awkward pause, he pondered whether to hang up, lie, or commit to this ill-directed course of action. He chose the latter.

"Sir, my name is Clayton Haley, and I am a vice consul at the U.S. Embassy in Paris, France. I'm calling to follow-up on a medical appointment I believe you have scheduled with a Mr. Mohammed Abdullah al-Qahtani." Haley, though with misgivings about the call, knew he was in his right to make it. In fact, given the frequency of fraud committed at the consular window, he and his colleagues often resorted to internet searches and phone calls to verify the veracity of conferences and workshops, the existence of certain educational establishments, and other bona fides to support claims made by applicants.

"I find it highly unusual to be contacted by the U.S. government about a potential patient. I must invoke doctor-patient confidentiality," claimed Dr. Hassan.

"Of course," said Haley. "I fully understand. My purpose in calling is simply to verify that you do have an appointment with Mr. al-Qahtani. Pending issuance of his visa, it would be helpful if you could confirm you will see him next month. He mentioned in my interview he is consulting with you regarding epilepsy?"

Dr. Hassan pressed back. "Again, I find this line of query very disconcerting and inappropriate, Mr. Haley. I will not discuss with you any potential medical issues I may or may not have with patients." He hung up abruptly.

"That was harsh," thought Haley. "I get the whole confidentiality concern, but he could have at least confirmed the appointment." Still, though, the guy was kind of right. The bottom line was the purpose of travel was clearly medical, as denoted in a letter from the Mayo Clinic confirming an open-ended consultation. It wasn't in Haley's remit to determine the nature of the treatment, only to confirm that he could afford it and would come back to Paris. Haley perused the file one more time. Al-Qahtani's clearance came in from Washington, so there was no reason to hold issuance up any longer.

"Still—" he pondered, "why is al-Qahtani seeking epilepsy care in the United States from an Iranian doctor, who specialized in . . . what was it?" Haley thumbed through his notes on Dr. Farhad, who specialized in *somatic . . . cell . . . nuclear . . . transfer*, he read slowly, trying to compel his mind to make sense of these words. "Why did I study humanities?" he groaned, having no idea what this meant. "Oh well, back to the internet," he mused.

Turns out per a couple of online scientific articles that Dr. Hassan's expertise was in the transference of a nucleus of an adult cell into that of an *oocyte*, or unfertilized and developing egg cell with no nucleus. Not understanding the process, Haley could only surmise this created some type of hybrid cell, which he learned began dividing when exposed to electric shock. This process formed another term unfamiliar to Haley, a *blastocyst*, which was then implanted into a surrogate mother. "This is mind-numbing," complained Haley, "maybe ol' Farhad is just a lab dweeb with no social skills." Haley was tempted to close the science tab and check college football scores instead, but an article with less scientific jargon caught his eye.

The most famous byproduct of this so-called somatic cell nuclear transfer was a sheep named Dolly back in the nineties. Haley was young but remembered this as kind of a big deal, and it certainly achieved widespread media attention. Again, the technical details of this cell transference were lost on Haley and his political science background, but amusingly, he learned the donor cells for the process were taken from a sheep's mammary glands, thus the eponymous homage paid to Dolly Parton and her own generous scientific endowments. "Seems the Scottish scientists had a juvenile sense of humor. Are there no famous buxom Scottish women?" mused Haley.

"But why would al-Qahtani consult with a clone specialist about his epilepsy?" wondered Haley.

***

The following day found Haley at his desk trying to clear files from his morning interviews. Jeffries leaned over the thin partition that separated Haley's cubicle from that of his teammates, startling him. "So, I see you issued the visa for your Kay-tani pal. I suppose his story checked out? Off for medical treatment at the Mayo Clinic?"

"Yep. His case was indeed straightforward. No reasonable grounds for 214b or other refusal, and he has strong economic and social ties to this consular district. All in all, an easy issuance. The story still bothers me, though," said Haley, still mystified by the odd nature of the case. He didn't mention to Jeffries the abrupt call with Dr. Hassan.

"Of course it does, but what can you do about it? We're charged with letting good folks into the States and keeping the bad ones out. It's a simple formula," explained Jeffries.

"Yep. All in all, it was an easy issuance. He and his nephews won't overstay and won't be a public charge. They have the requisite ties to our consular district here in Paris, so it's nice to put his case to rest," Haley responded, while wondering if he was actually trying to convince Jeffries or himself.

Chapter 10

"Please usher my guest in and cancel all my afternoon appointments," Dr. Hassan ordered the receptionist in his office suite. "And please prepare the special Arabic coffee brew I ordered recently from Detroit."

The rather plump but efficient receptionist complied, but the pace in which she did so suggested some annoyance at her rather needy and exceptionally nervous boss.

"*Ahlan. Ahlan wa sahlan, sidi [Greetings, sir]*. I am so pleased to see you," Dr. Hassan greeted his guest at the door and, holding his hand tightly, led him into his spacious and opulent office in an otherwise indistinguishable wing at the Mayo Clinic.

"*Ahlan fiik.* I am not stay long."

"Please, you must have coffee. And dates. I do not have proper dates from the Kingdom but have grown partial to the dates from California. The infidels succeed in growing that which has fed our ancestors for centuries."

The guest ignored him. "Please give update."

Dr. Hassan nervously sputtered details of his recent trip to Amman and his quiet meeting with Dr. Abdulaziz al-Onezi. "Dr. al-Onezi is very skilled and has much expertise. He is among the many accomplished doctors who fled Iraq during the American devastation. Jordanians recognize his talent, which helps them have more babies than they need. You know, for some odd reason, Jordan has one of the best IVF practices in all of the Middle East. Plus, they welcome the Iraqis like Dr. al-Onezi, who is boarded by the United States, Canada, and European medical systems. As you know, when you pointed him out to me, he had lost his wife to Saddam Hussein and his only son to the Americans."

"Yes. He has too much pain. I give him purpose." The guest stopped suddenly, and his light brown eyes looked with disapproval upon the entry into the office of the receptionist.

Noticing the disdain, Dr. Hassan abruptly intercepted the coffee pot and cups clumsily carried by the receptionist. Clearly, she was unfamiliar with and ill-equipped by gender on how to properly serve the traditional Bedouin repast. Seeing that she was being relieved of having to perform the menial tea service, however, she gratefully, yet haughtily sauntered out of the room, closing the door. Dr. Hassan poured the coffee, which was received with a quick sip, and then a shake of the cup to indicate refreshments were over.

"Is al-Onezi ready to travel?" asked the guest.

"Yes, of course. He only awaits instructions. When and where shall I tell him?"

"You tell him nothing, only be ready. I will communicate him."

"Na'am sidi. Of course. We are both ready. I have prepared my notes. He has all of my research, and I have detailed for him all he needs. I am confident we are ready to succeed."

"I am pleased. All must perfect. Is he ready take on task? Are you? We provide many volunteers for experiment. Some fail. Some hurt. Maybe this *again-ist* doctor promise?"

"If you mean the Hippocratic Oath we swore, I can assure you what we are about to embark on is of such vital importance to humanity, it exceeds all positive intentions required by our oaths to western medical practices."

"I am pleased," the guest repeated. "Before I leave, I need paper from you for *sara'*. My shake very bad at nights, sometime."

"Of course, it would be my pleasure. Many drugs are available that help reduce epileptic seizures and side effects."

"*Alf shukur [one thousand thanks]*," said the guest, signaling an end to the conversation.

Seeing the impending conclusion to the meeting, Dr. Hassan volleyed, "Did you, per chance, have difficulties securing a visa?" He explained a call from one U.S. embassy official *Clifton Harley*, not quite remembering the name correctly. "It was highly unusual for him to reach out to me directly, and I told him very clearly I would not violate doctor-patient confidentiality. And to ensure he pursues this no further, I contacted my congressman's office to report this gross misuse of power."

The guest's eyes flashed anger. "Why bring attention? I have visa. No need for more work. You make no decision without consult me. *Fahemtani [Do you understand me]*?"

"Yes. Yes, of course. I fully understand. I only thought to squelch this line of questioning, to play the American congressional system against the American government. It's how we divide them."

"I am decide how we divide them. I will divide them too much. I will look after this Mr. Clifton Harley." Al-Qahtani turned abruptly to the door without further acknowledgement.

Chapter 11

"You asked to see me up here?" Haley asked Abrams upon entering the space in which she worked. She was surrounded by her colleagues in a cubicle farm. The furniture layout afforded just enough community to engage her neighbors and just enough privacy to get her work done. Tacked to the partitions in her work area were pictures of an elderly couple, one of her with a former secretary of state, and of Abrams in various backdrops of lakes, mountains, and even a desert, all of which included a tall, dark haired man draped over her. Also stuck to her wall were simple crayon drawings.

"Yes, but first, let me introduce you to my husband, Adam," she replied, gesturing at the guy in the pictures. "Sadly, he doesn't get here often, but every chance we get, we Chunnel back and forth from London and Paris to see each other."

"I'm sorry you couldn't find work together in the same city. That must be tough. At least you have his artwork to keep you company and let you know he's thinking of you. By the way, is that a bear or a rather large toe in that drawing?" nodded Haley at one of the particularly incoherent scribbles.

"That is actually a self-portrait, done by my niece. I think she's quite talented. I'll bet you weren't much of an artist when you were three," she said, rolling her eyes. "Everyone's an art critic."

"Notwithstanding one of the ugliest masterpieces I've seen, you have a lovely family. Mom and Dad, I suppose?" he responded, touching the corner of the picture with the elderly couple.

"Yep. They're amazing. They've always supported me. It was nice seeing them these last few weeks while I was on leave. And by the way, before I left on R&R, I asked the desk to review archives of cables written in 1979 and 1980 to see if there were reports about the Grand Mosque seizure that would shed light on what Dr. Ibrahim shared with us."

Haley's interest in Paula's family waned as he focused on her update.

"I've printed off copies of what they sent me, all of which have been declassified now anyway. You're welcome to review all of this here in my office, but I think you'll come to the same conclusion as me—NSTR, as our military colleagues say, *nothing significant to report*. The files I've read, many of which were drafted as letters from the ambassador to the secretary of state, indicated chaos reigned supreme in Mecca during the seizure. Our people then, and later, were unable to determine the number of people killed and who all did the killing. My take is that the episode was so embarrassing the Saudis chose to move past it as quickly as possible. Thus the rash of beheadings in early 1980. All those in the al-Qahtani cult died at the hands of Saudi government forces, either upon retaking the site or in public executions. I know you still think there is more to the story, but at this point I believe you've been handed a platter of coincidences, albeit very interesting ones. It was fun while it lasted. I'll circle back with Dr. Ibrahim to see what he was trying to meet about but otherwise believe we've exhausted this story."

"Fair enough," replied Haley, as he started thumbing through the old State accounts of the 1979 events. These cables were essentially PDF photographs of the original cables, many filled with geographic tags and codes to ensure delivery to the correct interagency offices. In fact, nearly a third of the individual cables was taken up with classification markers, caveats, addressees, and other boilerplate information. Paula was right, he mused, after perusing the papers. The accounts of the event tracked largely with what he had already learned. Nothing he saw in any of the cables corroborated any mystery inferred by Dr. Ibrahim. There was certainly no mention of Medina, other than indications that many of the cult followers had earlier been enrolled in the university there.

He glanced back at the niece's self-portrait on the wall and hoped the kid's talent and looks would improve as she got older.

Chapter 12

Ambassadorial Residence, Paris, France, July 4.

"Mr. Haley, first, I congratulate you on your national day celebration, one I think you owe somewhat to your current French hosts," posited Dr. Ibrahim. "And, two, have you been avoiding me? I have an update for you."

"Dr. Ibrahim, it is so nice to see you. And you honor us by joining in on our July 4th party. I'm so glad you accepted our invitation. I'm a bit harried now as it's a working event for me, but I look forward to having a pull aside with you later to catch up," said Haley.

Haley made his hurried departure, regretting the brushoff, but he legitimately had a number of responsibilities in pushing and pulling guests onto the beautifully manicured lawns of the ambassador's residence. It was unusually hot, compounded by the requirement to be in full business attire. "Off to the dry cleaners this weekend," thought Haley as he reflected on how rumpled and sweaty his best suit was getting. Still, though, better than last year. His colleagues had explained to him the ambassador had chosen a uniquely American theme for the event, one which required the embassy staff to wear blue jeans, western shirts, ridiculous straw cowboy hats, and bolos. Bolos? To his knowledge, even Texans didn't wear bolos. That and serving hotdogs and hamburgers to the hundreds of French guests expecting more high-brow culinary delights likely made most of them regret General Lafayette's support to the early American revolutionaries.

It was well past his shift as a greeter, and requisite mingling, sampling the food and wine fare, and enjoying the music, before he could track down Dr. Ibrahim.

"Dr. Ibrahim, I am very sorry we haven't been able to connect since our last conversation. It's good to see you again," offered Haley, as they sidled up to trays serving what was advertised as "Tastes of New Orleans." Dr. Ibrahim politely declined offers of jambalaya, not knowing what it was or if it had pork in it.

"Anyway, I have a few moments now," Haley justified. "What are your updates?"

"Nothing you might find astounding, and frankly, a bit more on the conspiratorial side, but an update, nonetheless," replied Dr. Ibrahim. I followed up with my relative who lived in Medina at the time of my father. He and I are about the same age, and like me, he was susceptible to the charms of Mr. al-Qahtani, even to the point in helping out, to a certain extent, but never fully embracing the movement.

"My cousin refused to tell me this on the phone, insisting only that we meet in person. He traveled to Paris a few weeks ago for just such a discussion. He told me that about the time of the events in Mecca, he was posted by al-Qahtani's lieutenants on the outskirts of Medina to oversee the transfer of some package. He could not reveal the contents of the package but said in late November, he witnessed a group of young men carrying a box about two meters long, one meter wide, and one meter tall, covered in black cloth with ornate, gold trim. They transferred the box to an ambulance driven by a small team of middle-aged men, whom he described as laboratory officials or scientists. The ambulance drove away. The men who arrived from Medina and who delivered the box told him if he ever spoke a single word of this encounter, they would kill him and his family. Until he admitted this to me, he said he had never breathed even the slightest word about this. And two other things he mentioned: The men from Medina, he said, were wearing Saudi National Guard uniforms. The men in the ambulance, he added, spoke Farsi."

Dr. Ibrahim was right. This was a useless update. Besides, al-Qahtani and his companions had their visas and would be traveling to the United States soon—and perhaps were there already. Case closed.

***

Pascale Henri, the office management assistant, posted an update on Haley's Outlook calendar for him to meet with Embassy Deputy Chief of Mission (DCM) Andrew Stephens later in the day.

"Pascale, what is this appointment about?" asked Haley upon strolling over to her desk.

Henri responded in clear, but slightly French-laced tones, "I'm not sure. I was contacted by the DCM's office management specialist who simply asked that you meet him at 1300 today."

Haley was curious but imagined this related to his activities as a first and second tour officer and ongoing mentoring provided by the DCM. Given the hundreds of employees at the embassy, he did not know the DCM well but understood from his colleagues that he took mentoring seriously and he was invested in the career development for the next generation of diplomatic leaders.

Haley sat outside the Front Office at 1255, awaiting word from the DCM's OMS for him to see Andrew Stephens. Stephens was a senior, career FSO, and with his high-level posting to Paris, a shoe-in for an ambassadorship at his next assignment. According to rumor intelligence, or RUMINT, a vital information channel in the State Department, Stephens was looking to return to NEA, or the Near Eastern Asia Bureau. In addition to key European posts, he reportedly cut his teeth in Francophone Middle East assignments in Beirut and Tunis, including during the Cedar Revolution in Lebanon, and then the Arab Spring as it launched in Tunisia. He also started his tenure in Paris the first week of the violence pursuant to the attack on the Charlie Hebdo magazine offices. "Note to self," thought Haley, "don't follow this guy around."

The OMS showed him into Stephens' office around 1315. Stephens greeted Haley with an apology. "I'm sorry to keep you waiting, Clayton. The Ops Center, which monitors world events, pinged me for a comment regarding France's take on our trade policy. Reuters posted an article suggesting the French president was very critical of our imposing tariffs on French goods."

"No problem," stated Haley, impressed and now more acutely aware that so much of the embassy operations functioned beyond the consular purview. "I appreciate your taking the time to see me." He took a brief second to scan the room, which in Haley's perception exuded an efficient executive vibe. There were no pictures of Stephens' family and very few eclectic momentos one would find in the offices of diplomats who had served in numerous countries.

"Of course. I'm doubly sorry we haven't been able to connect much since you arrived. I have an engagement outside the building at 1400 so will need to jump right into our chat, if you don't mind. I wanted to flag for you that we received a congressional inquiry sparked by your actions."

Horrified, Haley suddenly realized this was not a mentoring session. "A congressional?" He had dealt with a handful of these since his arrival to consular work. Congressional was shorthand for a question or complaint made by a constituent to his or her congressman or woman. These raised issues such as slow visa adjudications or inappropriate freedom of information requests. They were typically letters drafted by congressional staffers and forwarded to the State Department for responses, usually requiring a pro forma answer within a few days.

"Yes," said Stephens. "A congressman in Minnesota conveyed a complaint that you sought to violate patient-private privilege between a doctor and a visa applicant. Is this true?"

Haley recounted the very short encounter between Dr. Hassan and himself, to which Stephens expressed satisfaction. "Can you please take the lead in drafting a quick, formal response, indicating that you were simply conducting due diligence and at no point were you determining anything but the veracity of the traveler's account? Something to that effect, OK?"

"Sure!" Haley was relieved it was this simple.

"Can I ask why you were taking special interest in this case? I'm glad to see when CONOFFS (shorthand for consular officer) do extra work to verify the bona fides of our applicants. Anything different with this applicant?"

Haley dove in. He summarized Dr. Ibrahim's unusual account and how it connected somewhat to the application of the elderly Mr. al-Qahtani. He also admitted he probably spent too much time on the case and had inflicted upon himself the ire of both

Scrivens and Jeffries. He tried to present just the facts, but in conveying them, he found it difficult to suppress his intrigue in the matter. Resignedly, he closed, "I've issued the visa now, so all parties are happy, and I can now move on to other priorities."

"You know, Ellen told me you had been 'snooping around' her team's political contacts. She was quite annoyed. I take it from you that your sojourning was fully coordinated with Paula?"

"Certainly, it was. She actually set up the meetings. It was a great experience for me to work with her and see her in action."

"Glad to hear it. Going rogue—or appearing to go rogue—in this business sounds the death knell on one's career. Let me pass along some advice?" Stephens didn't wait for Haley to consent. "Ellen and Steven were both right. You had other priorities and your sleuthing, as they perceived it, was a distraction that got you nowhere. Even you admit that, right? You should listen to section heads and take their counsel to heart."

Haley, defeated again, nodded his understanding.

Stephens looked hurriedly at two generic government issued, round wall clocks, one set to Washington, DC and the other to local Paris time. He then looked at Haley, whose body language proclaimed defeat. Stephens offered, "Will you indulge me in allowing a bit of my own reminiscing? You know I served in Amman, right? I was there in 2010 during Jordan's struggle with an influx of Iraqi refugees, in addition to hundreds of thousands of Palestinian refugees, and just before a huge wave of Syrian refugees. The Iraqis in Jordan weren't all destitute. Some were and wholly dependent on UN and NGO benevolence. Some were millionaires and built many of the hotels and industry in Amman. There were also Iraqi military pensioners, high ranking colonels and generals. I had someone on my team connect with these expats, who conveyed they would never return to Iraq; they were content to live out their retirement in the comfortable environs of Amman.

"They told us, however, that those formerly under their command—majors, captains, lieutenants, and the enlisted—were still restive and still had a lot of war in them. They were holed up in Syria, awaiting an opportunity to return to a more even-footed fight. They fought us in our 2003 liberation of Iraq, then joined popular uprisings against the Iraqi government once we disbanded the Iraqi military. They dallied with Al-Qaida, the Iranians, and the Jordanian terrorist Abu Musab al-Zarqawi. They saw themselves as freedom fighters trying to hold onto Sunni leadership of the country in the post-Saddam era of Iraq. In response to the General Petraeus-led surge in 2007, many of these warriors fled to Syria, essentially to wait us out. The Iraqi generals in Jordan kept in touch with them and advised us that a storm was brewing. My team wrote cables and emails denoting these concerns, but frankly, they came at a time when no one was interested in rumors of resurgence, not when things were improving on the ground in Iraq. Long story short, they were describing the formation of what later became the Islamic State of Iraq and al-Sham, ISIS, or *Daesh*. My top reporting officer consulted with both the desk in DC and Embassy Baghdad on what we should do about these accounts and the rising potential threat. Do you know what he was told?"

Entranced and confused as to where this story was going, Haley simply responded, "No."

"He was ordered to stop talking to these old generals. Verbatim. This officer was crushed. He knew he was on to something, something big, but he didn't know how to pursue it or who to turn to for guidance. Who knows. Maybe if he had shouted louder, or if

I had been more responsive, innocent lives could have been saved. Maybe we could have slowed down the *Daesh* juggernaut that wreaked its hatred on the various Iraqi ethnic groups, including Sunni Muslims."

"I see," said Haley, not seeing at all.

"My point is that you had a hunch and you followed it. Color between the lines, coordinate closely with your teams in consular and political, as well as the security and intel shops. We're overseas to protect and promote U.S. interests, keep our folks safe, and make them prosperous. You're paid for your judgment and to ask questions, not be a mindless bureaucrat. Use your common sense, but be practical. Ask yourself what we can or should follow from Paris on this account. Maybe it's run its course. Maybe there are still threads to follow, though. Let's you and I stay close on this. Please come and brief me if you hear anything else related to this series of seemingly disconnected coincidences. Deal?"

Haley felt oddly encouraged and chastised at the same time, and somewhat bolstered as he left his chat with the DCM. It seemed to him he now had a green light to keep pursuing the al-Qahtani concerns. Weird, but he sensed Stephens had conveyed he supported Scrivens' apparent risk aversion, but also kind of wanted him to bypass her. State Department folks were infuriating. He missed the more direct military approach of his fellow soldiers from his Army enlistment days. He didn't miss the deprivation, humiliation, and being treated like cannon fodder, though. "What was it that diplomats were known for? Saying 'nice doggie,' while reaching for a rock?"

Regardless, as he had told Stephens, he'd run out of options. He wasn't sure what other thread was there to pull.

***

Haley had no idea how to process his meeting with Stephens. His afternoon schedule was light, so he thought he would hunt down Abrams to seek her guidance. He would send her a text, but knew she wouldn't see it while in the classified section of the embassy where phones weren't permitted. He chose not to go to the political section because he didn't want to run across Scrivens. He decided instead to email Abrams from his iPhone to check when she was available. While walking down the stairs from the front office, he opened his Outlook application and typed a brief note onto his touchscreen pad. He realized he could have waited to get to his office rather than risk a tumble down the staircase, but knew that he would be distracted until he could somehow defragment and reorganize his mind.

As Haley reached his desk, his landline office phone was already ringing. It was Abrams' extension.

So as not to bring his consular colleagues into the conversation, Haley quietly recounted his DCM session for Abrams to get her thoughts and to see if she had any ideas about moving forward. "So, what do you think?" he asked. "Is there anything left to do, or should I simply leave this as is? By all accounts, I have some interesting coincidences strung together that only conspiracy theorists would love to pick at."

"That you do," said Abrams resignedly. "I've got nothing for you. Maybe it's worth you touching base with Dr. Ibrahim once again? He's the one keeping this running."

"I will," Haley responded. "And give my best to your niece. What's her name again? Is it Toe-face?"

"It's Jessica, and she's graduated from crayons to watercolors. I'll commission her to paint your likeness, using her dog's butt as inspiration," retorted Paula.

Chapter 13

One of many five-star hotels, Paris, France.

The broad-chested hirsute gentleman in an expensive-looking, dark business suit and no tie, welcomed al-Qahtani at the door of his palatial suite in one of Paris' finer hotel establishments.

"You are most welcome, my prince. I wish you peace and health. It is such an honor to see you in person," he conveyed in stilted classical Arabic, then continued in English, "I hope you were successful in your travel to the United States." He gestured to his guest to join him in sitting in rather ornate sofas in an opulent *majlis*, or parlor.

Al-Qahtani nodded and followed his host in taking a seat. He found it fascinating how Gulf wealth followed many of his kinsmen to the West and ensured even the fancy Parisian hotels were equipped with *majlis* furniture, so they could properly conduct business in the traditional Bedouin style. What he did not realize is that much of the quality furniture required for making these transactions comfortable was manufactured in the mountains of a state called North Carolina, in the United States.

Al-Qahtani reciprocated greetings in Arabic, but largely refrained from any business discussions until after traditional Arabic coffee and date service had been provided.

"Thank you, sir, for visiting me in my hotel," the host interjected, continuing again in Arabic once an Indian manservant dispensing the refreshments had left the room. I understand you're not comfortable with meeting in mosques or *hussainiyyas [Shia prayer halls]*, given that French intelligence regularly monitor our religious establishments."

"Of course," said al-Qahtani. "We have kept our operations off their radar for decades, but we must continue to be very careful. I'm sure I was picked up on their cameras here, but it is not unusual for me to meet with prominent businessmen, given the work I do in raising funds for charities. I do not believe my visit here will register with the authorities. I do not like to move about much, but now is the time to accelerate our operations and take more risks."

"What are you hearing about al-Onezi's visit to Wasit governorate in Iraq?" al-Qahtani queried.

The host replied, "His travel was largely a success. He met with your agent there in a town called Aziziyah. He helped him to make connections with the team in Sadr City, as well as Najaf. He confirmed that over the last few years he extracted enough material to proceed. With this science, the chances for success are minimal, so he developed as many as one hundred test subjects to best increase odds in our favor, and many are at various stages of development to increase the viability for the specimens. We have multiple options, but that is a challenge we can address later as needed. Al-Onezi spent much time traveling around the region conducting his clinics with many potential, um . . clients .

. . or patients. He met with the religious leaders you recruited as well, who played an essential role in convincing family members. He reviewed Dr. Farhad's notes and believes himself capable of continuing to manage the prescribed processes."

"I am pleased. What is next?" asked al-Qahtani.

"My Lord, you have been very, very explicit that these families must be true or *Arab* Arabs. Along with other considerations, this requirement creates complications in our vetting procedures, especially given the mix of tribes and ethnicities hailing from Iraq, Iran, and around the region, but I'm sure we have enough qualified candidates for our initiative."

"Again, I am pleased. You have been a faithful steward since the beginning. Since our 'phase one' so many years ago. We could not imagine even then how close we would come to achieving our goal. The Mehdi almost made his entrance during our stillborn revolution; there will be no doubt this time, and we will not be thwarted. We have waited a long time for technology to catch up with us. Now, with science and Allah's help, we are nearly ready to usher in our destiny," concluded al-Qahtani.

"Thank you, my dear Ali," continued al-Qahtani. "I have another task for you. I find some questions raised by U.S. Embassy officials uncomfortable. Twice now, a young man named *Clifton Harley* has surfaced with questions I find inappropriate and beyond his remit. I'd like for you to find out why and deal with it."

"*Bikul suroor, sidi [With pleasure, sir],*" said Ali, as he wrapped up the conversation with al-Qahtani. "With great pleasure."

Chapter 14

American Cafe near the Sorbonne, Paris, France, the following week.

"It's a pleasure seeing you again, Mr. Haley." Dr. Ibrahim said, continuing to remain formal in interactions with Haley. They both settled into the same seats at the same American cafe, both with espressos this time. Haley bought the espressos despite Dr. Ibrahim's protest.

"No. Thank you, sir, for seeing me. I have enjoyed chatting with you and learning more history about the events in 1979 that have impacted so many lives." Haley reciprocated the polite formalities, an easy task for him considering the age difference and good manners instilled in him by his upbringing. Plus, he did enjoy Dr. Ibrahim's kindness and wealth of knowledge. He was an easy guy to respect, Haley reflected. "I'm sorry Paula can't be with us today. She was called into an urgent matter at the embassy." Haley felt a tinge of guilt at this white lie. In order to keep Paula clear from Scrivens' displeasure, the two had agreed Haley would take this meeting solo.

"I am sorry Ms. Abrams was unable to attend. Please *tusalem alayha [give her my regards]* and my warmest greetings." He noted, adding, "And I apologize, but I only have a few minutes to spare, then I must get back to the university for a lecture on Islamic history. I'm sure you would find it interesting, but alas, it's in French, so might be a bit of a struggle for you."

"I would indeed love to attend the lecture, but I'm afraid it would be over my head. Even my poor, rudimentary Arabic has lapsed into disuse. I'll be mindful of your time and get right to the point. You've been very helpful in providing insight into the events of the past, and I think you and I agree that connections from 1979 somehow point to present day. And we cannot deny the odd coincidences that surround the unremarkable Neauphle-le-Château. But, what's next? Surely, in the days of Google and WikiLeaks, there has to be some way to determine what connects these disparate data points?" pondered Haley.

"As a millennial, I thought you would be just a bit more creative," mused Dr. Ibrahim, his eyes twinkling. "Let's consider again the attack on the Grand Mosque and who might have been an eyewitness, maybe someone who was there and participated in the liberation of the captives?"

Haley felt a slight desire to defend himself. "I'm sure there are many in Saudi Arabia who could speak to the operation back then, but for some reason, there've been few accounts of the event, at least in English. For something so traumatic, you would think there would have been more sensational news about this. I've searched quite a few websites, but there simply isn't much to go on."

Dr. Ibrahim interjected, "I do not mean to infer that you go to Saudi Arabia. The Saudis have been very careful to keep this quiet, and certainly no one there will wish to relive the embarrassing account again. Why not closer to home? French Commandos allegedly participated in the operation, correct? Surely some would be here in France after all this time. I imagine that many would be known to your own military colleagues at the embassy, no?"

Chapter 15

Haley certainly had not considered looping in his Department of Defense colleagues in unraveling this mystery. After Dr. Ibrahim and he parted ways, Haley called on the Army attaché at the embassy. Colonel David Richt had worked in the Defense Attaché office, more commonly known as the DATT or DAO, for nearly six months. He reported to the senior defense officer, a brigadier general who oversaw the U.S.-French Army, Navy, Air Force, and Marine bilateral military and security assistance portfolios. He and his colleagues worked on various forms of military cooperation with French counterparts, both in terms of weapon sales and in sharing covert and overt information.

"Colonel Richt, thank you for seeing me." Haley, despite having been an enlisted soldier prior to joining the State Department, was still a little shy about conversing directly with senior military officers. His engagement with officers in the Army had been largely limited to the platoon and company level, meaning he rarely interacted with officers above the captain level, except when receiving a Purple Heart for injuries suffered in combat in Iraq.

"Please, Clayton, call me Dave. I like keeping things informal, especially when I engage with you State folks. Y'all remind me what it's like to be in the real world, away from all the military command structure, order of battle, beans and bullets, etc. I've actually been looking forward to chatt'n with you."

"Thanks, Dave," Haley said in uncomfortably familiar terms. He glanced around the sparsely furnished office, noting on the desk a U.S. flag framed in a triangular box, which he presumed was a gift from Richt's previous command. On the wall, Richt also showcased a few award certificates, including a familiar-looking one from the State Department. He also sported in a glass enclosed cabinet what looked like a Maasai war club, making Haley wonder if Richt had served in Kenya. Otherwise, the office had the standard olive drab look so often associated with Army fashion and color schemes. "I appreciate that you're very busy, so I can simply get right to the crux of the matter. Any chance you ever come across old French Foreign Legion commandos who might have served in Saudi Arabia in the late seventies? I'm looking, in particular, for someone who might have helped liberate the Grand Mosque from assailants in 1979." Prompted by Richt's puzzled look, Haley regaled him with the backstory that he had pieced together, including tidbits from Dr. Ibrahim and some internet searches about how French commandos may have been part of the forces that stormed the mosque.

"That's quite a tale, Clayton," he passed, sounding very Texan. "Weird I ain't ever heard this. You know, I was posted to Saudi. Riyadh, to be exact. Nasty place. Unbearably hot. Not much for women, either. I've long suspected the country suffered from a severe pandemic of cooties—everyone afraid of getting the cootie germ from women. Too kindergarten playground for my taste.

"I served at USMTM (The United States Military Training Mission) there back around 2000. Not a bad assignment but tough to be so far away from combat *and* family. And to answer your question, maybe. I occasionally hang out at an aging warrior's club in the old part of Paris. It's home to a bunch of salty French war vets. Some of these guys served in nasty places, even dating back to Indochina days. Most are younger, though, and served in the Gulf War, Algeria, across sub-Sahara and some other gosh-forsaken places. They let me in because I saw some combat in Iraq and Afghanistan, and I tussled a bit in Mogadishu back when I was a young lieutenant with a fresh Ranger Tab. I go over to the club once every couple of months and smoke cigars and drink a little cognac. I hate the stuff, but it's nice to hang out with the ol' wardawgs. Let me ask next time I'm there to see if anyone served in Saudi."

***

Richt made some calls, and lined up an evening of drinks at the club. He swung by Haley's apartment in his Ford F150 King Cab truck. Haley sidled up to the truck with uncertainty, not knowing who might be behind the tinted windows and the wheel of this rather large land barge. Richt lowered the window and, eyeing Haley's startled look, said, "Yeah, it's me. Hop in. I know the truck sticks out a little here in France, but I like to remind the Frenchies just who saved their behinds in Dubya Dubya Two. I had just bought this during a domestic assignment when my orders were cut for Paris. I made it clear to my bosses I would go back overseas on two conditions: One, I go accompanied with my family, and, two, I go in style and get to keep my baby. The shipping folks in the embassy had to pull some strings, but it got delivered with little fuss."

Haley hopped in, and the vehicle thundered off on Parisian streets designed for horses and carriages and very small, quiet electric Smart cars. The night was dark, but as always, street lights quaintly lit the city. "And it was Paris," thought Haley. "This city's *joie de vivre* generated its own illumination." He wondered how he recalled this term, given his lackluster performance in high school French.

Haley and Richt swapped some old war stories. Certainly Richt's were pretty cool, but even Richt—with his significant combat experience across nearly two decades—appreciated Haley's accounts of his own hit and near misses in Iraq. He acknowledged, "In my early days, I saw some pretty nasty stuff, stuff I won't ever forget. The longer I stayed in, the higher I grew in rank, and the farther I became from the front line action. Sounds like you were in the mix, and accounted for yourself with estimable valor, Clayton, estimable valor."

Haley smiled with satisfaction, as he had never discussed his combat experience with anyone. Even his own father wasn't aware of all that he had endured. He wasn't ashamed, but it just wasn't something that came up organically in conversation. Very few people had connecting points of reference on such encounters. Richt, on the other hand, seemed well-versed in combat, and they spoke comfortably as they moved from busy thoroughfares into the older parts of Paris where the streets narrowed. Haley wondered if "Colonel America" and his rather large tribute to American engineering could fit in the cobblestone passageways of old Paris. He'd read Vikings actually raided this part of Paris, and given the swagger of his chauffeur, queried mentally if the local denizens would respond in the same fashion as their forebears.

Chapter 16

French Foreign Legion Club. Downtown Paris.

They parked the truck and entered a narrow establishment that looked to have once been an old house or tavern. A weathered sign above the door detailed *Les Anciens Combattants des Guerres Étrangères*. Haley's French wasn't good, but he could just make out what must be the equivalent of the VFW (Veterans of Foreign Wars) club in Walhalla. He recalled from his childhood the occasional WWII and Korean War veteran wearing his VFW Garrison Cap in church on Memorial Day and Veterans Day. It hadn't occurred to him that as a veteran, he had actually joined their rank and file. And now, here he was in the French version of a VFW.

"Girard, this is the young fellow I told you about on the phone," said Richt, somehow seeming more American than usual in the club's distinctly French atmosphere. Haley took in the joint. It was dark and run down, and smelled like cigarettes, beer, and body odor, all well past their expiration dates. Most of the furniture was wooden and encased in black lacquer and, along with the bar, displayed gashes and scuff marks denoting long time use—potentially abuse. It was a delightful blue collar contrast to the urbanity and *savoir faire* that was the rest of Paris. Haley loved it and felt at home.

Richt introduced Haley to retired Colonel Girard de Castille. "I'll vouch for his right to join the old warriors club, and I tell you, you'll want to hear his story." "And Clayton," Richt turned to Haley, "Girard tells me he was in Saudi back in the 1970s and saw some real action there."

Haley and Colonel de Castille exchanged pleasantries, with de Castille sizing Haley up to determine if the young man warranted his attention and time. While making this determination, he shoved a cigar and a snifter half full of cognac at him.

Haley politely deflected the drink and cigar but ordered from the barkeep a *jambon beurre*, and at Richt's prompting, narrated for de Castille the depictions he had of the accounts of the seizure of the Grand Mosque, the role of the original al-Otaybi and al-Qahtani, and how young men with the same family names appeared at his consular window recently. His account got off to a rocky start with him stammering a bit and befuddling some of the details, but as he spoke, his mind cleared, and he began connecting to his aged French counterpart, as denoted by the gentleman's increased attention.

"Zat's quite ze story," de Castille cleared his throat, emphasizing the *ghi* sound, in the second syllable of *story*, paused, and finally said, in clear but heavily accented English, "Now let me tell you mine."

***

"Oui, I was zere," de Castille began, intermittently coughing or clearing his throat. "It was November of 1979. I was on my first mission as a commando in the *Groupe d'Intervention de la Gendarmerie Nationale*, the elite French police tactial unit covering counter-terrorism and hostage rescue, under Captain Paul Barril, deputy commander of the unit. I was the equivalent of your ranger, all salt and vinegar, and not a little Cognac," he nodded at the sifter. "I was ready to make war in the daytime, and it was none of your business what I made at night. A real *fils de pute*, an SOB as you might say, though your English term doesn't express the sentiment as well as French."

"This guy is a living, breathing cliché," thought Haley.

Richt seemed preoccupied with the menu, but his body language suggested he would pay just enough attention to determine if de Castille's story would be of interest.

"I was actually quite jealous of my brothers-in-arms who went to the battle fronts in Algeria, Mali, Chad, and other hot spots," continued de Castille, not noticing his audience's waning attention. I believe my assignment to Saudi Arabia was akin to a prison sentence. Who wanted to go there? There was no war, no insurgency, no rebellion, no need for my special talent. And my squad was to report to a National Guard unit comprised of spoiled Bedouin unfamiliar with the business end of a rifle."

He continued, "To my good fortune, as I believed at the time, some cult took over the Grand Mosque, led by your *Gah-ta-NI*," wrongly emphasizing the last syllable, as the French are wont to do. "At the outset, it appeared we wouldn't see any action unless the rebel forces departed the mosque fortress and attacked us. We were told as non-Muslims, it was Haram—forbidden—for us to enter the mosque. We were essentially support services for the very inept Saudi National Guard and their Pakistani troops who were apparently Muslim enough to enter the holy site. They were also non-Muslim enough to carouse with us after hours, as I recall—

"After the first week, however, it became clear the rabble inside the Mosque was more committed to their cause than the rabble on the outside. My team was called to create a diversion and attack through the old city's underground sewers. The National Guard and the Pakistani commandos, meanwhile, would circle around and storm through the front gate. Plans were made. So were prayers, both Christian and Muslim. All of us non-Muslims were required to convert to Islam before we could enter the city. It was simple and performed by an Imam in a hasty ceremony. We had to make a statement declaring the desert Bedouin Mohammed was the prophet of the only God, and we had to pray, orienting ourselves toward Mecca. That one was quite easy. It was in front of us. We had to go on hajj to Mecca as well. We were about to check that box, too, but instead of circling the Kaaba, we were to round up those who laid siege to it. There was no time for the final two Islamic pillars—fasting and giving to charity. It certainly took less time to become a Muslim than having to read through catholic catechisms as a child. And I should say it didn't take long after the inevitable apostasy to set in. I hope my priest back here in France was able to repair any spiritual damage done by my temporary conversion," he smirked.

"Anyway, my team entered through the sewers, which led us into an open courtyard. By the time we got there, it was a bloodbath. Bodies everywhere. I could not distinguish between rebel, guard, hostage, or innocent bystander. The Saudi National Guard simply killed everyone in its path. People shot at us; we fired back. We gave chase to anyone we found alive. Snipers shot at us. I'm not sure from which side. Someone even used poison gas. I don't know who. I still have difficulty breathing, and it nearly cost me my military career. It was the worst use of military tactics ever."

De Castille recounted for Haley and Richt details of the melee, depicted by its lack of planning and ensuing chaos. He estimated that some 500 people died, and it was unclear to him how many of this number consisted of the cult members.

Despite the bluster and bravado, de Castille's account seemed to match that of the details already familiar to Haley. "That's an amazing account, sir," he added politely. "I'm sure it was very traumatic, and the Saudi government moved quickly to recover, rebuild, and forget this event. Certainly, I've never heard of the accounts that led to the seizure of the mosque. Weird that it's never talked about."

"Non. It's not weird that people don't know about the events of 1979. The Saudis covered it up. They decapitated most of the survivors so no one would know about the event, and so no one would ever inspire another uprising. They also silenced any attempt at an investigation," said de Castille reaching for another cognac.

"I'm sorry, but to clarify, you said the survivors were decapitated. You meant the surviving rebels, no?" asked Haley.

"He's clever," de Castille nodded to Colonel Richt, who had found his own cigar more interesting as the conversation droned on. "As I said, the Saudis didn't care who died and who lived. They wanted to end the gun battle at all costs and were willing to sacrifice anyone who might have been associated with the rebels. Almost anyone, I mean."

"Again, sir, you're being opaque. Did some of the cult members survive?" asked a growingly animated Haley.

"I am not able to say more. I was compelled to sign what we call an *accord de non-divulgation (a French non-disclosure agreement)*, which I am bound to until this day. I can tell you, however, that not only did some rebels survive, but we were ordered to smuggle some of them out of the country and bring them to France. My unit was charged with turning these individuals over to the *Direction de la Surveillance du Territoire,* an intelligence agency that disbanded nearly ten years ago. To my knowledge, this service relocated some of the survivors to a small town about an hour west of Paris. I believe with some certainty you met one such survivor at your consular window."

"Are you saying what I think you're saying? That your team smuggled al-Qah—"

De Castille forcibly and angrily interrupted Haley. "I said I will not say more. I gave you my story as a favor to mon ami Colonel Richt, and because I have regrettably had too much to drink. You are not to share this except through your embassy classified channels. It is an old story with no relevance today. I will not jeopardize my pension by violating the trust placed in me to safeguard this story. I will tell you, however, if you wish to explore yesterday's news further, you should research the name Muhsin Bin Laden."

Chapter 17

On the ride back to his apartment, Colonel Richt waved off Haley's profuse apologies. "You have nothing to be sorry for. You clearly tapped into some old war memories. That's the most animated I've ever seen him. Well done. Weird that he's still holding on to some secrets dating back to a forgotten event in the 1970s. You musta hit a nerve."

Haley nodded a disingenuous acknowledgement that Richt's words had registered with him, but he was already googling one Muhsin Bin Laden on his iPhone. "It never occurred to me that Bin Laden had brothers. I wonder how they turned out," he thought, almost audibly.

"I'll bet the apple didn't fall far from the dang tree," replied Richt, he seemed to sound even more Texan as the night drew on. The rumbling of his truck's all terrain tires amplified on the uneven cobblestones. Richt kept one eye on his GPS, one on the road, as he capably navigated his way west.

"So according to Google, the Saudi Binladen Group is the world's largest construction firm and grosses $2 billion a year,"

Haley announced. "I guess business wasn't hurt by siring one of the worst villains in modern history. You want to know something else? The Bin Ladens aren't even Saudis; they're Yemenis who were lucky enough to become Saudis before World War I. The patriarch of the family, one Mr. Mohammed Bin Laden, secured a bunch of construction contracts for King Abdulaziz, AKA Ibn Saud, who was pretty much the founder of modern Saudi Arabia. One of his sons sits on the throne there. Turns out, Mohammed Bin Laden scored big time in contracting for renovations in . . . guess where? Mecca! He made his fortune on holy site restoration, including at the Al-Aqsa Mosque in Jerusalem. And get this—by the time the guy died in 1967, he had fathered more than fifty children. Talk about some unsupervised horseplay in the genepool . . . I'll bet lil Osama has some major daddy issues. These are some seriously messed up people."

"Fifty?" blurted Richt. "Ain't these fellers ever read the Old Testament? If so, they'd know that having multiple wives only created multiple problems. Just ask Solomon or David, right? Dang it!" he swore. He was caught up in Haley's narrative, and missed a turn, and now had to wait while the GPS recalculated.

"Let's see. Let's see . . ." Haley muttered as he scrolled through other articles to get details on Muhsin. "Sorry I keep getting distracted, but what I'm seeing here is so much better than fiction. Get a load of Osama's messed up origins. Not only was he one of fifty kids, his mother was essentially a prostitute; concubine is the nicer term for it.

"Hang on." Haley was completely immersed in this internet search. "Wait a second—" he said while inputting Osama- Bin-Laden- Mother- into his browser. "Here's an article from *The Guardian* a year ago saying she was a young Syrian girl named

Hamida, who may actually have been Alawite—adhering to the same political, religious, and ethnic class of the chinless monster in Damascus, Bashar al-Assad—and his father with the peanut-shaped head, Hafez. The article doesn't describe these two megalomaniacs as such. That's my editorializing," joked Haley.

"Yeah. I figured that," responded Richt. "Tell me more."

"OK. Let me see. Same article. Hamida in the interview said she was married at age fourteen and was Mohammed Bin Laden's tenth wife. Gracious. Quite the randy old chap," Haley erupted with an abhorrent attempt at an English accent. "I'll bet her ancestral village was awarded some nice construction projects for offering her up to the old geezer. Since Islamic rites dictate a man can only have four wives at a time, old Mohammed divorced her after the birth of Osama, likely to add another young girl into the rotation.

"Osama grew up not knowing his father, but the apple didn't fall far from the tree, as you predicted. He married his own cousin when she was only fourteen and had his own stable of temporary wives."

"If Islam allows this, how is this religion not a sex cult?" Richt asked rhetorically. And do the Saudis not prosecute pedophilia? And what dark place on earth it must be for these young women sold into sexual slavery by their families! They certainly didn't ask to be pimped out like this!"

"Agreed but let's keep looking for our new BFF, Muhsin. Sorry I keep getting distracted," Haley apologized.

Richt replied, "Not at all. After our chat with de Castille, I'm feeling extremely ignorant about these events that seemed to have shaped countries we call our closest friends and foes."

Haley continued to scroll through various articles about the Bin Ladens while Richt navigated the streets of Paris, working their way west and out of the older parts of the ancient city.

"What?" Haley squawked loudly, jarring Richt who took his eyes off the road momentarily.

"Turns out, Muhsin Bin Laden may have been one of the cult members himself. And according to a couple of different websites, he may have used the Bin Laden construction trucks to smuggle in weapons for the al-Qahtani rebels. He was arrested by the Saudi Authorities, but somehow he was not among the dozens publicly executed for this horrific attack on the country. Instead, he was exonerated and took over the family business in Medina, home to the burial site of Mohammed and one of the top holy sites of Islam! Talk about having some family connections! His fellow conspirators—if these online accounts are true—literally got the axe, while he continued to live in extravagant wealth."

"I wouldn't be surprised if he carried on with the other family business, the one which entailed ruining the lives of young women. I hate these smug pedophiles," griped Richt.

***

Richt's large truck pulled in front of Haley's apartment. Haley was sure his neighbors in the apartment building could hear the rumble of the dual exhausts. Still uncomfortable in calling a colonel by his first name, but buoyed by a fascinating account and revelatory research, he said, "Dave. This has been a tremendous night. I gotta thank you," he noticed for the first time his own reversion to his natural dialect and wondered about the re-emergence of the long dormant diphthong in the second person pronoun.

"No, Clayton. I need to thank you. Sump'n don't smell right, and I tell you, you got the sniffer of a blue tick hound dawg. Don't you let up, you hear?"

Chapter 18

Mobile phone conversation.

"Sidi, we've been able to clone his mobile phone and see he's been speaking to an Arab professor at the Sorbonne. This professor is one Dr. Ibrahim Mustafa, a Palestinian and son of Mustafa Khalil al-Othman, who worked in Medina back in 1979," conveyed young Ali al-Qahtani in hushed Arabic tones. "We traced the doctor's phone as well and know he's made calls to his relatives who are still in the Kingdom."

"Mustafa Khalil al-Othman," the respondent muttered. "You said he was in Medina in 1979? And his son is in Paris now? This coincidence is too, umm . . . coincidental. I need you to track his movements and ensure he does not meet with anyone from the U.S. Embassy again. Do what you must, but we are too close to launching our plan; we must not have any distractions. You are authorized to take any action you deem necessary."

"Na'm, sidi Ali. I will take care of it," replied the younger Ali.

***

MESSIANIC REVEAL

U.S. Embassy, Paris, France.

"I'm sorry you won't be able to make it, but given his class schedule, Dr. Ibrahim is only available for morning appointments this week," said Abrams to Haley in coordinating a follow-up with their key interlocutor. "I need to see him anyway for his insight about an Arab League initiative, so I already have prior approval from Ellen. Why don't you provide me some questions to raise after your meetings with the Foreign Legion guy? I'll be careful not to source him but do think it useful to touch base regarding your pal Muhsin."

"Fair enough," replied Haley, not thinking this was fair at all. Unfortunately, he was swamped with interviews every morning and could not leave the visa window. He was quite anxious to follow-up on the Bin Laden angle but admitted knowing the Bin Ladens had potential ties to the cult did not really change a thing. Osama was dead, and his brother had reportedly been cleared of any wrongdoing for forty years. Plus, the elderly Mr. al-Qahtani had made a seemingly uneventful trip to the United States and returned, presumably to his residence in Neauphle-le-Château. At this point, Haley remained intrigued about the series of potentially tied accounts, but to what end? He dropped in with DCM Stephens from time to time, but other than regaling him with cool stories, he just didn't have much to report. Maybe Abrams meeting with Dr. Ibrahim would shed some light on the matter or simply close the loop and allow him to go about his job without further distraction, he mused.

***

"DUCK AND COVER! THIS IS NOT A DRILL. REPEAT: DUCK AND COVER. MOVE AWAY FROM THE WINDOWS. SECURE ALL CLASSIFIED."

Wailing, deafening sirens across the embassy's intercom system interrupted the next morning's visa interviews. Drills were pretty commonplace, so Haley took this on as more of an annoyance than a harbinger of something serious. Haley groaned at the aural intrusion, and sympathized with neighbors of U.S. embassies, who also must be inured to these routine occurrences.

"Not another drill!" complained fellow consular officer Craig Skople. "We had one of these last week. And why are the Marines doing this during our peak window times! They know we have people in the waiting room. What are we supposed to do with them?"

"Are you sure it's not a drill?" yelled Haley over the siren. Given the sudden movement of activity and colleagues trying to speak over the alarm, much of the import of the message was lost on people in the section.

"THIS IS NOT A DRILL. REPEAT: THIS IS NOT A DRILL. DUCK AND COVER. MOVE AWAY FROM THE WINDOWS. SECURE ALL CLASSIFIED."

"I guess that answers your question," projected Skople as he moved a little too casually toward his desk and crawled under it.

Haley followed suit, quickly grabbing his phone in case he was stuck for a while without communications. While under his desk, he opened his phone to look at any WhatsApp messages he missed while at the window.

P. Abrams-5/23 0945

Hey Clayton. Tks for your msg. Ert
to coffee shop near sorbonne. Will
pass your regards to ibrahim. He was
expecting you at the meeting? Will ask
him about muhsin. Who knows? Maybe he'll
have some scoop on him too. Paula

***

After thirty minutes, the regional security officer ordered Post One to issue the All Clear. Turns out there was no immediate threat to the embassy. The embassy alarm had been triggered by an external incident. Given terror attacks in recent years in Europe, the default for embassies was to go into lockdown when receiving credible threats. It was still unclear if there was any direct targeting of the embassy, but rumors were already circulating there had been a shooting downtown, perhaps near a school.

Haley checked online. No details yet, but the ticker on CNN, FoxNews, Sky, and other outlets confirmed what he already knew—an attack took place. Consul Jeffries was summoned to an Emergency Action Committee meeting chaired by the DCM. These meetings were convened each time an event occurred that required a review of the embassy security posture and to determine what message should be extended to American citizens in the community to ensure there was no double standard in terms of what precautions should be taken in the protection of American interests.

Haley went back to the adjudications at the windows. The applicants were perplexed but seemed oddly pleased that whatever the concern was didn't impact their schedules for the day any further.

Jeffries returned after approximately thirty minutes. He was pale and shaky. He assembled American Citizen Service team members for a quiet huddle. After which, they all got on their phones or left hurriedly.

Jeffries then spoke to the larger consular section. "Folks, I don't have a lot of details yet, but there appears to be a shooting near the Sorbonne University. An unknown number of gunmen apparently shot up a coffee shop there. Initial reports are that there are fatalities. I've asked the ACS team to connect with our security guys to get positioned at the relevant hospitals in case there are any AMCITS among the dead or wounded. For us, let's clear out the consular section and reschedule appointments. Let's also review our SOPs from after the Charlie Hebdo attack to make sure we have our bases covered. OK?"

***

Haley fired off a quick WhatsApp message to Abrams. He was annoyed his mind had run to a couple of worrisome conclusions. "She better respond soon," he hoped.

Clayton Haley—5/23 1032

hey Paula. Weird stuff going on. Call
me? Hope you and Dr. Ibrahim were able
to link up. C

Realizing worry was nonconstructive, he fired off a quick message to one of the assistant regional security officers, Danny Rossini, a friend with whom he had enjoyed watching some of the March Madness NCAA basketball tournament, at least until his beloved USC Gamecocks got knocked out of contention.

    Clayton Haley—5/23 1036

    Danny. I know you're busy, but are
    you able to detail a location re the
    shooting?

    Danny Rossini—5/23 1036

    Can't talk now. On way to site. Seems
    bad. Don't have deets yet, but some
    Jihadis shot up a cafe next to the S.U.

    Clayton Haley—5/23 1038

    POLOFF Paula Abrams was meeting a
    contact at one of the coffee shops near
    the U. I can't reach her. Can you track
    her down to ensure she's OK?

Haley was thoroughly distracted now but knew he needed to stay focused. He approached Jeffries and informed him there was a possibility a colleague was in the vicinity of the shooting. Jeffries thanked him but proffered that it was useless to speculate on such matters, and that under double standard rules, the embassy could not take measures on behalf of an employee above that of any other AMCIT involved in such an incident.

"We just have to wait. Keep your phone handy for when she calls," he offered hopefully.

Haley felt no comfort from Jeffries's words, and he couldn't shake a sense of terrible foreboding. Something wasn't right.

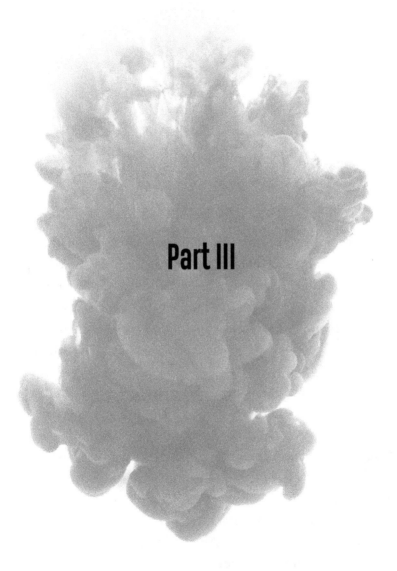

Part III

Chapter 19

"Next of kin has been notified," Rossini stated pragmatically. "I know this is tough for you. It's tough for all of us to lose a colleague. We here in RSO [Regional Security Office] take this hard. Since we adopted a 'Fortress America' outlook after Benghazi, our record has been good; we haven't lost any diplomats since then. Do you know why she was there in the coffee shop and with whom she was meeting?"

Haley realized the conversation was half colleague consolation, half deposition. He found it hard to focus. It had been a day since the attack but word had already gotten out that Abrams, Dr. Ibrahim, and at least two others were killed in what was being billed on news networks as a "brazen terror strike in the heart of Paris." Plus, given Consular's AMCIT remit, it was his friend Skople who bore the unpleasant task of identifying Paula's remains and notifying her husband. After fulfilling his gruesome task, Skople took administrative leave, not ready to come back to work.

Haley disclosed Dr. Ibrahim had been a mutual contact of both Abrams and himself, and that if it had been possible, he would have been at the same coffee shop when it was attacked. It was difficult to speak. He felt nauseous and thirsty at the same time. He wanted to be somewhere else, but couldn't identify where. He did not wish to speak at all, or to anyone. He didn't trust his mind to order cogent thought and certainly didn't trust his voice, which trembled and prevented him from speaking above a whisper. He struggled in his account to Rossini of why he and Abrams were interested in Dr. Ibrahim, never imagining the slightest possibility anyone would be gunned down so cruelly. Once finished, he excused himself to regather his composure.

"So what exactly happened?" Haley said after a break and a long drink of water. "You said Jihadis attacked them?"

Rossini replied, "We're still gathering information, of course, but yes, it appears that two assailants on high-powered dirt bikes drove up to the coffee shop, pulled out AK-47s, and fired through the window. They hit your friend, Dr. Ibrahim, seven times. Paula—" he lowered his voice to finish the sentence, "was mortally wounded with just one round through the neck. You know, this is a big embassy, but I knew her. I feel horrible. I spoke to her husband. He's not dealing with this well."

"Of course not," muttered Haley. He didn't know her husband Adam, only that he was a hedge fund investor in London. Sadly, life as a diplomat meant especially talented or skilled spouses often had to make career sacrifices. Adam Abrams was able to get a job in London, which was a lot closer than New York, the only consolation for their mutual pursuit of careers. He and Paula were still far apart, but at least they had been able to see each other on the weekends.

"You said that two others were killed?" Haley inquired.

"Yep. One was the barista, the other a customer on her way out. The barista survived her wounds only for a few hours before succumbing. She, too, was hit once, as was the other customer. A few other customers complained of injuries related to flying glass and the panic that ensued. The French are investigating but so far, have few leads. The assailants got away on their motorbikes. We're hoping to take a look at video footage but don't expect much. They wore balaclavas and were at the scene and gone within only a matter of seconds, just long enough to yell *allahu akbar* and wave an ISIS flag."

"I don't think this was an act of terror," posed Haley.

"How can you say that?" pressed Rossini. "It's Charlie Hebdo all over again."

"No, it's not. This is good old-fashion murder. A hit on someone who knows too much. Dr. Ibrahim was the target. He's a devout Muslim himself, though not one to curry favor with ISIS, Al-Qaeda, or other terrorists. He was the target because of what I told him. I got him killed. I got Paula killed too."

Chapter 20

"Why do you claim you got Paula Abrams and a Dr. Ai-bra-him Mus-TA-fa killed?" asked the agent in charge, annoyingly mispronouncing Dr. Ibrahim's family name by emphasizing the second syllable. Haley really had a lot of other things that should have consumed his thoughts, certainly not a simple mispronunciation. He looked at the agent across the conference table and then around the embassy's secure conference room. In his state of shock and sadness, his attention was hyper-focused on unimportant details— the agent's ugly tie, the ring of condensation from the agent's diet soft drink on the varnished table, and mildew stains on the ceiling tiles, indicating a leak from an air conditioning unit. The room was supposed to be fool-proofed against eavesdropping, and with its vault-like door and insulated walls, Haley felt that he was instead in either a prison or psyche ward.

The FBI team was already assembled to investigate the supposed terror attack. In fact, they were on the ground within eight hours of the incident and had joined with the embassy RSO and Legal Attaché teams. Also present was a guy Haley saw in the cafeteria from time to time but had never met.

"Was there a sick perversion to them or did they somehow enjoy this kind of work?" thought Haley. "Their bloated sense of self-importance had somehow enhanced their swagger, the way they spoke, and even the way they sat. But that's not fair," he chided himself. "They're here to do their job. They don't know or care about Paula, but they do care about justice," he consoled himself.

"Yes. I believe a line of questioning I was pursuing got them both killed. Paula was a dear colleague of mine, and Dr. Ibrahim a very kind, patient interlocutor. He was helping us contextualize, in modern understanding, an event that occurred in 1979, something to which he had a personal connection." Haley launched into his narrative of how the al-Qahtani/al-Otaybi interviews had provided some simple threads to pull. His audience, however, was short on attention and patience. Agent-In-Charge Stern—"his look, not his name," thought Haley—cut him off.

"I understand from Abrams' rater, one Ms. Ellen Scrivens, that Dr. Ai-bra-him was a regular interlocutor, and it was not unusual at all for them to meet. They met before your arrival to Paris, in fact. And their issues of common interest covered . . ." he glanced at a small green notebook then read, "the Arab diaspora community, their assimilation, their political involvement, remittances to countries of origin and so on. In fact, Scrivens described your connection to this matter as 'peripheral.' Sounds like you might be elevating your importance in the matter."

"Weird. Scrivens to the rescue?" Haley smugly thought but proceeded to verbally articulate, "That may be, but they met on this particular occasion at my behest. I had some questions to run by Dr. Ibrahim but couldn't make the appointment. Paula promised to raise them."

"That may be the case, but her notes found at the scene seem to focus mostly on Arab League issues, not unrest dating back to the 1970s. I'm finding this a waste of time. We would be better served studying the forensics at the scene," asserted the agent. And then turning to the RSO, "When will the French let us have access to the coffee shop?"

"I've met Dr. Ibrahim twice at the very café in question. The French have assessed this to be a terror attack, correct?" Haley asserted.

"Yes. An assessment I agree with so far," said the agent on his feet, in mid-step toward the exit.

"How is it that the spray of automatic gunfire was zeroed in on just Dr. Ibrahim?" pressed Haley. "According to press reports, both assailants fired into the coffee shop, yet Dr. Ibrahim appeared to take the full brunt of the attack. I think maybe Paula and the two other victims were collateral damage."

"We'll call on you when we need a visa, Mr. Haley," dismissed the exasperated, unintroduced agent, turning with his entourage of fellow G-men to the door.

***

Haley remained in place. He had the room to himself. He reached over and ran his index finger through the condensation ring left behind by the FBI guy. He was numb. He didn't know what to do or where to go. He wanted to be by himself, but did not want to be left alone with his thoughts. He should call home. Mom and Dad were worried about him. They had exchanged texts so knew he was OK, but would want more of an account than he was prepared to share. He knew he wouldn't be able to control his voice or thoughts now anyway.

With nothing else to do, Haley resignedly pushed back his chair. He entered his passcode on the keypad and turned off the lights in the secure conference room. He marveled at just how black the room could be. He opened the vault door and exited, only to be met by the "cafeteria guy."

"Clayton, can you hold up a sec?"

"Sure, what do you need, uh . . . I'm sorry, but I don't recall your name," Haley muttered, still numb from the shocking deaths of two people he cared about.

"Wilson, Wilson Edger. I work upstairs, you know, with various colleagues." Haley didn't know Wilson but had been to his office from time to time to ask his colleagues about questionable consular hits on applicants. Wilson's colleagues had occasionally been able to provide useful background to Haley regarding regional political trends, helpful at times in adjudicating visas for applicants from countries outside of Europe.

"What can I do for you, Wilson?" responded Haley.

"I'm more than a little curious about what you didn't say in the mini-deposition," Edger said, noting, "but first, I'm really sorry for your loss. Our friends in law enforcement are here doing their jobs but should have started with consoling you. You've taken a big hit. Please let me know if you need someone to talk to or to pray with. I can't imagine what you're going through, but in times of uncertainty, my take is it that we should fall back on God's peace. Let it console you and clear your mind. If you'll allow me, one of my favorite Bible verses is 'Peace I leave with you; my peace I give you. I do not give to you as the world gives. Do not let your hearts *be troubled and do not be afraid,'* from the Gospel of John. Pretty good stuff, no?"

Oddly, these kind words, which seemed sincere, soothed Haley. It was weird though, for someone in the very secular and quite liberal Foreign Service apparatus to express any type of faith-related sentiment. "Thanks, Wilson."

Catching him before he walked away, Edger asked, "Why do you think this was your fault? Clearly, Paula met with your Dr. Ibrahim on several occasions. Why would this have been different?"

Not feeling like talking, but needing to be heard, Haley replied, "You heard about the bullet spray. Clearly both guns were pointed at Dr. Ibrahim. Otherwise the whole place would have been shot up. There's not a chance in the world this was a terror attack. This was murder. I know it. Paula and Dr. Ibrahim were there following-up on questions I had. Believe it or not, the questions were about one of Osama Bin Laden's brothers, a real piece of work who may have joined a cult to overthrow the Saudi establishment back in 1979."

"You mean the Grand Mosque seizure?" Edger asked incredulously.

"Sure. You've heard of it?" replied Haley with equal incredulity. "That would be a first. I've been pulling on various threads of coincidence for some months now. Every time I try to close the book on my stupid conspiracies, another storyline manifests. Dr. Ibrahim believes the big uproar in Mecca was a diversion for some kind of theft in Medina, one that caused the death of his father."

"Hmm. This is kind of heavy. Certainly not the usual stuff we get from consular," Edger said eliciting the semblance of a smile from Haley.

"Nope. And nothing I asked for," moaned Haley bitterly. I was simply following leads in order to close a particular consular case, not bust conspiracies wide open."

"I get you, my friend, but still, you shouldn't blame yourself," Edger said comfortingly. "By the way, any chance you read Arabic?"

"Yes. Not great but enough to get by. Why do you ask?" queried Haley.

Edger inputted his passcode on his smartphone, swiped to his pictures, and brought up a photo of a crumpled and stained notepad. Notes on the pad were written mostly in French, with some English woven in. At the top of one of the pages, however, was what appeared to be three words scrawled in Arabic script. The author had circled the words and enclosed them with asterisks.

*** علي حسين الصدر ***

"Do these words mean anything to you? French intel shared them with me, noting they were found in a notebook in your Dr. Ibrahim's possession," conveyed Edger.

"Yep. This is a name." Haley's voice involuntarily crescendoed as his temperature rose. "The name of an Iraqi or perhaps Iranian Shia who may have helped provide refuge in Iraq for Ayatollah Khomeini in the 70s; who may have shacked up with the Ayatollah in a commune about an hour west of where we're standing right now, prior to the nut job's triumphal return to Iran; who may have been part of the al-Qahtani uprising at the Grand Mosque; who may have been complicit in stealing some unknown item in Medina; and who may have killed Dr. Ibrahim's father, and maybe now, Dr. Ibrahim himself. Yes, I can read the name. It's Ali

Hussain al-Sadr, one of the biggest conspiracy threads connected to this huge knot of confusion and intrigue."

"Let me suggest you have your phone wiped to mitigate any potential hacking—just in case," whispered Edger.

Chapter 21

The ensuing days were a blur for Haley. The embassy was abuzz with the investigation follow-up and the memorial service for Abrams. Her husband was a wreck. Haley couldn't offer any comfort, given the guilt he still harbored, so he shamefully avoided him. An immature tack for sure, but it was his way of coping. He was placed on administrative leave, primarily for his mental health, according to DCM Stephens and Jeffries in consular, but also for his physical wellbeing. After Haley's rather emotive eruption with Edger, Edger consulted with the RSO and the FBI folks. They didn't believe Haley's "wacked-out conspiracy" held any water but couldn't discount the possibility that his "goose chase" may have ruffled some feathers. Besides, as the days went by, little evidence presented itself that the murders of the coffee shop victims was fueled by Jihadi hatred. The reality was Clayton may have introduced himself as a target, meaning he may still be in danger, along with those around him. And it was unconfirmed, but the IT guys at the embassy did identify some indications that someone may have tampered with his phone.

"We're going to ask for your voluntary curtailment," said Stephens. "Please don't take this the wrong way, but I've talked to the regional medical officer, RSO, and HR, and it's best for you, your safety, and your colleagues. Go on early Home Leave, regroup, defragment your mind, and get back to work. What happened to Paula and your friend is unforgivable but not your fault. Before you leave, please give Wilson and others you trust the full dossier on your suspicions. I'm not saying I buy into your notions, but I think we would be foolish to ignore the many coincidences. Keep in touch. Godspeed."

En route to follow-up with Edger, Haley wondered again if Stephens was endorsing or punishing him. He pressed the buzzer and looked up at the camera just outside the unmarked office in which Edger worked. He mused at how Edger's folks blended into the embassy fabric, weaving a latticework of bureaucratic normalcy with surreality and mystery. After a good three seconds, the lock clicked open, and Edger opened the door. He noticed cramped workstations, offset by a number of humorous posters ridiculing Osama Bin Laden, Ayman Zawahiri, Abu Bakr Baghdadi, and other terrorists he couldn't recognize.

"Hey Clayton. How're you holding up?" Edger led him to a small windowless room with three computer monitors, an especially ratty sofa, and a large, five-drawered safe. He gestured for him to sit on the sofa.

"I'm fine," muttered Haley untruthfully, still feeling numb. "I'll be heading out soon. I guess it's fitting to get fired after killing a colleague."

Edger shook his head. "Can I offer you some advice?" Not waiting for a reply, he said, "You need to get over yourself. You had no way of knowing Paula and Dr. Ibrahim would get killed at the coffee shop. This isn't your fault. I don't deny that you may have poked a hornet's nest, but we're hired to use our judgment, right? You followed the path dictated by your intellectual curiosity."

Haley couldn't help but wonder if Stephens had coached Edger on this pep talk.

Edger then asked Haley to provide the backstory and the various leads he had accumulated. After which, he said, "Let me ask you a simple question. Do you think the coincidences you picked up on are connected?

Haley embarrassingly looked up and replied. "Yes. It's all I can think of. It consumes me. Ever since I learned my visa applicants hail from the same town as Khomeini. None of this makes sense. My mind has tried to move past it, but in my heart or spirit or gut or wherever, I can't let this go."

"I'm glad you said this. Let's dig deeper." They reviewed Haley's account of Ali Hussain al-Sadr again. Then Edger did some keyword searches on one of his classified terminals. Edger said, "It's gonna be tough to word-search this guy as there are thousands of Alis, Hussains, and al-Sadrs. I'll keep looking into this, but we need some way to narrow the search."

Haley thought for a second. "From the various accounts I have, he can be connected to Neauphle-le-Château," now pronouncing the name of the town perfectly, "Medina, Saudi Arabia, and various cities around Iraq. And now Paris, given that he showed up in Dr. Ibrahim's notebook.

"But I mentioned him to Dr. Ibrahim months ago. The guy Paula went to speak about was Muhsin Bin Laden. Got anything on him? Or was he one of the Bin Ladens that disavowed Osama?" Haley continued.

"Let me get back to you," replied Edger, "but first, do you mind if I pray for you?"

Haley shrugged while Edger joined him on the sofa, put his hand on Haley's shoulder, and began praying a short prayer, touching on words like peace, comfort, rest, and solace. "It solved nothing," Haley bitterly thought afterward, but he did acknowledge a reduction in the din of white noise in his mind and a dose of courage to face what lay ahead.

Chapter 22

"Your nephews' actions at the coffee shop were a bit more public and high profile than desired but got the job done. They missed the 'Carleton Hurley' in question but dispensed with Dr. Ibrahim. With him, his ties to Medina and what happened there also died," said al-Sadr, again hosting his guest in his fancy hotel majlis. "Plus, given the frail sensibility of the Americans, they are sending the young visa officer back to the States. Our tap on his phone reports no other action. He is quite saddened by the loss of the young woman. These Americans rain down death and destruction on our people but can't withstand the inconsequential loss of one life."

"Yes, the publicity was regrettable, but the boys successfully completed their mission and left nothing that can be traced back to us," replied al-Qahtani. He finished his second cup of Arabic coffee and sampled dates, which had recently arrived from Saudi Arabia.

***

U.S. Embassy, Paris, France.

Edger didn't get back to Haley. In fact, Haley's curtailment orders were issued the following day, and he found himself en route to Walhalla for rest and recuperation. He knew he wouldn't hear back from Edger while he was away from his classified network so didn't anticipate any updates before heading back to Washington. He looked forward to catching up with his family and putting Paris and his suspicions behind him. He might even visit the flea market again to see if the vendor had any more children.

Part IV

Chapter 23

"*Ahlan wa sahlan,* sir. Welcome to Baghdad. My name is Abdulrazzaq. I am embassy expeditor and driver," said a squat, impressively mustachioed, rather rotund, bow-legged gentleman in a dark, cheap suit.

"*Ahlan fiik,* Abdulrazzaq. My name is Clayton," said Haley after spying the individual who was speaking to him, noting with a bit of embarrassment a large sign with his name grossly misspelled: *Harvey Klington.* "Close enough," he guessed. Abdulrazzaq's portly belly precluded the buttons ever closing on his suit coat, reminding Haley of the "beer gut bubbas" from back in Walhalla.

"Abdulrazzaq," mused Haley meant *Servant of the Sustainer* in Arabic, or maybe Farsi. Either way, a pretty noble name for the jolly gentleman greeting him. He briefly reflected on how his own name had no real meaning he knew of, certainly no one in his family was named Clayton. He had wondered from time-to-time if his Dad chose the name from the chief protagonists from his many Edgar Rice Burroughs books on the shelves back home.

Abdulrazzaq snapped Haley back to jet-lagged reality, grabbing his bags and moving toward the airport's large doors. This wasn't Haley's first time flying into Baghdad, but the welcome this time was certainly different. During his previous Army-deployed sojourn, he traveled in full military battle rattle—he would never forget the strange sensation of flying with a weapon on a plane. He also recalled his welcome. Instead of Abdulrazzaq's generous smile and hospitality, he was greeted by a very snooty personnel clerk who seemed to relish the inordinate power she had over the platoon-sized bodies of what appeared to Haley as fettered lemmings. Nope. Life as a foreign service officer certainly had its advantages, dignity among them.

As Haley and Abdulrazzaq exited the airport, he inhaled the first blast of Baghdad heat. He felt as if he had been drawn into a giant hair dryer set to scorch. He could almost feel his skin crack as all moisture evaporated from his body. He even sensed the cilia in his lungs were starting to melt. "How do I even remember the word cilia, and what do they actually do?" he pondered, again regretting his educational bent toward the humanities. "I wonder if I could fit myself into an oven to cool off," Haley mused. He and Abdulrazzaq loaded his baggage into an armored suburban, again a far cry from the Rhinos, Blackhawks, HMMWVs, MRAPs, and other vehicles he traveled in as a soldier.

It had been nearly a year since Abrams' death. As they headed toward the U.S. Embassy compound, Haley reflected over the recent months . . .

***

After a few weeks at home with family, Haley had returned to Washington and was assigned to help out in State's Near Eastern Affairs (NEA) Bureau on the Iraq desk, covering political issues such as human rights, elections, tribalism, and other concerns. It was interesting and therapeutic. He had contacted Abrams' parents and conveyed to them his high respect and admiration for her. They were gracious in receiving his condolences and hoped he would call again. He probably wouldn't, at least not while he was wracked with guilt. He dove into his work in the ensuing months and enjoyed the respite from al-Qahtani, the Grand Mosque siege, and the other conspiracies that had so distracted him in Paris.

Haley registered one small news blurb that pertained to his conspiracy file, however. He read some traffic sent out to the wider NEA distribution that an AMCIT with the name of Farhad Hassan had been among several hundred fatalities during the last Hajj in Mecca. It was remarkable given it appeared to be the very Farhad Hassan with whom Haley had spoken, per a memorial on the Mayo Clinic website, but otherwise not significant given that deaths, especially due to fires and stampedes, were, sadly, rather commonplace in Mecca during the execution of the holiest of Islamic rites. "I suppose, if you're gonna go out, go out in style and as close to one's own paradise as possible." Still, he pondered, "Death due to trampling? Really?"

In this particular account, Dr. Hassan was one of some 225 victims, three of which were Americans. No further information. He filed this tidbit away in his mental "delete bin," deeming it noteworthy, but not something he wished to dwell on. He simply didn't have the capacity or will to reflect further on the details of the visa case which still haunted him.

Chapter 24

The ride to the embassy was thankfully uneventful. Haley and Abdulrazzaq cleared a number of checkpoints before finally arriving at his new quarters for the next year or so, with an option to extend. Once on the safe side of the twenty-foot high Alaska barriers, the compound looked like a cross between a modern, stately university and a maximum security prison. Built in 2008 at a whopping price tag of $750 million, the massive yellowish and rectangular brick edifice was protected by mylar coated glass frames designed to lessen the impact of rocket attacks. Perpendicular to the embassy lay the living quarters. Haley's apartment was structured like college dorm rooms, but a bit more spacious, and with more amenities. Just a short walk from the embassy was a gym—which included an Olympic sized swimming pool—and a dining facility, or "DFAC" pretentiously called *Delfacios*, to suggest it was a bit more than it actually was.

"Certainly not Paris," he thought, but he believed he would be quite comfortable, notwithstanding the extreme heat and dustiness, the concrete bunkers that riddled the place, and the sheer isolation from the surrounding area.

From his room, he could just make out a bend in the Tigris river and hoped the security folks might let him sneak out to the river's bank to drop in a fishing line. He had brought a collapsible rod and reel for just such an opportunity. He recalled from his Army days the very delicious dish called *mazgoof,* and hoped he might have some again soon. Mazgoof, the national dish of Iraq, is a style of cooking Iraq's river fish, some say akin to a carp, over charcoals. The Iraqis had reportedly been cooking mazgoof in the same fashion since they were known as Mesopotamians, maybe even Sumerians or Chaldeans. At any rate, it was an ancient dish that had never lost its appeal over the millennia. That, and Iraq's fabled kebabs, could make the monotony of life at Embassy Baghdad a bit more bearable.

***

The ensuing weeks witnessed Haley's in-processing, accessing his classified and unclassified accounts, and starting his first assignment as a political officer, a far cry from consular work in Embassy Paris. He was anxious to get into his first stab at analytical work. His portfolio was rather broad, covering municipal and national elections, tribalism, governance, LGBT persecution, sectarianism, human rights, and religious freedom. He yearned to get outside of the embassy as well. The security situation had improved just enough for highly coordinated jaunts to certain destinations pre-cleared by RSO to meet with clients. Most of the work, unfortunately, had to be done from "Fortress America," as the embassy was sarcastically known.

Haley was paired with brilliant local embassy staff members, experts on political files he would cover: a young Iraqi woman named Ghada al-Jibouri and an Egyptian expatriate named Sami Yacoub. While al-Jibouri helped him with the broader governance and sectarian files, Yacoub researched and covered the onerous Human Rights, Trafficking-in-Persons, and International Religious Freedom reports. Al-Jibouri was a *muhajiba*, meaning she wore an *abaya*, or loose fitting gown (or "*moo moo* as they're called in Walhalla trailer parks," thought Haley) and rather colorful *hijabs* covering her hair. Haley noticed she allowed just enough strands of hair to escape the hijab to denote that though conservative by ideals, she was just rebellious enough to show she would not be controlled by any mores imposed upon her. Yacoub, on the other hand, tended to go a bit overboard with his Coptic iconography to show the world that though he was Arab and Middle Eastern, he was Christian. Both Yacoub's and al-Jibouri's ethnic and religious differences and streaks of nonconformity should have pitted them against each other, but somehow, due to mutual respect by two professionals and a determination to influence U.S. Middle Eastern policy for good, both were collegial and even fun workspace colleagues. Due to Yacoub's jovial and rather loud disposition and non-stop joking, al-Jibouri nicknamed him *tharthar*, or "chatterbox." Al-Jibouri enjoyed goading him with this moniker, especially given that "th" sounds are difficult to pronounce in the Egyptian dialect—a reverse lisp, so to speak.

Haley sensed each in their own right would be a handful, but knew he would enjoy working with them. Plus, he was smart enough to realize he had much to learn, and these two would serve as excellent instructors. His three-week diplomatic tradecraft course, prior to his travel to Baghdad, illustrated the relationship between Foreign Service officer and local expert reflected somewhat on the military relationship between a young lieutenant and seasoned enlisted noncommissioned officer. Haley, with his military background, understood the need to respect these protocols.

Frustratingly for Haley, his enthusiasm for networking and contact building with Iraqis was stymied by his need to cover a number of visitors. CODELS and STAFFDELS, (Congressmen and Congressional Staff delegations), respectively, along with senior U.S. government delegations kept the mission busy. It often fell to the political section to manage these visits. Haley's new boss, the political counselor, afforded him several opportunities to serve as control officer. He didn't mind, however, as it forced him to learn his brief on bilateral relations, network with Iraqi counterparts, and meet with his own senator from the upstate region of South Carolina, a Baghdad frequenter.

With Congress in recess, the embassy currently hosted a number of visitors to ensure they got face time with senior Iraqi leadership and their precious photo ops with the troops. This played well back home and established for them an image of congressional valor. The mission rationalized the large strain on personnel in hosting the visitors as worth the hope they would return to Washington better informed on the critical nature of U.S.-Iraqi relations. Some visitors valued input from the country team, or embassy section leaders, while others enjoyed the free booze and meals and generous per diem allotments afforded to them as esteemed American legislators.

Haley perceived the busy stream of visits coupled with his new reporting obligations just the right medicine for him to put Paris finally behind him and to get his diplomatic career back on track.

For the first time in over a year, he felt whole. Ironically, he felt this peace in one of the most dangerous cities on earth.

Chapter 25

"Ghada, can you please give me the 101 on current Sunni-Shia relations in Iraq?" asked Haley of Ghada al-Jibouri, hoping to get insight on a cable he was tasked with drafting about the upcoming Ashura commemorations. They arrived at a table with coffee on their trays in the very spacious, but thankfully somewhat empty, *Delfacios*. The dining facility showcased the architectural creativity of a warehouse, with an inspirationally matched monochromatic white interior design. Accoutrements of the building included only tables, chairs, a salad bar, and a bar for diners to receive their hot food items. A few motivational military posters affixed to the walls provided the only splashes of color to the otherwise drab, sterile facility.

"Of course, but to understand current relations, you must know history, and if you don't mind me saying, you Americans aren't very good history students. I think you spend more time trying to make history than studying it," she said with a twisted smile and a clear but distinctly heavy Iraqi accent, emphasizing the *r*'s in particular.

Given the number of Civil War reenactments, or "re-engagements"—as some of the more spirited devotees perceived them—he had witnessed in South and North Carolina, Haley was on the verge of disagreeing with al-Jibouri. He thought better of it, however, especially as he reflected on how his grandfather was born in a home, not a hospital, without electricity or running water and attended a one-room schoolhouse for most of his childhood. At that time, Baghdad was a thriving, developed metropolis, skilled in advanced education, medicine, arts, diplomacy, and sciences. "I probably have a little to learn from those who've already enjoyed their time in history," he surmised and allowed the jab.

"Let's first discuss the upcoming Ashura holidays," she ventured. "You may think that Ashura is only for Shii," pronouncing the last syllable's deeply guttural 'ein in a way that despite years of practice, still eluded Haley. He noted that al-Jibouri often swapped the terms Shia and Shii interchangeably, but understood the latter to mean the singular form of the term. "You said 101, right?" rolling her eyes a bit in impatience, having already educated three of Haley's predecessors.

"As you know, Ashura comes on the tenth day of the first month—Muharram—of the Islamic calendar." He didn't. She continued, "The Sunna also mark this holiday to, how do you say, to rememberate?"

"Commemorate," corrected Haley.

"Yes, to commemorate when Musa saved 'ebrieen from Egypt Fero' so they could cross the Red Sea."

Musa, knew Haley, was Arabic for Moses. He also knew that 'ebrieen was Arabic for Hebrews and was astonished at the etymological spelling differences between the words Hebrew and Arab, roughly noted in their three letter root spelling 'i-b-r versus 'a-r-b. He wondered if Abraham had any inkling his offspring would be so divided by this bout of dyslexia. "Fascinating," he thought and marveled also at how the Arab/Muslim world got the same Sunday school lesson he did about the Red Sea crossing. A loud, off-key Walhalla Presbyterian Vacation Bible School rendition of "the horse and rider thrown into the sea" went through his mind . . .

"Some Sunna also mark Ashura as the co-mem-oration" she emphasized "of Prophet *Nooh* leaving his ship with animals, and others, the arrival of Prophet Mohammed to Medina al-Munawarah. But for the Shia, they mark the murder of Hussain bin Ali, the grandson of Mohammed, at the Battle of Kerbala some 1300 years ago. Arabs have long *'co-memories.'* Shia also mark Ashura in Iraq, Iran, Afghanistan, Pakistan, Bahrain, and other places. Very famous in Lebanon, too. They commit *'flatt-u-la-tion'* to whip themselves as punishment for failing to save Prophet Hussain."

"I believe you mean flagellation," corrected Haley enjoying some brief comical imagery.

"You can count in Arabic language? What do you think Ashura means?" she asked suddenly.

Haley quickly touched his fingers counting, "*Wahed, ithnain, thalatha, arba', khamsa, sita, saba', themaniya, tisa', ashira. Ashira?* Really? *Ashura* means ten?"

"Of course, Arabic language not so difficult," al-Jibouri smiled again. "Muharram the tenth. The tenth day of the first and forbidden month. No warfare is allowed to take place during this holy month."

Al-Jibouri went on to provide details of the battle of Kerbala that *schismized* Shia and Sunni Muslims. To the best Haley could grasp, the seat of Islamic power some fifty years after the

Mohammed's launch of Islam around 630, had shifted from the Arabian Peninsula to the *Bilad al-Sham*, what is now known as greater Syria, which included all of Palestine, Syria, Lebanon, and large parts of Iraq. Made sense, she inferred, given Damascus' geographic centric role of connecting the world's religious, political, and commerce power bases. According to al-Jibouri, a character named Yazid bin Mu'awiya ruled the Umayyad caliphate, which at the time, seemed to treat Christian and Jewish populations under Islamic control fairly, as long as they paid the *jizya*, or tax for being left alone. These dues, along with the *zakat*, Islamic charitable giving required as one of the five pillars of Islam, largely financed the *imperialization* of Islam.

This Yazid, she explained, whose mother was a Christian, supported religious assimilation of the considerable Christian populations in the greater region. As such, he and his father before him were popular with their expansive power base and made wealthy by their focus on commerce. Al-Jibouri further explained that given this accumulation of wealth, Yazid's father allegedly broke a promise to return his now consolidated political support to Hussain bin Ali instead of his own Yazid. Hussain, for his part, sought a return to what he perceived were the pure interpretations of Islam as laid out in the sayings of his grandfather Mohammed, still being drafted at this time, eschewing economic and commercial growth.

Yazid's inheritance left him a powerful political and economic ruler, and Hussain now bereft of his promised spiritual and birthright caliphate, could not let that stand. "The Shia believe that Hussain was denied his rightful role as leader of the faithful due to usurpation and political expediency," al-Jibouri summarized.

"Islam's spread across the desert gave Yazid's people enormous power and wealth. Maybe sand flows richer than blood?"

"I'll bet Jeb Bush and Hillary Clinton could sympathize with this guy," floated Haley.

Al-Jibouri further explained that as Yazid further consolidated his power base, largely through payoffs and treaties, Hussain bin Ali refused to declare his allegiance. And he undertook an ill-advised trip to Kerbala, Iraq where he was met and killed by forces loyal to Yazid. The battle was largely seen as a lopsided massacre, filled with hateful, vengeful atrocities against Hussain—"they cut off his head"—and his small group of followers. It was followed by seemingly unnecessary and vindictive pillaging of Medina, burning of the Kaaba, and laying siege to Mecca. "Again, Yazid was more determined to establish a political and military empire, not manage a religious following," al-Jibouri clarified. "So began the rift between Sunni and Shia Muslims.

"Since then," she resumed, "Shia pilgrims visit the site of Hussain bin Ali's tomb in Kerbala in the holy month of Muharram, on the tenth day, and again forty days later, often under persecution by Sunni political leadership. They do this to show their devotion to the 'true heirs' of Mohammed. The Ashura commemoration of his death is very important to Shia adherents, who consider Hussain bin Ali, the third Imam, as the sole and rightful successor to Mohammed. They still resent what they see as the highjacking of Islam by Yazid and his conversion of the religion into a political and military authority. Hussein's brutal murder and his martyrdom is seen by his loyal devotees as a struggle for religious purity. The Sunnis, they perceive, used their forceful military and economic colonization of countries to impose their spiritual ideology, denying the organic growth of the true faith."

"I get it," said Haley, not really getting it. "Najaf is front and center the Vatican, or Mecca as it were, for the Shia Muslim world, because it's where the tomb of Hussain is and where his role in establishing a caliphate—connected directly to Mohammed's family line—was so abruptly ended. Islam, like Christianity and Judaism, had an exceptionally violent beginning, no? And for faiths that prided themselves on following God, they all seem a bit preoccupied with graves of the prophets and founders," Clayton added, considering Mohammed's resting place in Medina and Peter's Basilica in Vatican City. "Weird," he thought, "Jerusalem is holy to Christians because it houses not one but two tombs for Jesus—both empty, however."

"Sadly, yes," replied al-Jibouri. "Determining the destiny of Islam was torn between those who supported Mohammed's religious/political legacy—the Sunna, and those who supported his bloodline, the Shia. Adding to their sense of martyrdom, you should realize that four of the first Shia caliphs were assassinated. Thus the overwhelming devotion to Hussain's and his father Ali's tomb in Najaf. To add more mysticism to their claims, the Shia also believe that the remains of Adam and Nooh are also buried in Imam Ali's mosque or tomb in nearby Kerbala."

"Wait. Noah and Adam are buried in Kerbala?"

"I don't believe so, and I don't care. But I am from Sunni Islam, so it's just not what I believe. I'm only saying this to speak to the mistrust between our faiths. Many from my side believe the Shia to be *kafir*, or heretics. I don't feel strongly about it; my family, the al-Jibouri, have many Sunna and Shia. In fact, my mother's family is all Shia. I'm Sunni because my father is."

Al-Jibouri continued, "What's important for you to know is how important Najaf and Kerbala are to the Shia in Iraq, Iran, Afghanistan, and all over the world. This allegiance has threatened the Sunna for generations since the beginning of Islam. Iran wishes to control Najaf and Kerbala, and Saudi Arabia desires to erase these cities, like the Taliban did to the great statues in Afghanistan. They really hate each other. In the early 1800s, for example, on Muharram the 10th, the Wahhabis from the brand new House of Saud sacked Kerbala and destroyed the tomb of Hussain bin Ali. Similarly, under Saddam Hussain, Shia were prohibited from pilgrimages to these cities. He greatly feared anything that would inspire and coalesce the Shia masses.

"The Shia preach that on *yom al-qiyama*, judgment day, the prophets and most devout buried in the Imam Ali Mosque will raise from the dead. Think of the powerful symbolism of this place. One day, so many of the leaders of Islam will be resurrected and usher in a new era of governance. Who knows, maybe the Mehdi will come from there? Where do you think that Iran's Ayatollah Khomeini got his inspiration? He spent fourteen years in exile in Najaf before going to France."

Haley's head was spinning again. Why hadn't he chosen a Western Hemisphere assignment? Or the Far East. He knew in Iraq he would encounter some of the same conspiracies he stumbled upon in Paris, but instead of being a third party observer, now he perceived himself a front row participant—again.

To clear his mind, he decided to hold on drafting a think piece on Ashura. Instead, he and al-Jibouri would simply compile data points on any violence, protests, and persecutions. The analytical piece could come later, he concluded. "And what's the deal with big moves in the Islamic world taking place in the month of

Muharram?" he asked, thinking again back to the 1979 siege of Mecca and how one of the verdicts against the rebels was the crime of "violating the sanctity" of this holy month.

Haley also tasked Yacoub to put together some questions to raise and to explore setting up meetings with public officials and NGOs outside the embassy to discuss what might be an uptick in honor killings. As part of his duties in covering human rights, he was required to monitor how national and provincial governments responded to reports of these killings. The murder of daughters or sisters by family members was a blight and ugly mark on societies in the Middle East. It was not common but had not been eliminated either, and the State Department was required by Congress to report on such atrocities. Per Yacoub, over the last few years, several dozen young girls ages fourteen to eighteen had gone missing from towns and cities surrounding Baghdad, mostly to the east, north, and south. Sadly, with violence prevalent in Iraq, disappearances were not unheard of, and the police reportedly had no leads.

Chapter 26

Five-Star Hotel, Paris, France, the same week.

"I advise against it," al-Sadr stressed, from a different majlis, in a different luxurious hotel in Paris. There are too many unknowns, and even with our resources and devotees, Iraq is still unsafe. Even I, with all the protections offered by the al-Sadr clan, have difficulty entering and exiting Iraq."

"My mind is made up," replied al-Qahtani. "Do you think I would be absent from personally handling the last stages of our glorious initiative?" I want to bear witness myself to the arrivals and to ensure that we pick just the right individuals for our noble venture. I've been awaiting this for forty years. Nothing will prevent my participation."

"I understand and will, again, take care of the arrangements."

"Good. What are the concerns you mentioned in the text you sent me?"

"Namely, that my name has been raised in French security and intelligence channels. I don't believe it is of concern, but my sources believe Dr. Ibrahim passed information about me to the Americans. There is, for sure, no connection to you, but there appears to be some questions about my financial assets and ties to a number of ventures I control in Beirut, Kuwait, and, of course, our sizable holdings in Dubai. I would rather these not be uncovered, especially as they link our network to Tehran and Qom."

"Yes, this is serious. Keep me posted. I want no distractions now."

"Agreed. And this is why I had Dr. Farhad eliminated. He was too jittery, too nervous. He had served his purpose and was no longer needed. His work in Jordan helped launch our program in Iraq, so there was no further need to keep him on board."

"I agree, but you should have consulted with me first before deciding on his disposition. It may be that we would have further needed consultation on his expertise. This is a new science. Our Jordanian and Iraqi friends may struggle without his guidance. What's done, however, is done. And it's very appropriate that he ascended into Paradise while on Hajj in Mecca—where this all began, and where it all will end."

***

U.S. Embassy Compound. Baghdad, Iraq.

"Sami, I'll clear it with RSO, but can you please start reaching out to NGOs and local governance in Aziziyah to explore the reports of disappearances of young girls to see if there is any honor killing nexus?" Haley enquired of Yacoub. The two sat in Yacoub's office. Given that Haley worked in the classified section of the embassy, Yacoub could only visit him while under escort. Haley found it more efficient and personal to meet Yacoub and al-Jibouri on their turf. Yacoub, predictably, had Coptic paraphernalia on display in his office. Catching Haley's eye, in particular, was a slightly cartoonish, seventies-era printing of a very caucasian Jesus ascending into heaven, surrounded by cherubim. Just next to it was a modern, framed photo of the Egyptian national soccer team. Given the Arab world's passion for soccer, at near fever pitch and equivalent to that of the American South's love for SEC football, Haley thought this an accurate prioritization of devotion.

"Of course, boss," Yacoub replied energetically. "I've been in touch with several contacts; they know you'll be wanting to see them. We'll need to leave around 6:00 a.m. to ensure we make our meetings and get back to the embassy by nightfall."

Trips outside the capital, beyond the Green Zone, had only recently been authorized by RSO, which meant they could easily be canceled should concerns arise regarding the safety of the mission staff. Travel to Aziziyah was especially disconcerting, given that it entailed travel just south of restive Sadr City and then through a lengthy stretch of Diyala governorate. Diyala's western portions formed the eastern angle of the fabled Sunni triangle, the domain of notorious thug and terrorist, Abu Musab al-Zarqawi, the nom de guerre for Ahmad al-Khalayleh, a Palestinian Jordanian who bombed and beheaded his way throughout the region until his death in 2006.

"*Diyala, Wasit,* still very nasty places, boss," posited Yacoub. "Zarqawi's legacy, it's very, very bad. Many people still celebrate him because he stood up to the Americans and the Iranians. Even if your RSO says it's safe, it's not safe. Many bad people. For me, the world is better without him. Your people killed him in a small town in Diyala called *Hibhib.* When he died, I yelled *Hibhib,* hooray!

"You don't have to worry though," Yacoub quickly went on, ignoring Haley's eye-roll at the bilingual pun. "You and me, we'll be just fine. RSO has M-4 rifle, you have RSO, and I have Saint Dasya the Soldier," vigorously rubbing a Christian medallion he wore around his neck. "Plus, the people of Wasit hate Iraqi government more than they hate you now. Too much corruption. Too much Iran. You'll pay me overtime, right?"

"Of course we'll pay overtime," Haley responded. "And don't worry about the danger. RSO will coordinate closely with Ministry of Interior counterparts to ensure all is well before they approve our little adventure. We have more chance of dying of boredom on this trip than anything else."

"No chance for boredom," Yacoub exclaimed. "On the way to Aziziyah, I'll teach you all the bad words in Arabic, so you can learn our best insults. We Arabs have the most polite language but also the coarsest, very useful to expressing our true emotions. English, not so much. That's why Qaddafi only cursed in Arabic."

***

Sadr City, Iraq.

"What do you mean that he's here in Iraq?" burst al-Qahtani, this time from a *majlis* in one of many safe houses in Sadr City Iraq. "This is too much of a coincidence. It's unacceptable," he continued, clearly uncomfortable as he eyed the religious iconography hanging on the walls, commemorating Shia devotion to Hussein and Ali. Such devotion was deemed heretical in Sunni circles. "Soon," he thought to himself, "such issues won't matter."

"We cannot confirm his presence, only rumor of his presence," al-Sadr responded. Our people in the Interior Ministry provided me a business card of one of the human rights officers at the embassy. These Americans love to proclaim their role of world savior to the many people whose lives they destroy with their weaponry," he said while buying time rummaging through his pocket for the card, which was printed in both Arabic and English. He handed it to al-Qahtani.

"Glai-ton Ha-ilee," al-Qahtani read aloud, pronouncing the Arabic spelling phonetically, in his Gulf accent. "You must determine if this is the same person from Paris. If so, I will not tolerate any further interference into our efforts. Do you understand me?"

"Of course, my prince," said al-Sadr already thumbing through his smart phone for just the right contact at the Ministry of Interior.

Chapter 27

En Route from U.S. Embassy Compound, Baghdad to Wasit Governorate, Iraq. Three days later.

Haley and Yacoub departed with packed lunches from *Delfacios* and some extra water bottles and snacks, just in case the journey took longer than expected.

Their armored suburban was driven by embassy driver, Abdulrazzaq, the same squat expeditor who met Haley at the airport. Riding shotgun was one of the several assistant RSOs, one Jeff Stearney, who had been in the country all of two weeks longer than Haley. Stearney had made several trips out of the Green Zone, but the trip to Aziziyah was his longest to date. His nervousness showed: he fidgeted, kept glancing at his watch, and drained his water bottle as if he expected plenty of restroom breaks. Haley sat just directly behind Stearney in the customary, prestigious seat typically reserved for principals in motorcades and other official movements. Yacoub kept referring to this place of honor irreverently as the "kill seat," readily and giddily yielding it to the American officers he often accompanied.

True to form, on the long trip though check points and on the road to Aziziyah, Yacoub tutored Haley on Arabic profanities and other topics, such as life growing up Coptic Christian in Muslim Egypt, his love for food, drink, and women—in no particular order, and the loss of status of Egypt as the leader of the Arab and Muslim world due to the rise of the Muslim Brotherhood, or "al-Ikhwan al-Muslimeen," as he referred to the group in Arabic.

"But you must distinguish between the nasties in the *al-Ikhwan* and the '*al-Ikhwan al-Muslimeen*'. You should hate them both, as I do. The *al-Ikhwan* were the forebears to *al-Qaeda* and *Da'esh*, some real nasties," he said repeating his epithet. "These were the Bedouin militias the House of Saud used to consolidate its power base by eliminating rivals. They committed countless atrocities across the Arabian Peninsula, the thieving band of murderers. Once the Saudis realized they could no longer control them, they turned on them, and then turned to the British Empire to put them down, like one would a pack of dogs. Justifiably so. These militias all but disappeared around a hundred years ago but have re-emerged from time to time to challenge the Saudi establishment's religious claims. Back in the seventies, they even assembled an Army and took over the Grand Mosque in Mecca." Haley listened attentively, but opted not to chime in on this data point, something he knew a little about.

"And, you know where much of the inspiration came for the other group, the 'al-Ikhwan al-Muslimeen' or Muslim Brotherhood? Yep. From America." Without waiting for an answer, he pushed on. "In Egypt, we all know the story. Hassan al-Banna founded the group to try to sway corrupt, Western Pharaonic leaders back to Islam. You may know there is a debate in the Islamic world regarding the promotion of political versus religious power. Al-

Banna's acolyte, Sayyid al-Qutb, studied in the U.S.—Colorado, I believe—and became disenchanted by what he perceived was American superficiality. Americans, he believed, weren't happy; they were corrupt and without Allah. Yep. He and al-Banna tried to launch their cult in Egypt. It floundered a bit for a while but then took off with King Farouq's deposing and some high profile assassinations, including that of Anwar Sadat. They both were hung as murderers and traitors, and with their executions and the poverty that beleaguered the average Egyptian, the popularity of the group took off. Everybody loves martyrs, no? And now, you see these idiots in governments and parliaments across the Arab world and even in Turkey. I hate these guys. Curse them and their long beards . . . and the mustaches of their mothers. I'll bet if they ever had American barbeque and dated American women in Colorado, they would have never become radicalized."

"Can we please focus on the meeting at hand in Aziziyah?" deflected Haley, though he was torn between his piqued curiosity about the two *Ikhwan* groups and his desire to avoid stories of conspiracies and intrigue.

Haley glanced out his window to see the vehicle moving from urban residential neighborhoods to brown, rocky, sandy terrain, interrupted only occasionally by swathes of green as the road took the passengers in the vicinity of Tigris River oxbows.

***

Aziziyah, Wasit, Iraq.

"It is an honor to host you in our humble city," Yacoub unnecessarily translated into English for Haley, whose Arabic had picked up since he arrived in Baghdad. "You are most welcome."

"Thank you, sir. It is a pleasure for me to visit you here," replied Haley in Arabic, showing off a bit, continuing, albeit with a slight strain on truth, "Your city is quite beautiful."

He also omitted a side data point he had actually traversed Wasit governorate while deployed to Iraq during efforts to stamp down *Da'esh* insurgencies. Though he had escaped his deployments mostly unscathed, it felt awkward for him to have served as a combatant in a city he now wished to conduct civilian business. "No need to bring that to their attention," he thought.

The meeting between Haley and His Excellency Saeed al-Koukou, Mayor of Aziziyah began in the faux opulence of the majlis in the mayor's office. After Arabic coffee and dates and then a round of piping hot tea served in small glasses on cheap but ornate trays, the delegations moved into a larger sitting room, so they might conduct business over lunch.

Haley looked forward to this part of his job. Iraqi food was quite good, and given Iraq's historical emplacement in the center of the known world, the country benefited from the import and sampling of spices and various cuisines across millennia. Iraqi lamb, in particular, enjoyed regional renown as the highest quality, and the obesity numbers of the men who enjoyed kebabs and chops added veracity to this claim.

Irreverently referred to as a "goat grab" by his old Army pals, he enjoyed the scene of how grown men would squat around the floor on plastic sheets while large trays of goat, *mazgoof,* lamb, or chicken were brought out over more than ample servings of rice. Complementing the banquet were small dishes filled with salads or fresh vegetables, and of course, hummus, baba ghanoush, and mutabbel. The lack of eating utensils proved no deterrent to Haley, or, for that matter Yacoub and Abdulrazzaq, both already up to their elbows as they dug deep into the food platters for the choicest handfuls. He appreciated that Arab hosts always insisted on feeding drivers and staff of visiting delegations, as well as the principals. Stearney kept his distance, surveying the feast while nervously sipping on a soft drink and pinching off pieces of the amply supplied clay oven-baked breads.

The hospitality and banquet-style dining experience, Haley assumed, was a carryover from thousands of years of heritage and tradition, though he noted the anachronisms of the all too essential Kleenex brand tissues and the ever present cans of Pepsi and 7 Up. "I'll bet the Abbasids in the early days of Islam never washed down kebabs with fizzy drinks."

He also noted the lack of Coca-Cola products in settings like this and wondered if this was due to a ridiculous rumor that holding a Coca-Cola can to a mirror reflected what some rather feeble-minded individuals believed to be scripted in Arabic, "*No Mohammed, No Allah.*" He recalled similar "backmasking" conspiracies floating around Walhalla in his youth, including allegations that Christian music star Amy Grant's music played backwards somehow glorified the devil. "People are genuine idiots," he thought, while relishing the food and the company of his kind and generous hosts.

Snapping back to the well-fed present, Yacoub picked up his interpretation duties while Haley asked a series of questions about reports of missing girls.

"Your Excellency," Haley began, addressing the mayor, "Again, I thank you for your kind hospitality and accessibility for our research into human rights across Iraq. As you know, the world judges all of us not by how we treat our friends and those most favored but how we treat those who oppose us, minorities, and others less advantaged. That's why we work with nongovernmental organizations and governments alike to explore how various religious sects, minorities, women and girls, the LGBT community, prisoners, and others are treated by society. Our research and mandates are broad, required by Congress, and I can assure you, we subject ourselves in the United States to just such vigorous reviews. As government officials, we believe strongly in our accountability to those we serve."

Al-Koukou responded graciously, again welcoming Haley and his entourage. He reminded Haley of what he characterized as atrocities committed by U.S. forces, notably at Abu Ghraib prison in the early years of the deposing of Saddam Hussain. Haley often heard such arguments and couldn't refute them given the horrible behavior demonstrated by individual service men and women, people he deemed unfit to wear the uniform of the United States military. He acknowledged the horrific mistakes made and lamented over how the behavior of these few cost the United States dearly in terms of loss of moral authority, and sadly, lives of honorable American and Iraqi citizens.

Having satisfactorily "told the Americans off," al-Koukou opened the discussion for a frank exchange of views. "You're most welcome here. We are very transparent; we serve the people in *Muhafitha [Province], Wasit,*" he interjected proudly in English.

Haley reviewed a number of the more banal questions regarding human rights and religious freedom and then asked, "What do you know of the reports of the disappearance of young women from around Iraq?" Al-Koukou replied he, too, had read reports but believed them to be exaggerated, saying should there be truth to rumors of missing girls, the mothers and fathers would be in the streets protesting against him and the police. "We hear too many story, but it no true," he again rattled off in his broken English. It always amused Haley to hear how his Arab friends confused the words "too" and "very".

Haley sipped on his tiny and ornate glass of scalding tea, served by the mayor himself. He knew from previous experience Iraqis prided themselves in finishing off a heavy meal with a hearty and sugary repast, brewed very dark with loose tea leaves. He had heard tea consumption coupled with dates contributed to the high rates of diabetes, and noticed that most Iraqi men were a bit paunchy. Maybe this was true? As he caught himself casting judgment, he reflected briefly on how every restaurant in Walhalla offered only sweet tea. Ordering unsweetened tea in some establishments was considered insulting. He mentally jotted a note to himself to invest in the import of all-you-can-eat buffet-style restaurants in Iraq, if the country ever stabilized.

Noting Stearney's signal to depart, Haley and Yacoub thanked and complimented the mayor for his hospitality, and made for the door.

"Be careful my friend," said al-Koukou, thickly rolling his r's. "Iraq still very dangerous place. Safety now, but too many daesh hate amedika too much."

Chapter 28

Return trip to the U.S. Embassy Compound, on the road from Aziziyah to Baghdad.

Loaded in the suburban and moving north, Haley pulled out his notepad and reflected on a conversation he had earlier in the day with an NGO in Aziziyah headed by a Dutch woman who arrived in Iraq only four months prior. He and Yacoub had peppered her with broad human rights questions and agreed to swap notes with her on anecdotes and data they collected, but otherwise this meeting revealed no real significant updates, especially regarding reports of abductions or families engaged in behavior akin to honor killings.

Unfortunately, the afternoon meeting with a second NGO, *Arrahma,* was canceled abruptly because the director was caught in traffic across town. "That's really disappointing," Haley passed to Yacoub. "We came all this way and really needed to see these folks. Remind me of the director's name?"

"It's Khalil Mehran, boss" said Yacoub, still texting his contact at the NGO to express his disappointment at the sudden cancellation. "I'll let them know this visit required much coordination, and it will be nearly impossible to reschedule, unless they wish to visit us in Baghdad."

"How did we come across this group in the first place?"

"Mehran is a dual-citizen Canadian-Iraqi. He's quite well published on issues ranging from human rights legislative reform to family law. We've not met him, but your predecessor spoke to him on the phone, and they connect via video conference from time to time. He's very active and seems to be well-regarded around the governorate."

"I spoke to him earlier to confirm our arrival and to ensure coordination with his office and that of local police, just in case we needed to make a quick exit," Stearney spoke up. To Haley's recollection, they were his first words of the day. "He's a no-show, so let's pack it up and get the dew out of dodge. *Ab-dul-RAY-zak*, let's turn this ship around and head home."

"Clearly, Stearney isn't disappointed our meetings are cut short," Haley whispered to Yacoub, who responded, "What is a dew and where is dodge?"

While the armored suburban lumbered north, out of the city and onto the main thoroughfare toward Baghdad, Haley and Yacoub began typing up their notes onto their government-issued iPhones.

Twenty minutes later, the vehicle approached a checkpoint. Haley reached into the back seat for bottles of water to pass around to the other passengers.

The water bottles never reached their intended recipients.

***

Impact.

An intensely loud and significantly shorter than staccato . . . **boom**. Definitely not a ka-boom, like in the cartoons, and there were no reverberations. It was deafening, but then so was the silence that followed, except for the ringing.

"How can a sound that loud be so short?" Haley was confused. Disoriented. He felt nothing, almost as if he were floating. A searing blast of heat flashed across his face.

He sensed nothing. He felt a need for urgency but not the will for it—not any will.

Time ceased. It was irrelevant.

Dust hovered, and even nearby flames burned in slow motion. He saw everything but noticed nothing.

He was stunned. He couldn't move and didn't want to. He was oddly aware he had no awareness.

Then Haley was suddenly mindful of the split-second transition from deep sleep to waking up in the morning. With this realization came an overwhelming flood of thoughts, perceptions, feelings, urges, and knowledge. Too much, too fast.

He couldn't take it in; he couldn't analyze or process the sudden information dump of data points.

"Pain. Ok, that's real. And so are the smells. What are they?" Flavors came to mind, all unpleasant. "Acrid, iron—or is it copper?—sweet, putrid."

Suddenly, his mind began interpreting the visual signals transmitted by his as yet focused eyes.

More descriptive terms challenged his hazy thoughts. "Carnage, blood, charred, smoke, devastation." His auditory skills had yet to come online, and locomotor movements were either unresponsive or in revolt.

He realized he was actually upside down, dangling but for his seat belt's unyielding grasp.

Hands were grabbing at him. Ripping. Cutting. Yanking. Dragging.

The smells again. A growing din of noise—too much cacophony to distinguish one sound from another. Voices, perhaps? Burning? Engine revving? Radio? Shots fired?

He felt his body being dragged across the ground. His mind was trying to interpret what his senses were failing to detect. Where was his shoe? Was his father there? Who was carrying him? Was he asleep?

Searing pain suddenly and finally forced his mind into gear. He still couldn't focus, but he began to realize he was being jostled about. The pain was in his leg, or was it his arm? The smell of copper so strong he could taste it.

He looked to where he had been dragged. He couldn't focus but observed blurred yellow flames and billowing black smoke against a rather empty desert backdrop. He passed out.

Part V

Chapter 29

Floor of room in an unknown location.

"*Istayquth [wake up]*," said an unfamiliar voice.

Haley felt a hand grab and shake his shoulder. "*Istayquth*," the voice repeated.

He tried to reach out, but his arms didn't work. He was met with the realization he was restrained. His arms were tied behind his back, and he lay on a cushion on a hard surface. As he struggled with the bonds, the pain returned. This time, he could indeed trace it. An excruciating sear flared from his left arm. Clearly something was wrong with it. He had never broken any bones so didn't understand the sensation. He just knew it didn't work correctly. And it hurt.

"*Ana Umstayquth*," Haley replied, not knowing how he knew the word for awake, and who it was he was informing about his growing consciousness. He couldn't see, but as more of his senses came online, the clearer it was that efforts were underway to block them. Going by the musty, dusty smell of canvas, a hood was over his head. And what was he laying on? The hard, cold grittiness of its surface suggested he was on a poured concrete slab. Why was he not in a hospital? Or back in the embassy? Or better yet, home in Walhalla with Mom and Dad and his brothers and sister?

Despair co-mingled with his fear. Then concern for Sami, Abdulrazzaq, and Stearney. Where were they? "Anyone here?" he called out in a nearly unrecognizable, raspy and strained voice.

"*Ikhras, haymar!*" snapped a disembodied voice. Haley knew that *haymar* was a common insult in Arabic, meaning idiot, or more literally, "*male donkey.*" *Ikhras*, he also knew, was a crude way to tell someone to shut up. He continued anyway, "Where am I? What am I doing here? Who are you?"

He couldn't be sure if he heard or simply felt the subsequent and painful "thunk," and he immediately descended into oblivion.

***

Haley awoke in considerable pain and even more discomfort. He still couldn't see. His arm hurt. His head throbbed. His head was congested, making it hard to breathe, compounded by the dust in the canvas draped over his head. He noticed and was comforted a bit by bandages on his head and his arm, which was also in a rudimentary splint.

He tried to recall the Bible verse of encouragement that Edgers shared with him. "Something about peace?" He thought back to Sunday School for other verses of encouragement. His memories came in garbled, but he recalled a bunch of Old Testament verses extolling courage but couldn't remember if they were from Judges, Joshua, or was it Deuteronomy? "Seems like there was a bolstering verse from Isaiah as well. Something about 'Be strong and take courage. Do not fear or be dismayed. God will strengthen and uphold you…' Something like that." His mind was still a jumbled mess of sensory inputs and hazy outputs. Pain both honed and dulled his thoughts.

"Finally, you are wake," said a heavily accented voice, apparently relishing the 'r' in "are."

"Who are you, and where am I?"

"Of course, you are scared to your current situation."

"Again, with the 'r's," he thought, but instead said, "Where are my friends?"

"Pomb kill your American friend. We execute Iraqi traitor. We have Nasrani." Haley knew there was no "p" in Arabic, making the "p" and "b" sounds interchangeable in English.

Haley gasped. "You killed Abdulrazzaq? He only wanted peace and stability for Iraq, a better life for his family than Iraqis had under Saddam Hussain. He was a good man. Why would you murder him?

"And Sami may be Messihi," Haley hastily continued, "but doesn't your belief system offer protection for *Ahl al-Kitab?* Let him go!" Haley recalled some in the Arab world still referred to Christians as Nazarenes, or Nasrani. He hoped by referencing *People of the Book*, he might evoke a smidgen of sympathy for Yacoub.

"I no care for *kafir* [unbeliever] Saddam Hussain," the voice responded in disgust. "We have more big plan for *al-Iraq*, for Muslim World."

"This kind of zealotry could only come from Daesh acolytes," Haley bemoaned to himself. "I'm dead," but wondered at the same time how and why ISIS elements—now on the run—were so far south and in the Shia part of Iraq. He posed aloud, "So what are you going to do to Sami and me? Put us in your stupid orange suits and behead us like the ISIS animals you are?"

"Do not insult me. I have no care for Daesh terrorists."

"Then who are you, and why did you kill my friends?"

"Maybe you remember me," he said, pulling the canvas hood from Haley.

Haley's groggy glance met the gaze of familiar-looking honey-colored eyes. "I know you. You applied for a visa in Paris."

"Yes, Mr. Haley. You know me. Better than you should. You ask many questions. You create many problems," said Mohammed Abdullah al-Qahtani.

***

Haley was stunned. It had been nearly a year and a half since he interviewed the gentleman in Paris. It had been a short encounter, but given the attention he had put into this case, he did indeed recognize the man.

"But, but, why are you here? And why am I here? I, I don't understand any of this," Haley stammered and muttered.

"Oddly, you understand more than you know. You and your questions have been, how do you say . . . inconvenient. You have caused me to take too much difficult decisions, too fast. I cannot let you interfere more. I hope for your sake you will answer many questions."

Al-Qahtani left the room. He also didn't bother re-adorning Haley with the canvas hood. This didn't bode well, considered Haley. As al-Qahtani departed, Haley could just see through the door opening and into a larger room, styled like a majlis, but more functional than opulent.

Hanging on the wall was what appeared to be a tacky portrait of Jesus. He quickly realized, of course—mainly from his previous tour in Iraq—most Shia adorned their homes with pictures of Hussain or Ali, who often very much looked like Western portrayals of Jesus, a rather good looking, dark haired and bearded image, almost always on a backdrop of cheesy black velvet. Haley flashed briefly as he recalled similar "artwork" images of Elvis Presley or dogs playing poker in some of Walhalla's more well-established trailer parks.

He also caught a slight glimpse of a rather rotund, black and gray-bearded man wrapped in black and wearing a black turban sitting in front of a television screen. His mind still groggy from the shock of the explosion and his encounter with al-Qahtani, briefly flittered into nonsense, calling to mind an embarrassing account when he asked an Imam in Arabic why he wore black trash on his head. From then on, he was a bit more careful to recall the distinction of *Umama* (turban) versus *Qumama* (garbage). The Imam was gracious and forgave him his faux pas and then went on to explain to him those who wore black turbans were Shia and considered themselves direct descendants of Mohammed and his relatives who succeeded him. These reverends, to borrow a Presbyterian term, liked to be called Sayyid, or "Lord."

Haley's mind warped between the here and now, distracted by the flickering of lights on the wall of the room in which the Sayyid sat, matched with sounds akin to popular battle games on Xbox or PlayStation. Just as his mind began to comprehend the scene he had glimpsed of a revered Sayyid playing Call of Duty, the door closed, locking him in his room and his thoughts.

Haley looked around. His arm and his head throbbed. It was hard to focus, but he couldn't determine if the shock he felt was from the bomb, or "*pomb*" as al-Qahtani had called it, or from his encounter with the real life specter of the man. The room in which he was incarcerated was small, maybe, ten by twelve feet, with no furniture. He lay uncomfortably on the concrete slab floor that seemed to draw moisture somehow from the dry room, feeling wet to his touch. The walls, all of which were painted white, had no pictures or windows, certainly no velvet Hussains. Overhead was a simple light fixture.

He then looked to himself. He found it hard to focus and was frustrated that his mind struggled to register signals his eyes sent. He noticed one shoe was missing, for example, but couldn't reconcile with why this mattered, given his current predicament. "Man," he moaned, "these shoes cost over one hundred dollars," lamenting the damage to his favorite Florsheim wingtips, the same brand his father and grandfather wore before him. Old-fashioned for sure, but somehow, Haley convinced himself these shoes becoming of a diplomat. Similarly, his dress pants were ruined. Fortunately, they were from one of his older suits, but still, he knew replacing it would set him back several hundred dollars. Maybe Jos. A. Banks will have another end of year sale?

He was thirsty and needed something to drink. He strongly suspected his captors were not interested in his well being. He saw blood smears on the floor. He assumed it was his but couldn't divine from what injury. His ears rang, and he felt dizzy. He thought about his girlfriend in college. He had wanted to marry her, but she said she couldn't follow him in his military enlistment. She was afraid he would be sent far away to lands unknown, perhaps as far as Fort Hood or San Angelo, Texas. She couldn't leave her Mama and Diddy in Walhalla. She dropped out of college her junior year to marry the music minister of her church. They had two children already and had moved into her parents' home. He missed her and still cared for her but acknowledged at the moment, she appeared to have made better life choices.

His mind continued to race in slow motion.

He tugged at the wrapping of the splint on his left arm. Sharp stabs of pain indicated he was not likely to get much use out of this arm. He only hoped no permanent damage had been done.

Chapter 30

U.S. Embassy, Baghdad, Iraq.

"Yeah, this is Lamar. What's going on?" Lamar Leverette, one of the assistant RSOs, took the call from the Marines at Post One, the embassy's security command and control station.

"I'm not sure, sir," replied Marine Lance Corporal Jennie Lerner. "The tracker on Suburban number 14 just flipped off. I cannot reach A/RSO Stearney. Per security protocol, he called in on the top of the hour each hour since he left this morning, driving a team south to a city in Wasit governorate, ummm, one *A-zi-zi-yah*. His last call was at 1400, and he mentioned he was en route back to the mission, anticipating an arrival between 1600 and 1700. He missed his call-in at 1500. I've been calling him since but no response. I'm getting no signal from the transponder in the vehicle. I can send you the grid coordinates for its last known location."

"Yes, please do," Leverette ordered. "I'll contact the Iraqi Interior Ministry for updates. They were supposed to have a chase vehicle keep tabs on our guys from a distance."

***

Once Leverette learned the Iraqis had reported an explosion on the main thoroughfare from Wasit to Baghdad, he alerted the DCM, who called an emergency meeting at the embassy so team members could coordinate information and determine what action, if any, should be taken.

In the meeting, which was convened within fifteen minutes, Leverette laid out what he knew, essentially little beyond the timetables provided by Post One, and that communications with A/RSO Stearney were down. He mentioned he had called the cell numbers of the others in the vehicle, but they, too, had gone unanswered.

The senior defense official, an Army Colonel, offered to coordinate with the nearby U.S. military command to "scramble some Black Hawks to reconnoiter the area," an offer approved by the leadership.

***

Interrogation room. Unknown location.

Haley tried to fight the strong hands as they lifted him and tied him to a newly materialized chair in the middle of the room.

"I am no interest to see you suffer yet," said al-Qahtani with faux compassion. "Please to tell me what you know about Dr. Farhad, and why you ask questions about me?" He gazed at Haley, who was quite unable to answer at the moment, given he was now gagged.

The gag was a dry dishrag. It was forced into his mouth with such violence Haley could taste blood in the back of his throat, the only moisture he could summon at the moment. The mustiness of the room blocked his nasal passages, and Haley despaired he would die of asphyxiation before the real torment could even start. "Whatever they have in store for me has to be better than the panic I feel in not being able to breathe," he thought. He had no choice but to clear his nose, blasting mucus and snot onto his already disgusting shirt.

Perceiving he might be ready to account for himself, al-Qahtani ordered the removal of the gag. A nearby thug complied, but not gently, and he punched Haley in the cheekbone for good measure.

A constellation of stars erupted into a million more lights. Haley sustained consciousness, but just barely. The thug whispered roughly in accented but clear English into Haley's ears. "I'm just getting started, dude. There's no place I'd rather be." His breath smelled of garlic and cigarettes.

"What. You didn't expect to hear *American* here in Iraq?" he queried, seeing Haley's stunned look. "I went to some of your finest community colleges in the States. Four years straight and not a single credit to my name," he bragged. "I did learn to box, though. I'd still be there if my uncle hadn't called me back. He needed my services."

"Where is Sami? Where is my friend?"

"He's alive. And he might stay that way provided you're helpful. My uncle, great uncle to be exact, has some amazing plans for the region and the world. He's been working on them since 1979. There's never been the slightest glitch in his plan, until you came along. What is your problem?"

Haley flinched and groaned as "Thug's" right fist came at him. The flinch worked and saved his face, but unfortunately, deflected the blow to his left shoulder. Excruciating pain seared through his body, but it gave him his first dose of wherewithal, and a newfound, irrational courage. "Why are you doing this? What is wrong with you? I'll tell you what you want to know."

"What do you know about my uncle, Mohammed al-Qahtani?" Thug pressed, while his elder simply looked on with approval.

"Nothing other than a string of weird coincidences. He's got the name and is about the age of a nut job Bedouin cult leader from Saudi Arabia who got himself and about 500 other poor souls killed laying siege to the Grand Mosque in Mecca. Those who survived got beheaded and are rotting below now, if the devil will take them."

Haley spoke to Thug but glared at al-Qahtani for reaction. Nothing so far.

"What do you know about Dr. Farhad Hassan?"

"Only that he was rude, and now he is dead. Did you kill him in a Mecca stampede?"

"What do you know about his work?"

"He was a geneticist and an Iranian monstrosity who left his country behind to live the American dream, something you could have enjoyed as well, if you had been a better student. Like you, I'm sure he had a mother who loved him very much but still allowed a creepy uncle to molest him," he directed to Thug.

"What did he work on specifically?"

"I have no idea. I don't care. I only contacted him to verify Blotchy's bonafides." The moniker didn't register with al-Qahtani, but Thug seemed to understand the ridicule of the birthmark on his elder's face. He slammed Haley with a haymaker.

"I repeat. What did he work on specifically?"

"Removing heads of cretins like you from their fourth points of contact," Haley responded, his anger getting the best of him, while recalling a favorite phrase from his Army Airborne jumpmaster. The next punch loosened a tooth.

"Listen," Haley said, spitting blood at Thug's feet. "We're getting nowhere. Let me ask the questions. Did you have him killed in Mecca while on Hajj? Or was that an accident? And let's cut to the chase: Did you kill Dr. Ibrahim Mustafa?"

Thug held back his punch at a slight gesture from al-Qahtani.

Through swollen and now teary eyes, Haley asked, "Why did you kill him? He was no value to you. He only wanted justice for the murder of his father back in 1979." Staring directly at al-Qahtani, Haley kept drilling. "I'll bet you're best buds with an *ibn sharmouta* named Ali Hussain al-Sadr, no?" Haley couldn't resist using one of the crude insults he had learned from Yacoub.

Al-Qahtani glared at Haley with a look of malevolence tinged with amusement.

"Dude. You just signed your death warrant," threatened Thug.

Chapter 31

U.S. Embassy, Baghdad Iraq.

Leverette called his main Ministry of Interior interlocutor, who managed an operation and command center in Baghdad that oversaw a national security and emergency communications network. From his contact, Leverette confirmed that an improvised explosive device detonated at a checkpoint just north of the city of Aziziyah, Wasit. His Iraqi counterpart reported "*an Amedican Super Ban*—"a common Arabic mispronunciation of suburban— was destroyed, and emergency rescue units were deployed to tend to medical needs.

Given reports of fatalities, Leverette requested embassy permission for authorization to join the military's reconnoitering via helicopter. After a number of calls and completion of requisition forms, permission was granted, and arrangements were made with the local U.S. military command to taxi a Black Hawk to the embassy to pick up Leverette. He grabbed his "battle rattle"—a vest with inserted metal plates, Kevlar helmet, his Glock 9 mm sidearm, and a Remington 870 pump action shotgun for good measure. He moved to the helipad where he was met by his

Foreign Service National Investigator (FSNI), an Iraqi gentleman who had served at the embassy for more than five years, often at great risk to himself and his family. The two boarded the craft, noticing that along with five or six U.S. soldiers, Embassy Legal Attaché Ronald James was already on board and similarly outfitted. Leverette wondered how his colleague from the FBI even knew about the incident and how he knew about the jaunt to check it out. Nevertheless, "not a bad idea to have an extra set of guns," he considered.

After about forty minutes in the air, the helicopter descended onto a scene exactly as Leverette had imagined: a large, scorched crater next to the remains of a mangled SUV. He and the rest of the crew disembarked with his FSNI colleague moving straight to the Iraqi police who had already cordoned off what was likely a tampered with crime scene. The GIs set up a security perimeter. The FSNI got permission from the Interior officials to allow Leverette and James access to the site. They moved in gingerly, knowing that on occasion terrorists detonated secondary devices to intentionally kill emergency responders.

The scene reeked of burned tires and fabric. The remains of Stearney and the driver, known personally to the FSNI, were already pronounced deceased, removed, and sent to the morgue in Aziziyah's city hospital. Leverette noticed blood spray in the vehicle indicating that Abdulrazzaq was likely shot, possibly execution style, after the explosion. There was no sign of Yacoub or Haley.

***

Interrogation room. Unknown location.

"Who gave you the name Ali al-Sadr?" asked al-Qahtani, waving aside Thug.

"Who is he?" glared Haley.

"How do you know this name?"

Haley clammed up.

Thug stepped in again to demonstrate his interrogation acumen.

Haley felt slowly drawn into space. A large emptiness. Nothing registered and nothing was familiar. He thought he was calling out to someone, but emitted no sound, at least no sound he detected. His focus began to take shape, but the edges of his uncertainty remained blurry. Suddenly his own sentience signaled the danger in which he found himself.

"Are you ready to answer questions?" queried Thug, upon seeing Haley re-emerge from unconsciousness.

"No, I am ready to ask questions," emerged Haley, groggily indignant, realizing he had nothing to lose and nothing to prove. "Is your boyfriend Ali the creep who was in Medina in 1979 while your pal Gorbachev played Jim Jones with his fanatic freaks in Mecca?" Both references were lost on Thug and al-Qahtani, but insulting these two in the face of what he knew to be imminent death was gratifying in a defiant sort of way. "Was he the one who killed Ibrahim Mustafa's father?" Looking straight at al-Qahtani he continued, "And since I'm asking, what poor soul did you let die in your place so you could disappear all these years?"

"Maybe I can answer your questions," answered a third voice, in accented English. A large, hirsute gentleman, likely in his sixties and sporting an expensive looking suit—likely not Jos. A. Banks Clothiers—entered the room. "I've been listening to your interview. It's impressive that you gained so much from a silly visa interview. You are inquisitive and clever, and clearly we have underestimated you, a problem we will fix shortly."

Haley sensed this new guy was more interested in ending the conversation that gleaning more information from it. He struggled helplessly at his bonds, knowing even if loose, his left arm simply didn't work. Escape was impossible. Especially if Thug was still around. His only hope for succor was his wit, which at this moment, he believed was failing him. "Are you a member of the Qahtani religious fanatic kafir cult?" he asked, instinctively wanting to keep antagonizing his hosts.

"Sergeant Clayton Haley, of Halvallah, Sous Carolina, age twenty-eight. Graduate of Sous Carolina Univers-ty. Enlisted U.S. Army. Military Intelligence. Arabic Linguist. Two tours al-Iraq, including Wasit Governorate, to fight Islamic State resurgence. Purple Heart for shrapnel. You saved your platoon commander's life, nominated for Valor Medal. Army Commendation medal. We ask questions too. Sergeant Haley, you do not matter. You are like insect on car windscreen. Wiper blades remove you. My friend, Abdullah here, will remove you."

"Impressive. Did you know I was in the high school band too? And my favorite musician of all time was Maynard Ferguson, with Phil Driscoll being a close second? Why did you kill Ibrahim Mustafa's father in 1979? You're the *ibn sharmouta* Ali al-Sadr aren't you?" he conjured, mentally thanking Yacoub for his lessons in Arabic profanity.

"I don't know, I don't care this Maynard Dri-xol," he responded, annoyingly and incorrectly enunciating the names, thought Haley. "You are brave man, and you are dead man, so I tell you why I killed Abu Mustafa. He saw me remove special item from Medina.

It was unfortunate. He was in, how do you say, wrong time, wrong place?"

"*Hamdu-li-friggin-la,*" exerted Haley, apathetically irreverent and sacrilegious. "So, it was you. What did you steal, and why does it still matter? What are you doing with it? And what could be so important that the Hadith worshipper like your boyfriend, Zuko"—referencing an oblivious al-Qahtani—"would team up with a twelver kafir like you?" It was his best attempt to insult both sects equally.

Ignoring Haley's list of queries, he simply said,"I will in turn ask a final, sadly for you, rhetorical question for you to take to your grave. What, or who, do you think could unite all of Islam?" al-Sadr responded, his turn to demonstrate apathy.

Al-Sadr chose this moment to take a mobile phone from his suit coat breast pocket. Clearly, he desired no response from Haley to his question. He uttered his guttural tones into the device. In Haley's disoriented state, he couldn't tell if al-Sadr spoke one of a number of distinct Arabic dialects, Farsi, or another regional language. Abdullah and al-Qahtani waited patiently and contentedly.

Haley's mind raced but in slow motion. He suddenly felt tired. That his minders simply ignored him added insult to considerable injury and further stripped him of his dignity and feelings of worth. He cast a thought to Yacoub, and hoped he might be faring better. They had said he was alive, but if in their care, Haley knew no help was coming.

The cadence of al-Sadr's call picked up, suggesting the close of the conversation. Haley watched him tap his phone once or twice and then turned to al-Qahtani, "My prince, let's you and I move north to check on our project."

Still ignoring Haley, he then spoke to Abdullah, "Abdullah, please find Mr. Haley a comfortable orange suit, one the Americans like so much for their public displays of our brethren in Guan-ta-NA-mo," irritatingly emphasizing the *na* syllable. And finally turning to Haley, "Good bye, my friend. You have been inconvenient, but irrelevant. You will die now."

The finality of al-Sadr's closing remark hit Haley hard. He knew his life was coming to an end. He moaned a bit, wishing he had married his girlfriend in college maybe had kids and done the white picket fence routine, procured a Sam's Club membership, and maybe even saved up for a fishing boat. He deeply missed his parents as well. From a still, quiet place deep within him, he looked at al-Qahtani, and then closed his eyes, took a deep breath, and resignedly and inaudibly mouthed the benediction with which his father closed every church service: "The Lord bless you and keep you; the Lord make his face to shine upon you and be gracious to you; the Lord lift up his countenance upon you and give you peace."

He had no idea what prompted this. He had hoped to recall something witty or brave, or from inspirational scripture about smiting one's enemies.

Such an odd, conciliatory sentiment to surface in front of three men who only wished for him the evilest of harm.

Chapter 32

Checkpoint. Site of Impact.

While Leverette investigated the remains of the crime scene, Captain Nate Philson poured over maps of Aziziyah with Warrant Officer Chip Reims in the operations center at Camp Taji, an anti-*daesh* coalition military installation about seventeen miles north of Baghdad. "I'm telling you, Chip, for a bag and drag operation like this, they had to use a large vehicle. Witnesses told the A/RSO a white van left the scene about twenty minutes after the explosion heading south, back to the city. ISR (Intelligence, Surveillance, and Reconnaissance) shows a van parked briefly outside of the *Baqiya Hussainiyya* in the city center," passing him a ten-digit grid.

"What do you propose? We can't go in there with a team. It's not like we blend in. People will freak out."

"Let's have one of the 'terps' call the local police and see if they've got anything," said Reims, referring to the interpreters.

"More than likely, that's a dead end. The police might be in on it as far as we know. We'll have intel folks call over to see if they have sources who know the Hussainiyya," Philson responded. "I'll talk to the JTAC (Joint Terminal Attack Controller) about coordinating air and fire support, in case we need it. Meanwhile, we hover out of hearing range above the city in prep for a quick stop and drop. Getting in and out of a city like this ain't gonna be easy, especially if the locals see us shooting up the place."

"The trick won't be the shooting. It'll be getting approval from higher for an operation this quickly," shot back Reims.

"Yep. Do what it takes. I'm getting this kid out of there," said a determined Philson.

"Waddup, sirs! Hot mish?" barked out an eager, ragtag soldier in khaki cargo pants, black t-shirt, and flip flops as he popped his head into the room. His voice was muffled by a "double horseshoe" of dip, otherwise known as snuff or smokeless tobacco. Though intended for use as just "a pinch between cheek and gum," the young man had stuffed the tobacco into his lips to such an extent they looked like a duckbill.

"Yes, you Nimrod. We have a hot mission today. Democracy will be expediently dispensed," said Philson.

***

Interrogation room. Unknown location.

"Yeah, I'm not putting that on," Haley warned Thug, whom he now knew as Abdullah. He eyed Abdullah, ignoring what appeared to be a wadded up orange onesie in his hands, which was also forebodingly covered in dark stains. "You could have at least washed it since its last use," he thought to himself.

Abdullah yanked Haley to his feet. He punched Haley in the gut with the hand that carried the bundle. Given his arms were still tied behind his back, the hit doubled him over and there was nothing Haley could do but grunt, while gasping to refill his lungs.

Once he straightened himself up again, he resumed his defiance. He determined that Abdullah would get no satisfaction from his death.

For the first time since they became acquainted, Abdullah seemed uncertain. He was committed to the task at hand but clearly did not want the hassle of undressing and redressing a resistant Haley in the jumpsuit. Apparently weighing whether the theatrical effects were worth it, he seemed to opt for the more efficient approach of eliminating Haley simply in the clothes he was wearing. He gruffly pulled Haley by the arm out of the room.

As they passed through the main parlor, Haley noted that the tubby, turbaned religious figure barely looked up from his video game.

"One request, Abdullah," he said pleadingly, as they made their way through the room. "Might I say goodbye to my friend, Sami?"

"Of course. In fact, he'll be joining you on your next journey."

Abdullah moved Haley quickly through what appeared to be a mosque, given the *mihrab* he noticed once they had emerged from the parlor and into a larger prayer room. *Mihrabs*, he knew, were alcoves in mosques, including Hussainiyyas, which oriented Muslims while praying toward the Kaaba in Mecca. Haley surmised it wasn't prayer time, as the hall was completely empty. "No one is coming to the rescue," he lamented as his confidence faltered.

The pair exited the hall and moved to a van, which Haley noticed was under a cover and out of sight of any drone or satellite surveillance. Abdullah ungently opened the sliding van door, and for the first time since his abduction, Haley saw Yacoub, who somehow looked worse off.

"Sami, how're you holding up?" Haley struggled to keep his emotions in check. He reached out to him, only to get clocked by Abdullah just behind the ear where it hurt the most. The pain blinded Haley, who felt the welcomed return of his rage. The punch pummeled him forward and headlong into the vehicle. Without much difficulty, Abdullah lifted and unceremoniously rolled Haley's body all the way into the van.

Haley now understood why Yacoub was untypically quiet; he was tied the same way as Haley but still gagged. He was clearly in a state of discomfort. He tried to communicate with Haley via glances, but whatever he was trying to convey was lost on him. Meanwhile, Abdullah had moved to the front of the vehicle and started the engine. Another body took up residence in the shotgun seat, and this individual threw some gear in a black bag back into the passenger part of the van. The vehicle's sudden lurch knocked Haley fully off balance, and he rolled across Yacoub's listless form. As he trundled over Yacoub, his good hand grabbed and removed the cloth tied to his friend's face, allowing him to take a huge gasp of air.

Color returned to Yacoub's face, as did his temperament. He launched quickly into a violent series of epithets at the driver, the passenger, their mothers, Iraq, Islam, Mohammed, the Middle East and its leaders, and then returned back to the driver.

"His name is Abdullah, if it helps you in your swearing," whispered Haley, who wished he had paid more attention to Yacoub's lesson on Arabic curse words. He was only able to pick up just a few choice morsels in Yacoub's tirade, but thought that if a tenth of a percent of what he said about Abdullah's mother was true, she had low standards and had made poor choices in life for sure. "*Iowa, matha qalla!*" reinforced Haley in Arabic—"Yeah, what he said!"

Chapter 33

Airspace south of Baghdad.

"We have a white, late model delivery van, on the move, departing the 'backy' Hussainiyyah and youth center, approximately 200 meters north of the 'A-ziz-yah' main hospital," crackled a Texan accented voice across the secure military radio channels.

"That's it, let's move," ordered Philson.

"There's no way you can be sure," argued Chip, already donning his gear.

"I'm prepared to be wrong but not late," concluded Philson. "Let's smoke some bad guys."

Two Black Hawk helicopters, already in the air having just departed Camp Taji, headed at top speed straight to Aziziyah, Wasit. The Special Forces element in the helicopters included the pilots and an assortment of Green Berets identified by their "18 series" occupation specialties. The alpha, was, of course, Captain Philson. His assistant detachment commander was known only as Chip, and he played the crusty, salty warrant officer role perfectly. The team sergeant, called "Dad" was already asleep. Given his seventeen years and nine combat deployments, he knew to grab shuteye whenever possible and did not get overly anxious about the frequent "hot mishes" his team conducted.

Tank, the team's bravo, was on his fourth energy drink. As the veteran weapons specialist, he stroked his M240B machine gun like an elderly woman tending to her cats. The team's charlie, unflatteringly codenamed "Nimrod" who regularly defended his name as "the Great Hunter, not the moron," was the engineer and explosives fiend. The combat medic, or delta's moniker, was simply "Doc," and the echo, "Joseph Smith," who coincidentally happened to be Mormon, was the comms guy and was always referred to as "Brother Joseph." Foxtrot, the intel guy, was affectionately called "Spook" by his teammates. The rest of the team members were only called "juniors," as Dad perceived them as not yet having earned identities or other forms of recognition.

"Hey Nate, don't fool with us. We're gonna get to spread democracy today, right? My M-4 has been itching for some converts to the American way of life," bellowed Nimrod into the microphone. Unlike regular Army, Green Beret soldiers rarely stuck to military decorum like saluting, respecting rank, shaving, and keeping hair within regulation standards.

"I don't know, you Nimrod," Philson replied, as usual, inserting the second person pronoun for emphasis. "Do I need to remind any of you knuckleheads of the rules of engagement?"

"Doc was engaged once," yelled Spook, adding, "he ended the engagement when he saw what she looked like sober."

"I'll bet Brother Joseph was engaged lots of times. How many wives you got, anyway?" asked Chip.

"Counting yours?" replied Joseph Smith, just dodging a loaded magazine thrown by Chip with lethal jest in the tight quarters of the aircraft.

"I was just trying to engage in conversation," recycled Spook.

The inane banter continued for the duration of the chopper ride, which was directed by Joseph Smith following a live video feed transmitted by an overhead drone, which never blinked, never took its eye off the suspected van, and which now moved south across a bridge over an oxbow bend of the Tigris River.

They watched the van head toward sparsely populated farmland, which could yield rich bounties of produce when not contending with floods or searing summer heat.

Chapter 34

Desolate landscape outside the city of Aziziyah, west of the Tigris.

"Iqtal al-Masri awlan, gidamoo [Kill the Egyptian first, in front of him]," Abdullah ordered his partner.

"No, you kill me first!" yelled Haley over Yacoub's continued torrent of invective and swearing at their captors. Abdullah and his friend shrugged their indifferent compliance with Haley's request.

Abdullah pointed to his partner a convenient spot about five meters from the van for the task ahead. The ground was hardscrabble rock and sand but backed up against a mound that offered just a bit of privacy from prying eyes, in case shepherds or farmers were roaming the area.

Haley and Yacoub subconsciously agreed they would make nothing easy for their executioners. They saw defiance in each other's eyes, which bolstered them. Their hopes dashed, however, when they saw Abdullah's friend opening the satchel he stowed in the van. The bag contained a machete and more foreboding, the unmistakable curved shape of a scimitar. "Who uses a scimitar?" thought Haley.

Most disheartening, though, was the scene of Abdullah's companion extracting a tripod from the bag. Haley had remained strong throughout the torture and beating, but he lost heart when he realized his death would be videoed. He didn't want his mom or dad to see his last minutes. Even if he remained stoic, the thought of the scenes from his death exploited and played out for propaganda by reporters on CNN and Fox feigning and vying for sympathy disturbed him. He wasn't afraid of death, as long as it was a private moment between his murderer, himself, and God.

Abdullah grabbed Haley by the back of his collar and dragged him with little difficulty across the five meters. Yacoub, still in the van, looked on helplessly. His tantrum now was replaced by tears. His voice raspy from yelling, now could only utter, *"Allah ma'ak, ya akhi*—God be with you, my brother."

Unable to respond and descending into a shock of disbelief, Haley simply nodded and allowed his eyes to flash Yacoub an assuring smile. His arms and legs incapacitated, Haley dismissed any notion of making a getaway. The best he could muster would be an undignified penguin-like flopping around, until his efforts exhausted him. He would be simple prey to Abdullah's sword.

"Have you guessed yet what will unite all of Islam and the world? Have you figured out what Ali al-Sadr stole from Medina in 1979 and has been in safe keeping all these years?" Abdullah whispered to Haley as he dragged him the last meter to a flat surface. "If your faith is correct, Christian, you will know in a matter of seconds, but you'll be dead. If mine is correct, and it is, you'll burn in hades and never realize the glories ahead for the followers of the Mehdi."

Haley's hopes were further dashed when he realized Abdullah had emplaced in the ground a stand, so to speak, so he would be forced into an upright position. He wouldn't even be able to struggle, he bemoaned.

Abdullah yanked and forced an upright pole between Haley's arms and his back and then kicked the back of his knees, ensuring he was locked into a kneeling, static position.

"May I have a minute to reflect and pray?" he struggled to speak, finding his voice unrecognizable and resenting himself for supplicating such a loathsome person.

"You have as long as it takes me to go to the van and get the sword I'm going to kill you with."

Haley's mind was blank. He couldn't focus on his thoughts. He should pray now, but for what? And what was the use? He hoped his parents and siblings were okay and wouldn't know how he met his death. He wondered what reality he would awake into, or if like a match, his life would simply extinguish. He tried to recall the Lord's Prayer, something about the Valley of the Shadow of Death, and righteousness, still waters, green pastures, dwelling in the house of the Lord forever. Another Vacation Bible School song came to his mind—"Peace Like a River."

Weird timing. From the small uncomfortable rise, with sharp rocks digging painfully into his knees, he could just make out a portion of the Tigris River, a still portion. Peaceful. *"Peace like a river in my soul."* He could hear his dad leading the church's rendition of this old spiritual hymn. He closed his eyes, inhaling slowly through his nose, taking in the smell of mud, car exhaust, his own grubbiness, the heat on the air, a fragrance . . . flowers, perhaps?

Haley opened his eyes to see Abdullah's partner affixing a video camera to the mounted tripod. Abdullah was conferring with him, scimitar in hand. Haley's head abuzz, he certainly couldn't decipher meaning from their conversation and found it beyond his ability to care. Their conversation apparently ended, as Abdullah moved to Haley and then circled behind him.

Haley's heart pounded. It was worse having Abdullah behind him. His ears were beyond use now, so active they heard every sound but failing to provide intelligent interpretation. Abdullah and his partner were seemingly arguing over the sound check, batteries, or something, but Haley was beyond reckoning of what this meant to him.

The partner ran back to the van but returned soon enough and fiddled with the camera. Haley knew that the red light on the camera, once it came on, meant his life would end. He glanced instead at the river. *"Peace like a river."* His heart continued to beat apace: *dub-dub, dub-dub, dub-dub.*

His heartbeat grew steadily louder, seemingly to beat out of his chest, even becoming so loud in his ears, it drowned out all other noise, including the fussing of Abdullah at his partner, the birds, the wind . . . *dub-dub, dub-dub, dub-dub.* The beating became louder and faster still, and then it changed sound, with no inserted pause: *dugga-dugga-dugga-dugga.* Even changing pitch: *dugga-dugga-tigga-tikka-tikka-tikka-tikka,* getting ever faster.

Haley remained in a dreamlike trance, trying to focus on the river and the peace promised from it; *tikka-tikka-tikka-tikka* continued to beat.

A sudden disturbance snapped him from his reverie. A whip of air. In slow motion, his sight moved back to the despised camera. The fateful red light was on, but the expression on Abdullah's partner's face was somehow at odds with the scene. What was earlier nervous frustration now appeared to be . . . inexplicable horror.

Tikka-tikka-tikka-tikka continued. Above it, rang a singular "pop." Haley's addled mind could not reach the conclusion this was the sound of a gunshot. The cameraman looked around to his left and right and then up in the direction of where Haley's elevated heart rate seemed to inexplicably source. Just as the apprentice looked up, Haley watched his head detonate. The man's body was intact but simply no longer supported a jaw, face, scalp, or most other components of a head. The body collapsed in slow motion, and Haley was mesmerized at the mist of spray that colored some three meters of hardscrabble beyond where the body lay. He stared at the detritus of the man's humanity, not feeling any remorse and even zoomed his focus on what he believed was a tooth, or maybe cartilage, only a few feet away. At that point, belatedly, he heard the fateful "pop" that had already ended the would-be assassin's life, recalling the speed of sound lagged behind the reality in front of him.

Chapter 35

"Are there other bandits nearby?"

"The guy in the van, friend or foe?"

"Leave him alone. He's in shock, severely dehydrated. I'll get him fixed up," said a voice full of assuring confidence.

"Joseph Smith, you and the Nimrod, set up a perimeter. Chip, check on the guy in the van. See if he's okay, but don't untie him until we get the greenlight from Haley here. Spook, grab the camera and anything else you see of value. Let's take some pictures too. And let's see if these jihadis have any ID on them; we're not gonna get much from facial recognition. By the way, nice shootin', Chip. I don't think we had much time to spare."

"Yeah, nice shooting, Chip, but next time, how about a heart shot, so we can at least see who we converted to democracy?"

Haley assumed he was in a state of delirium. The conversations around him made no sense. He felt a ruffling around of his clothes, and then felt himself being lifted and removed from the pole that entrapped him. Strong hands manhandled him, and he was too weak and in shock to fight back. He felt his bonds cut, and for the first time in longer than he could remember, blood reach his extremities. Equally sensational, excruciating pain surged through his left arm, right to his brain. While he tried to gather his senses, he felt a sharp but quick pain in his right arm.

"Hey buddy. We're gonna have you fixed up in no time. You're with friends now. Take it easy. You've had a rough go of it, but we'll have you dip-lo-matt-ing, dip-lo-ma-ting, dip-lo-ti-zing, whatever you do, in no time. The little prick you just felt was a saline solution. We need to rehydrate you asap."

"Who are you calling little pr—"

"Shut up, you Nimrod! How about a little respect?"

"Hey, I found some of this guy's teeth. Anyone want to keep them?"

"Yeah, you can use them for show and tell at your courts martial."

"Oh. I'm keeping this guy's sword."

"I say we give Sergeant Haley first dibs on that."

It had been a long time since Haley had heard his name associated with his last known military rank. He felt the coldness of the IV drip work its way up his arm. As it did, he lost consciousness again, but this time without dread.

Part VI

Chapter 36

Black Hawk ride back to U.S. Embassy Baghdad.

Haley was incredulous that he had survived what appeared to be imminent death and completely unclear how he ended up on what seemed to be a Black Hawk helicopter, if his memory served him right. He looked to his right and left to get his bearings. He tried to struggle but found that pain and leather restraints kept him in place.

Strong hands were again grabbing and pawing at him. This time, they seemed to force something over his head. Over the steady beat of the *tikka-tikka-tikka*, a new sound emerged, cracking at first and then coming into more focus over that of the loud propeller.

"Hey Buddy," said a vaguely familiar voice, but given its transmission through a headset, Haley couldn't place it. He tried to focus his eyes on the source of the sound but became aware of several faces hovering over him. One was smiling.

"L-T," he stammered. The face continued smiling but shook back and forth.

"Come on, Haley. It hasn't been that long. Don't tell me you've forgotten how to operate a push-to-talk radio. Brother Joseph, a little help here!"

"L-T," repeated Haley, this time pressing a button someone had placed under his thumb.

"L-T? What, are you kidding me? It's Captain now. And since you're a civilian, it's just Nate. I was never a stickler for Army rigmarole anyway," said Nate Philson.

"How did you find me . . . where's Sami?" Haley responded urgently.

"Second question first. Your friend here is doing fine. A little roughed up, but we'll have him up and cursing again in no time. He's got a rather filthy mouth and is certainly no fan of the creeps we left rotting in the desert. Say hey to him," nudged Philson.

Haley had to be propped up a second but could see Yacoub was lying only a few inches away, similarly trussed up but calm and wearing a goofy expression on his face. Haley suspected some morphine might be credited with Sami's newfound state of relaxation.

"First question. You have Joseph Smith here to thank for finding you. Some guesswork and Providence as well. Brother Joseph, not his real name, is a member of my team. I don't recall why we call him Brother Joseph—it may be that he's Mormon and wears magic underwear, or more likely, that he can't keep his hands off other people's wives, like the original."

"Apparently, his followers didn't take to him marrying their wives, thus his death at their hands. Let that be a warning, Jo-Jo. Stay away from Chip's wife," an unrecognized voice chimed in on the radio.

"You can tell by the embarrassingly shoddy uniforms, the marvelous hair, their irreverence, the total disregard for military decorum, and lack of respect for leadership, I now have command of an ODA team full of Green Berets," continued Philson, using the familiar jargon for Operational Detachment Alpha. "When we get you patched up, I'll introduce you to the team. We were assigned to one of the military outposts near Baghdad. We've been training up Iraqi special forces. Once we were briefed by the military folks at the embassy about your predicament, no way was I gonna let the frat boy frogmen handle this mission."

"And for you knuckle draggers, how about some respect for the former Sergeant Clayton Haley, who served in my unit when I was a very green second lieutenant."

"You're still green. And you're no longer a lieutenant?" crackled a voice on the radio.

"Yeah and you still like dudes, so basically nothing has changed," crackled another.

"If not for Haley, and his pushing me aside and taking shrapnel from an IED, I wouldn't be here today. I owe this guy my life," Philson reminisced, with an emotional pull.

"Get a room, sir, no one cares!" scoffed another voice.

"Thanks, Haley. Next time let Nate take his own shrapnel. It's what lieutenants do best," chimed in more sarcasm.

"What's this about Brother Joseph needing to stay away from my wife?" interrupted a voice, apparently belonging to Reims.

***

U.S. Embassy, Baghdad, Iraq.

It seemed everyone wanted a piece of Haley once he got back to the embassy compound, but they were kept at bay by a determined regional medical officer (RMO), who treated him for dehydration, a broken arm, and a number of lacerations, some of which required stitches. He was also put on a concussion protocol but immediate medevac was deemed unnecessary.

Haley wanted some time to think about what had happened. While grateful he and Yacoub survived, he mourned the loss of Stearney and Abdulrazzaq. Their remains were retrieved in the following days, with plans for repatriation to the United States for Stearney. The embassy planned a memorial service for them on the grounds of the compound, which both Haley and Yacoub hoped to be cleared to attend.

The ambassador and DCM came to visit him in the small medical clinic. They both wished him well and were grateful his prognosis was positive. They clearly wanted a debrief, but the RMO wouldn't allow it. Haley didn't want to provide it yet either. In fact, he was determined to recount it initially to only one person, Wilson Edger. He asked the nurse in the clinic to fetch Philson or one of his men, who had not been far away, since the return to the embassy.

"Nate, can I ask a favor?" asked Haley, moving past the awkwardness in addressing a former superior by first name.

"I'm not rescuing you again," Philson smiled. "That score is settled."

"That's fine. I don't plan on getting kidnapped again by megalomaniacs anytime soon."

"Listen," Haley continued. "I know half the embassy is teed up to get my debrief on what happened. I get it but need to get my thoughts together. What happened in Wasit wasn't a coincidence. It wasn't someone embarking on their junior Jihad in a fight with the infidel. And it wasn't a kidnapping gambit for money. It was much bigger than all that, and it was tied to some stuff I uncovered in Paris. Can you please track down an agency guy by the name of Wilson Edger? Your intel guy or the folks here in the building can find him. Please ask if he can fly out here. It's very important that he does. I think he'll be interested in connecting these dots."

Chapter 37

The memorial service the following day was duly somber but a bit contrived given that folks didn't really know either Stearney or Abdulrazzaq. Haley painfully recalled the very personal and deeply emotional nature of the service for Abrams. He attributed this lack of intimacy to the transitional nature of Embassy Baghdad, where tours lasted around nine months versus at Embassy Paris, where folks enjoyed three years at a time. Someone had the bright idea of planting two trees near the sports field to honor the sacrifices of the two colleagues. The high humidity and heat, well over 110 degrees, made this decision regrettable.

Haley wanted to properly farewell his two colleagues but found the uncomfortable glances of his coworkers unbearable. He was all too aware he had not fully grieved Paula's and Dr. Ibrahim's deaths, some eighteen months prior. The guilt from their murders washed over him anew. Now, two more coworkers were dead, thanks to him. Haley interpreted the well-intended wishes from his newer colleagues as indictments on his apparent and continued poor judgment. He reminded himself he had asked for none of this pain or the suffering of others.

Yacoub, for his part, was an emotional mess. He still looked beaten-up and trembled uncontrollably throughout the brief ceremony. Ambassador Doug Silverberg, the RSO, and the elected head of the Locally Employed Staff all said a few remarks, which were all lost on Haley who felt obligated to speak and answer everyone's questions about just what happened. He had nothing to say, however.

Al-Jibouri's kind touch on his shoulder assured Haley. "You know, we in Iraq, we have lost many of our friends and family members. This is not new to us. Please do not think us stoic. We mourn as deeply as you do but believe in God's will. Your lives, our lives, they matter equally. We live, and we die, we succeed, and we fail, as the God wills it. I don't know this Stearney man, but I knew Abdulrazzaq. He died an Iraqi patriot. By working for the Americans here, he believed as do I, that his work here could help al-Iraq emerge from the brutality of the Saddam regime, the corruption of the current regime, and from the threat from Iran. We see American involvement in rebuilding our country as the fastest way to be rid of you—no offense—and the fastest way to return us to our own sovereignty. Why do you think I'm always telling you what to do?" she smiled. "We are all in the hands of the God, and it is our belief in the Prophet Mohammed that unites us all."

Haley nodded his acknowledgement of her assurance. He genuinely appreciated her kind gesture and her encouragement.

"What was it she had said? *Our belief in the Prophet Mohammed unites us all,*'" Haley pondered if al-Jibouri's consoling could be the answer to the question posed by Ali al-Sadr: "*What, or who, do you think could unite all of Islam?*"

He needed to see Wilson Edger.

Chapter 38

"Good to see you my friend, but I wish our meetings could take place in less trying times and places."

"Likewise, Wilson, I appreciate your leaving Paris and coming to Baghdad. I realize this is an inconvenience for you and a drain on your travel budget, but before I provide my debrief to the gaggle of press, intel, legal, and leadership folks, I need your help in contextualizing what happened to me in Wasit," Haley hurriedly launched in. He had insisted the two meet in one of the secured conference spaces in the embassy.

"Okay, but I'm not sure what role I can play or how I might be of service. I'm not an Iraq expert, and honestly, I don't know the details of your experience. I was told you refused to brief out your ordeal unless I was present. Even to the ambassador. I'm not sure what—"

"The guys who held me and tortured me were Mohammed Abdullah al-Qahtani and Ali Hussain al-Sadr." Haley interrupted, knowing just the mention of these two names would shed all the light Edger needed.

He was right. "You have my full and undivided attention," Edger began scratching copious notes onto a standard State Department-issued spiral, flipchart notepad.

***

"Mr. Ambassador, I beg your forgiveness and appreciate your indulgence in allowing me some time to recover before I brief you on the events of the past few days. Some drug-induced grogginess, a concussion, and a bit of shock all precluded my readiness to give you full account of my experience," Haley said, glancing at some hastily scribbled notes of his own. "Additionally, I needed to consult with my colleague Wilson Edger here to ensure that when I did my outbrief, I included just the right context, as my capture was part of a bigger conspiracy, I am sure. And I believed I needed to accomplish some due diligence in order to head off questions of my credibility and/or sanity. I am grateful to the agency in allowing for Wilson to fly out to Baghdad on short notice.

"With your permission, I'll account for the experience suffered by Sami Yacoub and me while in Aziziyah, Wasit, but if you'll bear with me, I need to start in Paris, some eighteen months ago."

Haley glanced quickly at his scribbled notes, regretting his poor penmanship, and launched into the historical narrative accounting for his meeting Mohammed Abdullah al-Qahtani. The ambassador, and those behind him from the FBI, CIA, DOD, RSO, DOS, and others from the bureaucratic alphabet soup, leaned in attentively. It was nerve-wracking for Haley, as he did not enjoy speaking before crowds. He also found the eye rolling from some of the participants discomforting, all of whom were more senior than he. Edger, who also observed the skepticism, shot Haley a reassuring look, bolstering him to continue speaking. Several times, the ambassador appeared on the edge of interrupting or questioning him, but Haley plowed through.

Haley covered what he knew about Mohammed Abdullah al-Qahtani, from 1979 and again, in the current setting. He provided brief accounts of the strange connection to Dr. Farhad Hassan and the coincidence of various residents in Neauphle-le-Château, as well as what he gleaned from Dr. Ibrahim Mustafa. He could tell he was losing some of the more ADHD-inclined law enforcement folks, so he zipped ahead to the death of Dr. Ibrahim and Paula Abrams, including the tie-in to Ali Hussein al-Sadr. He then fast-forwarded to the trip to Aziziyah, his lunch with the mayor, and the cancelation of the meeting with the *Arrahma* NGO. He then slowed the narrative to provide details on the beatings at the hands of Abdullah and the interrogations by al-Qahtani and al-Sadr.

"Clayton, I appreciate your need to provide background on this account, which I have to admit, sounds quite incredible yet compelling. I commend your seeking out Wilson, whom I presume buys into this tale?" finally interrupted Ambassador Silverberg.

"Yes, sir, I do—much of it," said Edger. "There are simply too many coincidences to discount. Sami Yacoub's account, verified separately, also backed up the physical description of al-Qahtani, which we cross-connected to his visa application. It's the same guy. We can't verify much on al-Sadr, because, simply put, this guy hasn't really come on to our radar, at least not before Paris. By all accounts, he appears to be a money man who moves in and out of shadows, like so many financiers of Gulf money."

Haley was half annoyed that Edger's supporting details sounded less than endorsing, but he knew that for one to be taken seriously in the government, especially with State Department folks, one must come across as cynical or at least cast aspersions on beliefs espoused by counterparts. "It's a game," he considered, realizing Edger, his chief ally, was playing his part.

"Well, this is all captivating, but so what do we do with this information? I'm happy to accept your account was not a typical 'grab and bag' kidnapping for ransom, and it wasn't motivated by terrorist ideology. But other than simply being annoying, why are they targeting you, and what is it they're up to?" the ambassador directed at Haley.

"I don't know, sir. I honestly wish I had never heard the name of the supposed Messiah or his still-loyal henchmen. I don't know what any of this means but strongly believe all this is connected, and that what was started in 1979, some still hope to finish. As he gave the kill order to Abdullah, the last thing al-Sadr said to me was a question. He asked, What or who would unite all of Islam?"

"Then at a minimum, we need to have the Iraqis track down these two and get some background on this Abdullah character. Maybe some history on him could shed light on Qahtani and Sadr. Wilson, can you and your team take lead on this? Let's find these guys and turn the screws on them for a change. Haley, come see me directly and immediately if you recall anything else, okay? And please keep assuring your family back home all is well. I'm happy to authorize some emergency leave if you want to recover from your injuries surrounded by family."

Chapter 39

"I'll bet you're glad that's over," said Edger, as they walked toward *Delfacios* for lunch.

"I sure am. It's still painful to talk about Paula's death, and to be honest, I mean literally painful," Haley winced while adjusting his arm in its sling.

"I'll follow up and see if we can locate these guys, but don't hold your breath. If half of what you say is true, these guys have gobs of money and connections to unscrupulous actors across the region. I'll bet they can move in and out of Iraq, Iran, UAE, Saudi Arabia, and elsewhere in the region without so much as a blink."

"I'm sure that's the case, but we should do all we can to find them. I owe them both some payback," said Haley.

"And if I can suggest it, can you let me know if intel picks up any reports of disappearances? The reason I went to Aziziyah in the first place was to look into accounts of young ladies being kidnapped. We were hoping to dispel rumors of honor killings.

"Wilson," continued Haley, this time at a whisper. "Can you also have your counterparts in Riyadh and Jeddah press their intel and security interlocutors on a potential disturbance or significant theft from Medina in 1979?"

"Sure, but don't you mean Mecca? That's where all the action was, according to the account you provided."

"No. I think Dr. Ibrahim died because he suspected Mecca was a staged distraction for the real incident that took place in Medina, and it cost Dr. Ibrahim's father his life, probably at the hands of the hairy brute, al-Sadr. Something happened in Medina all those years ago. I'm convinced of it. Can you ask?"

***

In al-Jibouri's daily roundup of external media reporting, she included several articles from the Open Source Center, a U.S.-funded translation outlet to monitor key themes and articles in the Arab press.

She followed up with a call. "Clayton, I hope you don't mind, but I included several religiously-themed articles in today's roundup. I know we're supposed to follow Iraq's external political relations with Iran, Syria, Saudi Arabia, and other countries, but given your experience in Wasit, I thought you might find it interesting to hear of trending Messianic themes and religious rumors and bits of sermons from Friday prayers. This has been going on for some time with little regard but recently has been picked up on Al-Jazeera, Al-Arabia, and other big outlets. I'm sure you've heard this from Public Affairs too."

Haley had not. In fact, he had sunk himself into his work again, collecting data for the onerous human rights report and other congressionally mandated papers. He covered religious freedom but didn't often review articles on Islam, given the tedious rules and works-based nature of the faith. It was just too complicated, and Haley couldn't sort among the Hanafis, Malikis, Shafi'is, and Hanbalis, as well as others—and that was just on the Sunni side of the faith. He suspected most Muslims could not intelligently distinguish among the various paths either, so he didn't focus on what they taught. It was the same with Presbyterians, Southern Baptists, Lutherans, Methodists, non-denominational, and other churches in the States, he figured. His focus, instead, was simply whether governmental or societal pressures inhibited the rights of Iraqis to practice their diverse faiths.

He didn't wish to spend much time on the articles compiled by al-Jibouri but had learned early on that if she thought a topic important, he would be wise to give it due consideration.

Friday Prayers Hint at Messiah's Arrival (Al-Watan— Saudi Arabia): Imams in Saudi Arabia called on the faithful to be mindful of signs signaling the pending arrival of the Mehdi.

Throngs Amass at Al-Azhar for Guidance on Rumors of the Mehdi's Return (El-Ghad—Egypt): Scholars interpret for the masses end times signs, point to return of apostates to the Umma and to the great conflicts which destroyed Syria and Iraq.

Bashar al-Assad calls on Loyalists to Vanquish "Terrorist Dissidents" (Al-Thawra—Syria): Syrian President Bashar al-Assad made a rare public appearance, standing side-by-side with clergy, to announce that the Mehdi has arrived and he desires for the Syrian nation to cease fighting and recognize the Alawite legitimacy.

Cosmetic Surgery for Men on the Rise (Al-Ittihad—United Arab Emirates): Social media reports an increase in cosmetic surgery for men trends in large numbers. Online stories indicate men are seeking subtle markings on their faces to resemble the birthmark ascribed by the Hadith to the long-awaited Mehdi.

Astrology Growing More Popular in Arab Countries (MEMRI—Israel): Arab Astronomers are turning to modern practices of physiognomy to detect the reflection of the Mehdi's face on the surface of the moon.

And so on.

Having followed Middle Eastern news for a number of years, Haley was pretty much inured to sensationalism, conspiracies, and religious fanaticism. He also interpreted how one nation's media outlet would glorify its own leadership, while castigating that of its neighbors in a passive-aggressive manner to reflect on the shortcomings back home. He certainly saw this in how Saudi and Emirati press bullied Qatar, and how Qatar's Al-Jazeera punched right back. This perceived trend of Mehdi sightings didn't concern him, but it did puzzle him how so many accounts, according to al-Jibouri, had crept into prime time in recent weeks.

***

In addition to social media trends anticipating the arrival of the Mehdi, Haley had al-Jibouri keep tabs on tribal-relevant chatter. From his studies, he understood tribal fealties often ranked higher than national loyalties, and occasionally, devotion to Islam. Royal families in the Middle East included the Hashemites of Jordan, the Al Saud of Saudi Arabia, the Al Said of Oman, and most recently the Al Khalifa of Bahrain, in which an ambitious emir, or prince, promoted himself to king. Ruling regional families include dynasties of the Al Sabah in Kuwait, Al Thani in Qatar, and Al Nahyan in the UAE. In all cases, the royal and ruling leaders entered into a social contract of sorts, as the dominant or primary tribe, to provide state governance. The other tribes tended to fall in line and not become restive, as long as they enjoyed comfortable compartments on the gravy train.

Some of the trends detected and reported by al-Jibouri, however, demonstrated social media sniping among tribes, often pitting the *Hadhar*, or civilized, well-established tribes against their more provincial Bedouin counterparts, many of whom were nationals of particular countries solely because their grandfathers happened to be within border lines as they were drawn on maps over the last hundred years or so. Many were also among the *Ikhwan* radicals so despised by Yacoub. Most of these restive tribesmen had long been bought off by or assimilated into the modern powers, who recalled all too dearly the havoc they wreaked across the region when consolidating the Arabian Peninsula on behalf of the Al Saud. It was among these tribes that al-Otaybi and al-Qahtani had recruited so many zealots leading up to 1979, recalled Haley.

In fact, for many of the countries on the Arabian Peninsula, the ink was barely dry on the Rand McNally maps denoting their borders. Especially for the Bedouins who previously enjoyed freely traversing the region answering to no power but Allah. It certainly put them at odds with upstart political rulers. Given Haley's suspicion that al-Qahtani was activating his diabolical plan to somehow unite all of Islam, surely it would be through these less-refined, more religious, and more prone-to-violence nomads.

He asked al-Jibouri flag all media references to the 1979 siege of Mecca to see if folks were getting nostalgic.

Chapter 40

The Indian manservant discretely directed the guest into a *majlis* in a palace located in the al-Rawda area of Jeddah, Saudi Arabia. Waiting for the guest was a tall, thin man dressed in typical *Khaliji (Arabian Gulf) dishdasha* garb. Upon seeing each other, they hesitated for a second, and then the guest approached the host, gently sidling up to him and touched noses, offering generous greetings in the name of Islam.

"Are you ready, Abu Mehdi? Are all plans in place and set in motion?" the host, Muhsin Bin Laden, asked upon concluding a litany of customary greetings, which established that all was well with his guest's family, business dealings, the weather, and again, with his family, *God-willing*. Bin Laden was tall and had a long, wispy beard like his famous brother, but given they were from different mothers, bore only a passing resemblance. He was perhaps in his early sixties.

"Yes, thanks to your generous funding and the facilitation of your scientific and security networks in Europe and throughout the greater Middle East. Your people have been of enormous assistance, as has our access to medical facilities and clinics owned by you and your honored family business," gleefully replied Mohammed al-Qahtani.

"Of course. It is of great pleasure for me to support your endeavor. You and I started this journey over forty years ago. Allah has blessed my family with substantial contracts and wealth; to be good stewards, we must use our prosperity to usher in the return to the true path of Islam. We would have been successful in 1979 had it not been for the unbelievers in the House of Saud. But for their actions, the world would have already turned to Islam, and we would be the rightful rulers of the faithful," responded Bin Laden.

"I owe you a great debt that I can never repay," al-Qahtani urged. "And, I might add, it is wonderful to be back in the sacred city. I have not set foot here since you arranged for me to be smuggled out of the Grand Mosque all those years ago. I see that your company has advanced the beauty and grandeur beyond anything we could have imagined in our youth. I am glad that Allah has rewarded you, and I hope that you have been compensated for injuries you suffered on that fateful day, and of course, for the loss of your revered brother, Osama, who chose a more direct, confrontational course to rid our lands of the corrupt."

"Yes. My brother and I were never close; we shared different mothers, but I admired his fervor once he ended his time as a playboy and re-embraced our faith. He was stubborn, however, and brought attention to himself too soon. He should have waited and joined us now in our days of triumph. If he had been patient, he would share our impending glory and our considerable wealth. Instead, he opted to swat at the hornet's nest. In return for his efforts, he was stung," dismissed Bin Laden.

Al-Qahtani reminisced, "Yes. Even when we were yet young and foolish, we had our plan worked out. The siege was, of course, doomed to fail. Our losses, including that of my own brother back in 1979, were fully justified. I still miss him but admire his sacrifice in taking a grenade blast and my burial place so that I might live. My exile to France was tough, as I was married to my cousin and already had a son. I've not seen them as they believed me dead. They will see me in my exalted role soon, though."

"It was not easy securing and protecting the package. I am only too happy that our facilities were equipped with the right storage capacity until technology advanced so that we might embark on our noble quest," remarked Bin Laden.

"Indeed. Though I opposed it at the time, I see now the wisdom of reaching out to our Shia cousins, who were instrumental in preserving the revered package in Najaf, Iraq and in investing in the technology we needed and secreting me to France and setting me up in comfort so that I might effectively plan and launch the future. Their Ayatollah was very supportive. He never swayed from his errant convictions, but we developed a mutual respect for our individual fervor. Besides, we were co-conspiring only for a few years."

"Then I hope you weren't converted to Shia Islam," chuckled Muhsin Bin Laden.

"Oh no. Not me. I used to infuriate my cousins by stealing their worship aids, you know, their precious *turbah* stones, thereby freeing them from using superstition in their daily prayers. They were so angry but never caught me," smirked Mohammed Abdullah al-Qahtani.

***

U.S. Embassy, Baghdad, Iraq.

"NEA wants you and Edger to travel to Riyadh and Jeddah to brief your account and the details you've compiled to date. Both Foggy Bottom and the folks across the River are lashed up on this. This comes from the top—the assistant secretary. Simply go and share with the front offices and folks who need to know on the country team. Stay for a few days and do some consultations, meet with some academics or others who may have been old enough to remember 1979," ordered Ambassador Silverberg, "presuming you're up for the challenge."

"Yes sir," replied Haley. "I feel fine. My arm is still out of commission, but the med unit has cleared me from concussion protocols, and I'm otherwise good to go." He paused and then continued, "Can I ask just how idiotic Main State folks think I am?"

"I'll be blunt with you, Clayton," blurted Silverberg. "Your corridor reputation is damaged, possibly beyond repair. Whispers suggest you're a bit of a glory hound, you're reckless, and you have a flair for the dramatic. And that you're a danger to your colleagues. Three USG employees who were somehow connected to you have died. I'll be honest, I won't be disappointed to see you leave post, and I'll be requesting you don't come back. One, you held on to vital information until Edger showed up, and two, you're damaged goods. I'm telling you all this to provide context for you and inform you of what you're up against."

"So why am I even going to Saudi Arabia? Why not simply send me home?"

"Your former DCM in Paris was just named ambassador to Lebanon. He's back in DC serving in NEA while awaiting Senate confirmation. He apparently buys in to your story. This was his idea. The assistant secretary supports this."

Chapter 41

Packing up with only one useful arm was a challenge, but given that Haley had only been at post a few months, several of his boxes had never been unpacked. Feeling ostracized and not close to anyone at the post, he opted not to ask for help. He took a few days longer than was necessary to get his TDY orders cut for Saudi Arabia. He didn't even ask for orders stateside, so unclear he was regarding his future.

While sitting alone at *Delfacio's*, picking at an oversized serving of *chili mac*, he reflected on Silverberg's terse words. "Glory hound, really?" These words cut deep. He felt enormous guilt over the death of Paula and Dr. Ibrahim, in particular, as he knew them well, but also for Abdulrazzaq and Stearney. He certainly felt no satisfaction over the beating he took at the hands of the now dead Abdullah. He also thought how nice it would be to delete the images of Mohammed Abdullah al-Qahtani's honey-colored eyes and his faded birthmark from his mind. He felt himself spiraling into self-pity, mixed with intense guilt and doubt.

"Hey sir, how's it hanging? Do you mind if we join you?"

Haley, lost deep in his dark place, failed to notice an army of muscularly malformed Vikings invade his space. He was stunned by their size, made somehow bigger with their personas, as denoted by their loudness, laughter, good looks complemented by magnificent hair, and anachronistic politeness and good manners. Plus, it was very unsettling to be called sir by soldiers, Green Berets no less, all of whom outranked his last service marker.

"Of course, good to see you. How y'all doing?" Haley unexpectedly comfortable, accidentally reverted to his native dialect.

"Bored. The pain of our existence," replied the soldier Haley recalled as Nimrod.

"It's bane, you Nimrod, the bane of our existence," corrected Philson, slapping Haley on the back and throwing a dinner roll at the Nimrod, who deftly caught it in his mouth. "How're you, buddy?"

"Yeah, Bane, like the bad dude from Batman. Come on, you Nimrod, you should read comic books, not just look at how the babes are drawn," said Doc. "How's your arm, Mr. Haley? Mind if I take a look?" he asked but was already gently massaging and checking the damage on Haley's left arm. With concern, he added, "I'm afraid you're probably going to lose at least the hand." Doc then pulled out of his Mary Poppins-esque medical bag a large bonesaw. "Hahaha, I'm just messing with ya," Doc winked. "You'll be fine."

Tank, the weapons expert was eating Haley's chili mac. "You don't mind, do you, sir?"

The scene recalled for Haley an account from one of C.S. Lewis's books about some characters that were terrifying until you learned how comical and delightful they could be. "Duffleflumps?

Pufflepods, something like that," he struggled to remember, promising himself he would look up the exact term later.

"How are you, Nate? It sure is good to see you," said Haley.

The idiotic banter among team members continued, but Haley zeroed into a private conversation with Philson. He noticed, however, that Spook was throwing grapes into Nimrod's widely agape mouth. He also noticed Spook stealthily reaching into the unpitted olive tray, foreboding an upcoming scene that might involve choking or a broken tooth. Two others, code names already forgotten, were "slap boxing" until uber competitiveness set in and they began to box for real—in earnest.

"Same here. As you can see, we're bored. Never a good thing with a group like us. We thrive on action. The training missions pay the bills, but it's like hooking a race horse to a wagon. Race horses gotta run . . ."

"I'm heading out soon," Haley blurted out, not sure why.

"What's the deal?"

Haley chose not to recount his conversation with the ambassador but did inform Philson he would be moving on to Riyadh and Jeddah, with uncertainty for his return.

"I hate losing you, especially so soon after pulling you out of the fire. Turns out we're packing up too, though. We're still in theatre but will likely do some special forces training for other regional partners. We even have orders to build out a training schedule with the Saudis. Don't get into any more trouble, but if you do, know the team here will be looking out for you. I promise you, we will find you."

On cue, the Nimrod bit down on what he thought was a grape. He let out a loud yell and spat out the olive pit in Spook's direction, who was already doubled over in laughter and evading culinary missiles launched at him by his victim. Doc also got in on the food fight fun while Chip went back for more chili mac.

"Dufflepuds," Haley recalled. The terrifyingly delightful creatures were Dufflepuds.

Chapter 42

Haley provided his briefings to small interagency groups in both Riyadh and Jeddah. His audiences, comprised of political, public affairs, intelligence, military, and law enforcement officers attended the meetings largely out of curiosity, given that reports of Haley's capture and torture had made it into the press. In person, however, they seemed to find him a bit unimpressive and appeared skeptical and less than convinced regarding his story. Absorbing their doubt, Haley's pitch was admittedly not inspired or inspiring. He flagged for the groups the key names to watch out for but elicited only the smallest interest, not necessarily positive, in the Bin Laden brother.

The crowd in Riyadh listened dutifully, thanked him for the brief, and wished him well. They had visitors from Washington in town so signaled no desire for immediate follow-up. That was fine with Haley, he mused, as he boarded a flight to Jeddah.

***

"Come on!" groaned a worked-up political chief at the consulate general in Jeddah in response to Haley's brief. "People have been trying to bury Muhsin Bin Laden with his brother for years. One, there's no proof he was actually part of the group that took over the Grand Mosque in 1979, and two, if he was, the Saudis would have never let him stay on, enjoying privileges and wealth. And you keep talking about how the Sunni and Shia are collaborating in your grand conspiracy. They hate each other."

"I'm not here to condemn the Bin Laden guy or otherwise put him on trial. I'm stating matter of factly the line of questioning that led to the death of Abrams, Ibrahim, Abdulrazzaq, and Stearney, included mentions of his name. He is reportedly of the right age and had the access, wealth, and means to escape unscathed and help in the cover up. He was supposedly in Mecca at the time of the revolt, and his family's vehicles were used to transport mercenaries and weapons. And no one can deny there was a cover up. Can you imagine if the Vatican was taken over by a bunch of bloodthirsty zealots? This happened only forty years ago, the same year as the Islamic Revolution in Iran and just before the Iran-Iraq war and other events that set the trajectory for the last four decades of unrest in the Middle East. And somehow this pivotal event got omitted from most history books," responded Haley, getting a bit hot under the collar. "How many of you here even knew about this cataclysmic event? Not one of you, I'll bet," he asked and answered rhetorically.

"My conclusion and assertion is that what they started forty years ago, they aim to finish. And somehow, they're not sticking to the old Sunni versus Shia narrative. I've been the guest of some of these folks and can promise you they are reaching across sectarian lanes to plan something dastardly. They're not nice people and they have something big planned." His indignation was invigorating.

***

Haley found briefings with the intel folks much less smarmy, largely, he surmised, because Edger had precooked his account in reports to them. They didn't engage much but listened attentively and took notes. "At least they liked my bit of science fiction," he rationalized.

"First off, thanks for sharing and making yourself available for the briefing," responded Station Chief Mark Browning. "What a mess. We've read reports of your account and honestly find it all quite interesting but circumstantial. I think we—"

"I'm not here to convince anyone. I'd rather be back just doing my work at either of the last two jobs I've been fired from," Haley defensively interrupted. "I'm only here because Ambassador Silverberg thought I was dead weight in Baghdad and wanted me to go on this roadshow and simply, quote 'tell folks what I know,' end quote." He accompanied his account using rabbit ear gestures with his hands.

"Hang on. I'm not passing judgment, and I'm not second guessing you. I just need to process this. You've dropped a bomb on my lap, and I need to figure out what my responsibility for this information is.

"Here's the deal," Browning continued. "The truth is we've been picking up weird chatter lately that we don't know how to process. Our *mukhabarat* [intelligence services] contacts have, on the one hand, conveyed an uptick in unrest among many of outlying Bedouin tribes, those seemingly disenfranchised from the rest of society. The most these folks could ever hope for are jobs in the National Guard. Jobs that don't pay well and many of which have unpleasant assignments exposed to the elements. I don't have to tell you how hot it gets here. These poor saps don't have the same access to medical care or universities and certainly aren't among the billionaire playboys who fly to Paris, London, New York, LA, and, of course, their favorite haunts, Las Vegas and Monte Carlo. There are a lot of young men who see how the *Sa-ood* and other favored families live in opulence, while they struggle just to pay the bills. They can barely afford one wife at a time, while their rich compatriots maintain two, three—and sometimes that rotating fourth—wives and accompanying households. And, since women are pretty much cut out of the economic picture, these low-end security and military workers are the sole breadwinners, chauffeurs, shoppers, et cetera. Not a great life. No wonder so many of the foreign fighters and terrorists that Saudi Arabia exported to Afghanistan, and later Iraq and Syria, came from these ranks."

"And on the other hand?" queried an adjusted Haley, curious and enrapt in Browning's intervention.

"On the other hand," Browning hesitated. "Our intelligence cooperation has decreased. For years, our exchanges, training, and joint operations with our *mukhabarat* counterparts were great. In fact, we were regular visitors to the *majalis* of very senior officials, including the head of intelligence. We used to be quite welcome even by the former Crown Prince Mohammed bin Nayef. Since his ousting from power, however, our cooperation and therefore our visibility has significantly dropped."

Haley recalled from newspaper accounts and old cables that MbN, the moniker given to Mohammed bin Nayef Al Saud, was largely regarded as pro-western and anti-terrorism. He was among the Saudi leadership who awoke first in the wake-up calls that alerted the country to a threat from within. Haley knew an FSO assigned to Saudi Arabia in the early 2000s who had to be evacuated due to violence in the streets and terrorist incidents on Western compounds.

One such FSO had described the unpleasant task of identifying the remains of AMCITs killed in May 2003 attacks. Given the sense that the "bottom had fallen out" of Saudi Arabia in the years following the U.S. liberation/occupation of Iraq, MbN was largely credited for cracking down on homegrown terrorism. He paid dearly for it, however, as he was targeted for assassination multiple times. According to various reports, one such time, a young terrorist deluded by his own brother, detonated a device hidden in his rectum within feet of MbN. Fortunately, MbN survived while the misled young man found out instantly and eternally he had clearly been on the wrong path toward spiritual discovery.

"And of course," Browning said, shaking Haley from his reverie, "The Saudi journalist Jamal Khashoqgi's gruesome murder and our determination for accountability from our Saudi counterparts has had a deleterious impact on our bilateral cooperation, and sadly, trust.

"Still, I'll follow-up with Mukhabarat intel guys that still take my calls, and I would normally suggest you have political section colleagues follow-up with academics who might have been around back then, but folks are just not as inclined to speak to us of late. The new leadership seems not to trust its own people much."

Chapter 43

"Everything must be perfect. We need Hollywood-level theatrics. We can leave no room for doubt. So much work has gone into this. I want the occasion livestreamed and coordinated via social media. Each National Guard commander must know his very select time frame for action. All palace guards in Riyadh, Jeddah, Mecca, Medina, Taif, and elsewhere throughout the kingdom must be ready to respond. Beyond eliminating legitimate contenders to the throne, I want minimal bloodshed. We are about to usher in a new era of peace for all mankind; only imposters shall be punished," said Muhsin Bin Laden to an attentive Ali al-Sadr. They sat in Bin Laden's palatial penthouse office, only a few blocks away from the Grand Mosque in one of the many towers built by his family's construction empire.

"Yes, sidi. Plans are in motion," al-Sadr replied. "We have recruited hundreds of national guardsmen to take action at the Grand Mosque, and thousands more across the country are ready to respond to our signals. The House of *Al Saud* will end instantly; its century of rule will end with the slightest whimper. Our allies

227

will be the families ignored and neglected for so long, many of whom hail from the noble *ikhwan* who conquered the peninsula on behalf of the Al Saud, only to be betrayed. The *Rashaid*, the *Shammar*, the *Qahtan*, and so many other tribes will quickly rally to our beacon."

He spoke faster as his passion grew. "We will implement our plans, as decreed in the Holy Scriptures, on the tenth day of the month of Muharram. The launch will take place as soon as Abu Mehdi stops at the Kaaba. Abu Mehdi will be handed a microphone already connected to the sound system of the Grand Mosque. We will have cameras in place and connected to social media outlets already primed for live streaming. In the Hadith, Prophet Mohammed (Peace Be Upon Him) was recorded as saying: '*In the time of the Mehdi, a Muslim in the East will be able to see his Muslim brother in the West, and he in the West will see him in the East.*' Surely is not this a sign that the Mehdi will broadcast his arrival over social media?

"And when the scholars prophesied '*The face of the Mehdi shall shine upon the surface of the Moon,*' were they not referencing how the image of our Lord will transmit through space and bounce from artificial moons or satellites?"

Bin Laden sat back in his plush chair with his elbows resting on wooden armrests and his fingertips lightly touching each other and grazing his lips. He listened attentively and motioned al-Sadr to continue.

"And Abu Mehdi will recite *ayat* [verses] from the Holy *Quran* which speak to the return of Allah's chosen Mehdi. He will truthfully identify himself as the long-awaited savior who began his sojourn in 1979 and relate how Allah kept him in *ghaibah* for the last forty years, awaiting his glorious emergence. I'm sure that the significance of the 'absence' of forty years does not escape you. As you know, our Prophet Mohammed (Peace Be Upon Him), was forty years old when he received the miraculous revelation from Angel Jibril *[Gabriel]*.

"Abu Mehdi will announce our simultaneous victory over the House of *Al Saud* and call on the *ummah [global Islamic community]* to unite both Sunni and Shia, overthrowing the pretender secular and western regimes in Egypt, Jordan, Pakistan, Qatar, Iraq, Oman, Afghanistan, and elsewhere—in all countries that oppose the imposition of *real* Sharia law and the return to our traditional and pure path."

"And what about the ultimate announcement, the one that will set forth the new era of peace and stability and re-launch the golden era of Islam based on religious devotion instead of political and financial pursuits? This has been distorted for centuries by the Umayyads, Ottomans, and other dynasties. We have to get it right this time." Bin Laden already knew the answer but wanted to hear the rationale behind it, as it concerned him. So much was at stake.

Al-Sadr, accustomed to giving orders, equally excelled as a supplicant. He carried notes with him, but didn't use them. He was in the final stages of implementing a plan in play for forty years. He knew it by heart.

"Sidi, I have ecstatic news to report on that front. Our little *Mehdi* is nearly ready. We have chosen the right child for this task. He is the best of all the subjects we developed. He is intelligent, strong, and handsome. He has some health problems, but with care and attention, we can keep any concerns at bay."

"What health problems? Nothing must go wrong."

"Sidi, we believe he has what those in the west call epilepsy . He has had some seizures, but we have been able to manage them with medication. And of course, this may not be a coincidence, given that many people believe the prophet himself (Peace Be Upon Him), suffered from epilepsy. It was his seizures, some believe, that opened his mind to the divine revelations of Allah."

"I am aware of these suspicions. My concern is the fitness of the boy to withstand the pressures and attention and lead into the future over a billion of the world's Muslims."

"Sidi, that's what we are here for. We have assembled the finest cadres of scholars from various schools of thoughts. We will have, at the glorious launch, the top Muslim leaders from the Arab World, Pakistan, India, Indonesia, Asia, and even Europe and North America. Travel tickets, hotel arrangements, and other details are already taken care of. They believe they'll be in Mecca to consult with the *ulema* in a confab among Islamic sects, an event that we are billing as interfaith dialogue—as our western antagonists refer to such gatherings. Even ayatollahs from Iran and Iraq will be here. They will not know of the revelation prior but will be on hand to verify the claim of Abu Mehdi and our new Mehdi. Abu Mehdi will order a conclave, as the Catholics call it, and present the scientific and spiritual evidence for our project. As in the days of old, there will be swift retribution for any of these who bear witness to but doubt the convergence of scientific and spiritual progress."

"It appears you have planned this in excruciating detail."

"I have been working on this for forty years, sidi," replied al-Sadr.

Chapter 44

Steaks sizzled on the grill. Condensation bubbled on soft drinks and beer, half covered by ice in a cooler. The backyard was small, but given the searing heat, just big enough to keep grass and rampant bougainvillea watered. Despite which, Haley noticed the patchy nature of the grass, telltale signs of havoc wreaked on the yard by Browning's Jack Russell Terrier and his seven-year-old kid.

Browning suggested a small barbecue as an ideal way to connect with his interlocutors in the intelligence service and bring to their attention Haley's account. The three officials, garbed in *thobe, ghutra*, and customary sandals, anachronistically nursed their Mexican beers, with limes, like old pros. They put their cigarettes out carelessly on a sidewalk fashioned out of bricks inlayed in the sand. Haley opted for ice cold mint lemonade prepared by Browning's live-in Filipina maid. It was refreshing, but the ground mint choked him up at times during his narrative, which he relayed to his audience.

The three guests, all from various Saud family branches, listened attentively, interrupting occasionally to verify a point or two and to whisper aggressively to each other in their guttural Gulf dialect. Upon Haley's conclusion, they simply departed in a Toyota Landcruiser, not thanking or acknowledging Haley's time or Browning's hospitality.

***

Haley's hotel room, Jeddah, Saudi Arabia, Muharram the 8th.

Haley returned to his hotel room, not really knowing what he would do next. He had made himself available for other briefings, but so far, no one took him up on his offer. The Saudi intelligence guys had his cell number and that of the hotel if they wished to gather further information from him. The lack of calls suggested they didn't.

It was a Thursday night, and he planned to fly out on Sunday morning. Given the work week shut down on Thursdays, it meant he would be stuck in Jeddah through the weekend. He thought he might venture out alone, maybe check out one of the many American franchises around town. The Saudis and huge expatriate community loved American eateries, and nearly all the same restaurants available in Walhalla or even the nearby big city of Greenville, SC could be found in Jeddah, minus the bacon and alcohol, however.

Or maybe he would find a good Lebanese, Indian, or Pakistani restaurant. It had been a while since he had tasted good Moroccan tagine, so he considered that option as well. Whatever he opted for, he knew he would be on his own; he didn't feel like bothering his consulate colleagues and asking them to give up their precious personal time on a Friday or Saturday. A day or two reading a book on the beach did not sound at all unappealing.

While looking through tourist pamphlets in the room, smiling with the realization he wouldn't find a Gideon's Bible in this hotel, he thumbed through a few leaflets on Islam, reminding him he was only about an hour's drive from Mecca, central to the religious doctrine of a quarter of the world's population and to the mysteries he began unraveling in France over a year ago. He wondered at the appeal of the Islamic religion to non-Arab countries, recalling that Indonesia is the nation with the largest population of Muslims. Given that purists decry translating into foreign languages the Quran and the Hadith, Mohammed's sayings, it was on Imams and scholars to research, interpret, preach, guide, and sometimes even do the thinking for their congregants. Haley doubted Christianity would enjoy its meager preeminence in numbers if folks still had to learn their faith in Latin, Hebrew, Aramaic, or Greek. "Good thing King James sponsored the translation of the Bible," he thought, "even if he was motivated by political reasons."

He also recalled from his introduction into Islamic studies the misperception that Arabs are assumed to be Muslims. He reflected on acquaintances with a number of Arab Christians from Lebanon, Egypt, Jordan, Iraq, and elsewhere in the predominantly Muslim world.

Despite the Sunni-Shia schism and several other religious doctrines and paths in Islam, somehow the Quran still held sway over the belief system of more than one-and-a-half billion people. They all looked to Mecca and prayed in the direction of the Kaaba five times a day.

The Kaaba, Haley read in one of the pamphlets, was pretty close to a perfect cube, smack dab in the center of the Grand

Mosque compound, which was built to surround and protect it. The "House of God," it was called. Muslims were charged with visiting it at least once in their lives and *"cir-cum-am-bu-late"* it, Haley read with a smile, amused there was a word coined for circling an object seven times in a counter-clockwise fashion. He tried to remember from Sunday School if Joshua and his army *circumambulated* Jericho, or if there was another word for moving seven times in a *clockwise* direction. Either way, he could not imagine the scene of two million circumambulators at a time, each year, going around the Kaaba.

The Kaaba, one pamphlet also asserted, was built by Abraham (Ibrahim) and his son Ishmael as the first house of monotheistic worship. By Mohammed's era, however, pagans had converted the Kaaba into a polytheistic temple, much like had been done to Solomon's temple in Jerusalem. Mohammed and his followers destroyed the idols and restored it to its supposed original intent, and in the ensuing centuries, the seats of Islamic power built the surrounding mosque and galleries, enshrining it into a global attraction, and for many adherents, a seeming supernatural worship portal.

Haley saw this as a far cry from his own faith's evolution, shaped largely by folks at the Walhalla Presbyterian church he grew up in, trying to make it to the Sunday steak lunch buffet before all the tables were taken up by the larger local Baptist crowds.

Chapter 45

Grand Mosque courtyard, Mecca, Saudi Arabia, Muharram the 10th.

Stanchions were in place, as was the platform for the big announcement of the "emergence" or "awakening." Al-Qahtani still toyed a bit with his talking points as he mulled over the biggest speech of his life and, in his mind, one of the most important speeches in history. By nature he was a good orator, and he knew stage fright would not be an issue. He was good at reciting, as he had memorized the Quran as a child and could recite it verse for verse today and had taught hundreds of young boys to do the same. No, his speech would be masterful, he bolstered himself.

He spied on the arrangements from an alcove in the south gallery. A number of pilgrims were circumambulating the Kaaba. Their path was detoured by the stage setup and the connecting and subsequent disguising of wires, but they were otherwise oblivious to what would occur over the next few hours. Testament to this was the buzz of their recitations as they chanted softly various *ayat* from the Quran from which they drew inspiration or solace.

He needed to time his grand entrance well, ensuring he had critical mass. He wanted a full crowd on hand to witness and take part in the ushering in of a new era. He called his associate and co-conspirator, Dr. Abdulaziz al-Onezi, standing nearby and next to a young boy, approximately four years old.

"How is the boy?" he queried.

"He's fine and in splendid health. I believe we chose correctly. He's certainly outlived many of his brothers, and I believe that despite complications connected to his epilepsy, with the regular medicines I administer, he'll live a long, healthy, productive life," replied al-Onezi.

"His mother was returned to her family and has since been married to a wealthy benefactor. She is still young and despite the trauma she endured during our procedures, I reason she'll still be able to have more children. She believes her child died during birth; she'll make no claim. Once it became clear he would survive, I took the liberty of naming our young Mehdi, Mohammed. I'm sure you approve," he continued.

"Of course. We want no one to dispute our claims. I've gone over the talking points you prepared for me. Your jargon was a bit technical in nature, so I've simplified it, and when I speak later today, the world will be convinced that one, I have returned from *Ghaibah*, and two, accompanying me will be the prophet's (Peace Be Upon Him) progeny and first biological male heir.

"Science and religion converge today in a supernatural cataclysmic 'awakening,' or do you prefer 'emergence?'" al-Qahtani rehearsed, glancing at his notes.

"Emergence, definitely," uttered Dr. al-Onezi, reflecting on the "awakening" movement in Iraq that contributed to so many deaths in the days before Daesh took over large swaths of territory.

"And yes. The science is irrefutable," he continued. "The religious leaders gathered here in Mecca will be swayed by our facts and presentation. Since the Scots cloned a sheep in the nineties, the world has known that cloning of humans was possible. The Chinese have likely done this already. What will shock the world, however, is that we dared to resurrect our prophet, and that by Allah's guidance, we had the scientific and financial capacity to restore unto him his body and bring him out of hundreds of years of *Ghaibah*. And you, Abu Mehdi, will usher this new era in ending your own absence these forty years and reclaiming your rightful place in cleansing the flaccid House of Saud, taking over stewardship of the Holy Sites of Islam. No one will doubt you when you show them you are the rightful Mehdi, returned from exile, and standing with you, the prophet incarnate in this young, beautiful boy. And should anyone still doubt, you will prove your claim when you show them the contents of the coffin and the remains stolen from Medina at your command some forty years ago. You are ready, sidi. You were born and now reborn for this."

***

It was nearly midday with the sweltering sun bearing down on oblivious pilgrims as they sojourned around the Kaaba. They were focused on the euphoric mindfulness resultant from the awareness of being on holy ground, made all the more real by their indulging in breathlessly uttering of Quranic passages. Their thrill of approaching the portal to higher levels of existence made it a challenge for many to contain their joy. Such zeal even masked their vision and awareness of the surroundings, including that other pilgrims wore holy garments akin to togas called *Ihram*, essentially two white sheets wrapped around the body, exposing shoulders. Women wore similarly simple, loose-fitting attire, the key to all of which was to show no distinction among classes or wealth. So wrapped up in their circumambulating, each individual, among the millions, charted his or her own connection to God, shutting out all distractions.

In the throes of this worship, al-Qahtani made his way to the Kaaba. He moved with an entourage which included a young boy, Dr. al-Onezi, and two manservants pushing a gurney upon which lay a rectangular box covered in black and gold ornate tapestry. He joined the crowd of worshippers on the northwest side of the Kaaba so he might work his way to the center of the crowd in time to reach the southern face, or Yemen Corner, where his platform was already set up.

Al-Qahtani, nervous for the first time, ascended the two steps and moved straight to center stage. He half-smiled as he noticed the stage branding indicating it was built by the Bin Laden family construction company. The boy followed him, letting go of Dr. al-Onezi's hand for the first time. The gurney likewise adjusted into place on the platform.

Al-Qahtani's hands shook as he reached for the microphone. He calmed himself in prayer and meditation, knowing this moment as his destiny realized. A lifetime of planning and seeking fulfilled. He began singing the call to the faithful to assemble for *Dhuhr,* or noon prayer. As a lifelong *muezzin [religious leader who calls the "faithful" to prayer],* he had led calls to prayer tens of thousands of times. It was second nature to him. As a purist in terms of adherence to *Fus-ha [formal Arabic],* his pronunciation and tones in the utterance was impeccable, filled with a solemnity and earnestness in compelling congregants to pray. He held sway over the masses with his inflections and rubato, holding certain notes longer at the expense of others, opening his vocal cords and then closing them into nasal sounds in unique Arabic tradition, started in the 600s by Bilal, a former slave and then friend to Mohammed who began the tradition of the Islamic call to prayer.

It had been arranged via Muhsin Bin Laden's people in the Grand Mosque that al-Qahtani's microphone would be picked up over the normal transmission of the daily prayers. His transmission transfixed the faithful milling about the compound. Most sensed a variation of sorts from the usual *muezzin* and his calls to prayer, gently pulling them out of their worship and drawing to their attention that they were being addressed by an old man standing next to a young boy.

"In the name of God the Mighty and Merciful, my faithful brothers and sisters, I greet you in peace," he began. His voice was strong. He felt the purpose of his cause; all jitters were gone.

"I have been *absent* from this place for forty years, this Holy Ground, sanctified by Prophet Ibrahim (Peace Be Upon Him), Prophet Ishmael (Peace Be Upon Him), and rededicated to God's purpose, by Prophet Mohammed (Peace Be Upon Him). I have returned to usher in a new era of peace and stability, a Sharia rule by Allah, not by man. We have no King but Allah and no borders but that between the faithful believers and enemies of Allah. I am Mohammed Abdullah al-Qahtani, returned to you now because Allah and I deem you ready and now worthy to accept me. You rejected me in 1979, so I lived in *Ghaibah* all these years waiting patiently for your hearts to soften. Now, I return and I bring proof from Allah of my legitimacy."

The crowds on the west and south could see him but kept milling about. Those on the far side of the Kaaba could not, but hearing his remarks, they began moving to catch a glimpse of who was talking. They tried to remain focused on their spiritual mission, but given the holiness of the ground they trod, assumed the elderly imam was there for their enrichment. Many began increasing the urgency in their recitations of Quranic passages.

Al-Qahtani's remarks were also streaming live and being picked up by news channels that often provided coverage of Hajj travel. Typically, not an interesting view for audiences but broadcast by the pious in televisions, homes, lobbies, and waiting rooms around the Islamic world. Tribal cohorts strategically positioned around Saudi Arabia paid special attention to this viewing, however, awaiting al-Qahtani's signal and spiritual reveal.

"With me on this stage is Allah's endorsement of my claim. I have with me the seed and body of Prophet Mohammed (Peace Be Upon Him)."

The boy stood stoically on the stage next to al-Qahtani, gently twirling a tassel from the corner of the tapestry in his short fingers.

"You failed to recognize me in my first appearance, but as it was foretold in the scriptures, I would disappear until my emergence. After which I would take my rightful place in guiding you. I am now returned."

Al-Qahtani spoke to the crowds around him but looked into the heart of the Islamic nation via the video camera positioned directly in front of him. The small, red light on the camera signaled to him that his remarks were being broadcast via religious news channels across Saudi Arabia and the broader Middle East.

***

Abraj Al-Bait Towers, Mecca, Saudi Arabia.

Less than half a kilometer away stood the *Abraj Al-Bait* (Towers of the House of God) complex of seven skyscraper hotels, just to the south of the Kaaba. These towers comprised some of the tallest buildings in the world, and on the top of the 120-floor Mecca Royal Clock Tower, the world's largest clock face. Among other superlatives describing the complex, at a reported fifteen billion dollar price tag, it's the most expensive building in the world. And, like many of the improvements at the Grand Mosque, it was developed by the Bin Laden family construction company.

In addition to the clock hotel tower, the complex boasted other high rises that account for up to about sixty floors each. Among these was the Maqam Tower, accessible by air given its helipad on the roof, which had recently been used. Still waiting on the helipad was a Saudi government helicopter with its blades running. Its passengers had holed up on the fifty-fifth floor in a room facing north to the Kaaba.

"Hey Nate, you sure we're supposed to be here? We ain't supposed to convert to Islam before coming to Mecca?" asked Nimrod.

"Be my guest, but my understanding is if you switch religions, you have to zero out your deficits with the last one. You need to find a priest, rabbi, wiccan, shaman, imam, or other trusted clergy who can hear your confession, you Nimrod," interjected Doc.

"Hey y'all. I think Nimrod is asking a genuine question, and we need to take this seriously," chimed in Spook. "Nimrod, when we get back to our unit, let's you and me chat with the Chaplain and get you signed up for 'conversion therapy.' We can do it together. They'll appreciate it if we go in as a couple. We'll get you straightened out."

"Thanks for understanding, Spook. You can't be too careful with religion," he said, Spook's practical joke going over Nimrod's head.

Typically stoic, even Philson smiled at this exchange. "Alright, gentleman. Let's cut the chatter. Remember: We advise only. We're in. We set up. We troubleshoot. We leave. And for goodness sake, literally, we were never here. Any questions?"

"Captain Philson, Mr. Reims. I think we are all set up," said a thickly-accented colonel in the Saudi National Guard.

"Tank, can you please take over?" asked Philson.

"Sure thing. Alright. It's a sniper mission. In a typical kill shot, I would walk you through a number of conditions and variables, including round velocity, humidity, wind direction and strength, vegetation, blind spots, cover for the shot and cover for the escape. The good thing about this is we're so close, you can pretty much jam the rifle up the target's nose, and then facilitate his personal introduction to Allah," said Tank to a very nervous sniper trainee and his spotter who seemed to have no clue as to what he was saying and little understanding of English.

"The thing is, the M110 Semi-Automatic Sniper System, 'SASS', or 'Sassy', as I call her, will do all the work for you. This is pretty much a point and shoot. Aim a little low, and you'll be fine," instructed Tank.

The colonel whispered in the ears of his juniors, "May Allah guide your aim. Do not miss." He uttered something else to the shooter, inaudible to those around.

Tank noticed the uniforms on each of his counterparts and trainees had the name Al Saud embroidered on the breast pockets.

Chapter 46

Grand Mosque courtyard, Mecca, Saudi Arabia.

Al-Qahtani absorbed what he perceived as adoration from the crowd, which seemed transfixed by his words. The reverberation on the microphone dropped his voice, adding a depth he almost did not recognize, making his remarks stately, confident, and ordained. He felt empowered and powerful. The masses were eating from his hand. His words flowed without effort. Allah was clearly channeling al-Qahtani to communicate to His people in ways unparalleled for centuries. This must have been how Prophet Mohammed felt when he received visions from Allah, when the inspiration for *that which is recited*, the Quran, was conveyed by the angel Jibril and then throughout the ensuing centuries transcribed by holy men as a gift to mankind. Yes. The speech was going well.

In full control of his faculties while speaking to the cameras, al-Qahtani relished in the crowd's eagerness for the Word of Allah. He intermittently looked at them and back at the camera. He knew he must connect with both audiences. He looked into their faces, into their souls, as he spoke to the prophecies of the emergence of the Mehdi from Ghaibah, regaling them his own absence of forty years while awaiting Allah's signal to return.

Those in the crowd, for their part, were amazed at the exhibition. Most did not speak Arabic, given they came from so many different countries, so al-Qahtani's words were lost on them but not their impact. Clearly, in front of them, was a compelling speaker, and his confidence and the resonance of his tones, and that fact that he was speaking from a dais in front of the Kaaba, reflected on his religious authority. Surely, he wouldn't be given such a platform without the full blessing of the religious establishment and the custodian of the Two Holy Mosques, the King himself. They were enthralled.

Those in the crowd who did speak Arabic were also transfixed by his sermon. Many, especially those older than fifty, vaguely recalled his name but given the swift rendering of justice and even swifter cover-up of the 1979 siege, few could recall any details about the events from the past. Al-Qahtani referenced his former partner and relative Juhayman al-Otaybi, "a martyr murdered by a corrupt, heretical political leadership," which jarred the memory of some, who faintly recalled the national embarrassment of an armed attack on their holiest of holy sites. The tribal names al-Otaybi and al-Qahtani were very common, easily held by tens of thousands of men across the Arabian Peninsula, so they were not yet convinced this was not just any other Islamic scholar. They remained enrapt in his oration, but a nervous tension began sparking in a few, compelling some on the fringe of the crowd to begin scoping out potential exits.

Al-Qahtani reveled in his own words. He felt Allah's favor on him as he assumed what he believed was the true custodianship of the religion of the faithful. He had great plans for his people.

He knew those plans involved leading those who submitted to Allah back to their former glory, a glory built on service and obedience. Obedience which required a master. Key to his lifelong mission would be the legitimacy bestowed on him as regent in administering the rule over Muslims in the stead of the young boy beside him.

Now came the Messianic reveal. An excitement rose from within al-Qahtani. "Allah the Creator, is the God of all knowledge, of science, medicine, and technology. In my sojourn of *Ghaibeh*, my long term absence, I have been at work to usher in the new era of Islam. In this time of study, Allah has revealed to me His plan, which restores to mankind His Prophet (Peace Be Upon Him). In November 1979, while the corrupt, western stooges of the House of Saud interrupted our assembly and introduction to the world of my arrival here in Mecca at the Holy Grand Mosque, my faithful companions went to Medina to recover the mortal remains of Prophet Mohammed (Peace Be Upon Him). We were on a mission from Allah, and we knew that the prophet's body at the head of our procession would lead us to victory. Due to the corrupt establishment's interference, our mission was delayed, but it again bears fruit today."

"The body of Prophet Mohammed (Peace Be Upon Him) is here with me today," he gestured grandly toward the box on the gurney. The child still gently played with the tapestry's tassels.

This pronouncement sent waves of uncertainty throughout the Arabic-speaking crowd. Those unaware of the import of al-Qahtani's words also picked up on what they sensed was a shocking announcement.

"And the spirit and the body of the Prophet Mohammed (Peace Be Upon Him) is also here with me today," gestured al-Qahtani grandly again but, this time, toward the boy.

"Let this sit with them a second. Let's milk this pause for impact," thought al-Qahtani.

"Through the marvels of technology and medical science, we were able to extract from the holy remains of the prophet enough of his essence to facilitate Allah's creation miracle," resumed al-Qahtani after a pause.

"The boy before you is the miracle of that creation. I, your returned Mehdi, will serve as his regent in restoring Islam's rightful role as the true religion," he continued slowly for impact.

The Arabic speaking members in the crowd, which likely numbered in the hundreds of thousands, were stunned.

Al-Qahtani was pleased. The shock on the faces of so many in the crowd was what he had counted on. What he had planned for. What he had dreamed of for so many years. His plan was unfolding perfectly. All that waited for him was the pre-ordained signal for his Bedouin kinsmen to take over the administrative and military offices throughout the kingdom and then the peninsula and neighboring countries. Given detailed planning and near perfect execution to date, he anticipated only minor resistance and skepticism—which would be met with quick retribution—as recalibrated Muslim fervor yet again swept through the Middle East and the world. This time with the aid and speed of broadcast television.

Al-Qahtani looked at the crowds again, absorbing the energy they emitted. He then looked at the tapestry covered sarcophagus of Mohammed, sighing briefly as he reflected on his life's work. His eyes turned to the boy. He felt a flicker of guilt over the ordeal inflicted on his mother, a barely pubescent teenager herself, and that his life would be tightly controlled by al-Qahtani. He would certainly not have a normal childhood, but neither had Mohammed. The regret passed just as quickly as it came as he bolstered himself for the issuance of the order to launch his revolution.

His eyes still on the child, he noticed a sudden splatter of dark red across the boy's chest, upward to his as yet expressionless face, and on the ancient tapestry as well. Al-Qahtani's vision and his body were violently wrenched outward toward the crowd again and toward the enormous clock tower just south of where he stood. He began collapsing, losing consciousness. His view snagged for a second on the camera in front of him, the red light off, no longer indicating the transmission of the broadcast. He fell to the stage. The last image before his mental faculties shut down permanently was the boy writhing next to him in an epileptic seizure.

Epilogue

A full second later, the sound of the shot rang out across the mosque courtyard, causing a panic. Those on the fringe of the massive crowd were able to get to the exits quickly. Those closer to the middle, hampered by their loose fitting Ihram outfits, trampled each other in their rush to distance themselves from the sound and the odd set of events surrounding the speech and apparent assassination of the old man.

***

Dr. al-Onezi grabbed the boy, Mohammed, and quickly administered a shot of Carbamazepine, of which he carried a ready supply, to quell his seizure. Otherwise, the boy seemed okay, he assessed. He held the boy tightly, crawling through the crowd to take refuge against the wall of the Kaaba until he might make his escape. He racked his brain to come up with what to do next. He believed al-Qahtani's plan relatively foolproof so was unprepared to see it collapse so suddenly and violently. Still cradling the boy, who was now calm, he looked at the corpse of al-Qahtani, barely ten feet away. He had been shot clear through; it appeared the bullet had entered the left side of his ribcage and exited the abdominal cavity. Given his own battlefield experience, al-Onezi surmised it to be a large caliber round fired at high velocity.

Al-Onezi felt no remorse over his elder's death. He supported the religious fervor as a cause that provided distraction from his grief and substantial financial gain courtesy of the benevolence of Ali al-Sadr and Muhsin Bin Laden, but he didn't believe al-Qahtani to be any more of the Mehdi than was his former head of state, Saddam Hussein. As for the boy, al-Onezi knew he wasn't any more the second coming of Mohammed than was any other child.

As a competent medical practitioner, al-Onezi felt guilt at the painful procedures he had inflicted on so many girls at the behest of al-Qahtani, some of which resulted in their deaths, and the cover ups as honor killings by their family members. Given the payouts he received and the death threats one Mr. Abdullah kept sending him, al-Onezi believed he had no choice but to keep silent and do the bidding of his overlords, chief of whom lay sprawled in death a few feet away. He never had the heart to tell the old man that the material extracted from Mohammed's corpse was not sufficient to produce a viable clone. He held young Mohammed even tighter, as a father would a son.

***

Philson and his team of Green Berets arrived back at the Jeddah Consulate General after their training mission. "Fellows, we have one more task here in the kingdom we just saved, and then we're wheels up. I'll take care of it on my own. Then we'll meet at the National Guard base for our flight out of here. We'll let our Marine cousins have their house back," he nodded respectfully at the young servicemen with their closely cropped hair, all staring reverently and reticently at the ragtag ODA band.

Philson emerged from the restroom having changed from his army drab into smart casual civilian garb and punched the app on his phone to call a car service.

"Hey Tank, your Saudi buddy did a pretty good job with the one shot, one kill routine," said Doc.

"Yep. I sat in front of him to ensure he didn't close his eyes while he shot. So many times soldiers in these parts are afraid that Allah will condemn them for killing other Muslims, so even in the heat of battle, they'll close their eyes in prayer and shoot over the heads of the enemies. It's a miracle anyone ever dies, but somehow those bullets connect in Yemen, Syria, Iraq, and other hotspots," replied Tank, continuing, "but this time there was more incentive."

"What's that?" asked Doc.

"Young Lieutenant Al Saud told me later the commanding officer whispered in his ear that if the old geezer didn't die from the first shot, the colonel would kill the shooter and his family himself."

***

Philson showed up at the hotel where Haley was staying. He called up to his room from the register. No answer. On a lark, he thought he might check by the pool. It was a hot day, so Haley might have thought to get some sun or even take a dip, cast on his arm notwithstanding.

He walked out by the pool seeing men, women, and children frolicking. The men and children were wearing western style bathing attire, while the women were adorned in *abaya* and *hijab*—by all accounts, equally happy. "What a strange place," he thought.

No luck by the pool, but Philson noted a sole lounge chair occupied down on the beach, under the protection of an oversized umbrella. He approached the chair, noticing the occupant had a towel over his head and left arm and nursed through a straw the unmistakably green, lemon mint drink so popular in the Gulf.

"'Sup, dude?" Philson startled Haley. "How's it going?"

"Hey, Nate," replied Haley finding it more comfortable to address his former commanding officer by his first name. "I'm doing better. The arm is still sore, and I should get the cast off in a few weeks."

"That's not what I mean. How are you doing?"

"Really, I'm doing okay. It's been a pretty horrible year, but I'm going to be alright."

"Good. I'm glad to hear it. I can't discuss it here, but I want you to know that your efforts, in particular, your recent briefings to a few Saudi officials, let's see how I can say it . . . prevented the sudden, abrupt, and violent change of the course of history."

"I'm sure you're overblowing any role I might have had. In fact, I don't recall anyone even listening to me, much less believing half of the hare-brained nonsense I've been spouting."

"Listen, Clayton. You need to get over yourself. You were hired for your judgment, which you've used consistently and with high integrity. You've shown initiative and leadership. It's your physical courage that saved my life a few years back in Iraq"—Philson gestured at scars on Haley's legs, visible given that he was wearing swimming trunks—"and now your intellect and moral courage has exposed a nut job megalomaniac bent on world domination.

"I can't go into detail, but we got him. Your old pal is dead. Your visa interview is complete. Let's go home now. Go pack your bags. We're taking you with us."

A stunned Haley, who while at the beach feeling sorry for himself, was in a news blackout. He got the SBU (Sensitive But Unclassified) version of what happened while packing and making his way to a military transport to Amman, Jordan and eventually Washington, DC for extensive and classified debriefs and the presentation, in private, of a near-executioner's sword.

***

Saudi Arabian social media, television, and newspapers all reported widely on the *"tragic deaths at the Grand Mosque due to stampeding. Over 138 faithful met their Allah-ordained destinies as unusually large crowds in their religious fervor crowded the holiest sites in efforts to commune with Allah. Authorities for the first time in recorded history allowed the faithful to approach the consecrated remains of Prophet Mohammed (Peace Be Upon Him), which may have sparked the zealous rush at the mosque. Most of the deceased were elderly or infirmed. Religious authorities promised to put into place more safeguards to prevent trampling in the future."*

Individual accounts of the events differed, with some eyewitnesses reporting that an Imam promised the arrival from "his long absence" the promised Mehdi. Rumors of the assassination of an elderly scholar and a young child also abounded but were quickly attacked in social media as false by an army of bots.

***

"How could this happen? Everything was in place? Every contingency was covered!" yelled an angry Bin Laden at Ali al-Sadr. They were both seated comfortably on one of Bin Laden's Embraer Lineage 1000E luxury jets, replete with a 42-inch television, fully stocked liquor cabinet, dining room, lounge, bedroom, and full shower. "What went wrong?"

Al-Sadr was equally apoplectic but remained calm. "I don't know. We considered every angle. The House of Saud was somehow alerted to our plan. The only person who knew this plan was the American. I sent Abdullah out to the desert to kill him, but somehow, he must have escaped. My people in Aziziyah still don't know how this happened and what became of Abdullah and his driver. Even so, Haley did not know our final plan. All he knew were some of our names. I'm sure he wasn't aware of your role. Somehow, the Saudi authorities pieced together elements of our scheme and got lucky. This is a setback, to be sure, but if you'll hear me out. Not all is lost.

"Al-Qahtani's death was unfortunate, but his zeal was strictly toward the religious, whereas you and I have more politically ambitious plans. Al-Qahtani can be replaced. I have already alerted a Najaf Ayatollah of our plans and the existence of the boy. He believes the masses can still be rallied around the boy and the prophet's living legacy."

"Fine. Continue your adapted plan. I will connect with my allies in Iran, Syria, and my financiers in Dubai. Close up operations in France until the dust settles. Get al-Qahtani's nephews out of Paris. Move them to London. Give them new identities. I will relocate to the Comoros Islands where my money and influence will keep any heat from reflecting on me. The king's people could not touch me in 1979, and they will not touch me now, but I should keep my distance in the interim and then convince them I had no hand in this. Move the boy to Qom, not Iraq. I don't trust the Iraqi people, no offense, Ali, but if you couldn't manage a simple murder there, I don't trust you to keep the boy protected and under the rightful guidance."

"Of course, sidi. As instructed. What, may I ask, shall become of the American nuisance?" asked al-Sadr.

"Mr. Haley interrupted Allah's plan for ushering in a new era of Islamic rule. It's only proper that he meet Allah in person, and soon, and in the most violent and painful fashion," uttered Muhsin Bin Laden.

About the Author

Award winning author Ethan Burroughs has dedicated much of the last two decades to exploring the Middle East and slowly unraveling its mysteries. His encounters have taken him to Saudi Arabia, Iraq, Jordan, Kuwait, Israel, and the Palestinian Territories where he has studied the history, faith, cuisine, language, and culture of the lands which continue to grab our headlines as we search for an elusive peace. He has had the great pleasure of spending significant time with characters similar to those depicted in this account, including our unsung patriots in the Department of State. He is a U.S. Army veteran and political consultant.

Visit the author at Ethanburroughs@ethanburroughs.com

Reference Maps

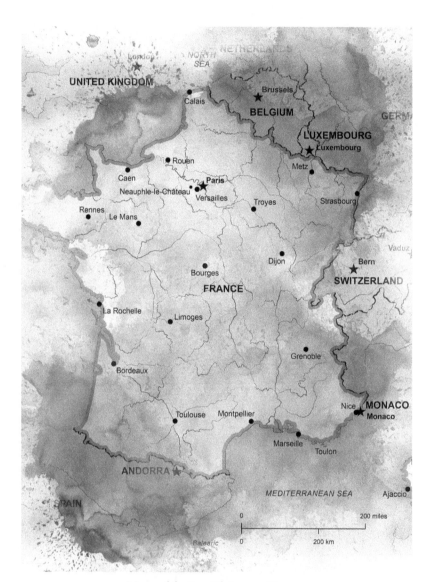

Neauphle-Le-Château, France

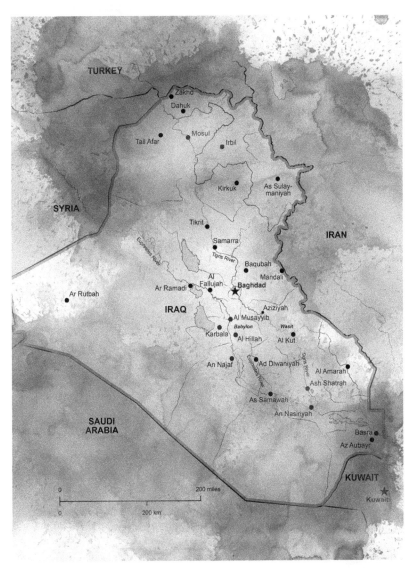

Aziziyah, Wasit, Iraq

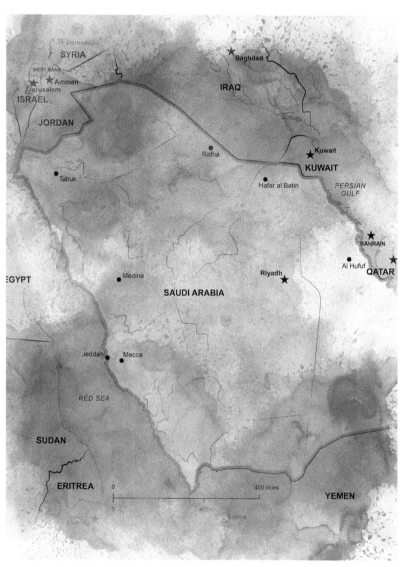

Medina and Mecca, Saudi Arabia

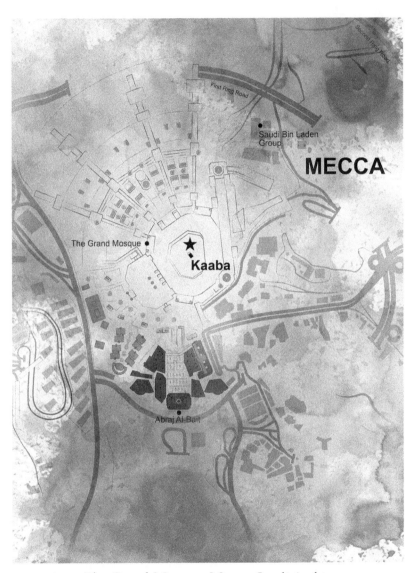

The Grand Mosque. Mecca, Saudi Arabia